Penguin Books
The Jacaranda Tree

H. E. Bates was born in 1905 at Rushton in Northamptonshire
and was educated at Kettering Grammar School. He worked
as a journalist and clerk on a local newspaper before
publishing his first book, *The Two Sisters*, when he was twenty.
In the next fifteen years he acquired a distinguished reputation
for his stories about English country life. During the Second
World War, he was a Squadron Leader in the R.A.F. and some
of his stories of service life, *The Greatest People in the World*
(1942), *How Sleep the Brave* (1943) and *The Face of England*
(1953) were written under the pseudonym of 'Flying Officer X'.
His subsequent novels of Burma, *The Purple Plain* and *The
Jacaranda Tree*, and of India, *The Scarlet Sword*, stemmed
directly or indirectly from his war experience in the Eastern
theatre of war.

In 1958 his writing took a new direction with the appearance
of *The Darling Buds of May*, the first of the popular Larkin
family novels, which was followed by *A Breath of French Air,
When the Green Woods Laugh* and *Oh! To Be in England*
(1963). His autobiography appeared in three volumes, *The
Vanished World* (1969), *The Blossoming World* (1971) and
The World in Ripeness (1972). His last works included the
novel, *The Triple Echo* (1971) and a collection of short stories,
The Song of the Wren (1972). Perhaps one of his most
famous works of fiction is the best-selling novel *Fair Stood the
Wind for France* (1944). H. E. Bates also wrote miscellaneous
works on gardening, essays on country life, several plays
including *The Day of Glory* (1945); *The Modern Short Story*
(1941) and a story for children, *The White Admiral* (1968). His
works have been translated into 16 languages and a posthumous
collection of his stories, *The Yellow Meads of Asphodel*,
appeared in 1976.

H. E. Bates was awarded the C.B.E. in 1973 and died in
January 1974. He was married in 1931 and had four children.

H. E. Bates

The Jacaranda Tree

Penguin Books

in association with
Michael Joseph

Penguin Books Ltd, Harmondsworth,
Middlesex, England
Penguin Books, 625 Madison Avenue, New York,
New York 10022, U.S.A.
Penguin Books Australia Ltd, Ringwood,
Victoria, Australia
Penguin Books Canada Ltd, 2801 John Street,
Markham, Ontario, Canada L3R IB4
Penguin Books (N.Z.) Ltd, 182–190 Wairau Road,
Auckland 10, New Zealand

First published 1949
Published in Penguin Books 1955
Reprinted 1956, 1974 (twice), 1975, 1977

Made and printed in Great Britain by
Hazell Watson & Viney Ltd,
Aylesbury, Bucks
Set in Linotype Times

1

As Paterson's boy Tuesday ran across the compound daylight
came up in long bars of orange and rose that faded almost at
once across the violet line of mountains. Light became tender
yellow on the dust, shining into a pale coffee face that had
something of the look of a handsome monkey with a perpetual
smile.

The boy was dressed in a pair of white duck shorts and a
faded football jersey of quarter colours that many washings
had bleached to salmon and brown, and he carried under his
arm a small radio set not much larger than a caddy of tea. He
carried the radio set close against his face, not only as if it
were very prized and very wonderful but also as if he were
listening for some sound to come out of it. His flat brown eyes
seemed profoundly to trust that it would. It did not occur to
him that it could ever be otherwise. Paterson had given him the
set. And it was impossible that anything Paterson did could not
be right. It was inconceivable that Paterson could not be
trusted. Paterson had also given him the football jersey and the
white duck shorts, and these simple things, together with
Paterson himself and the boy's eldest sister, the girl whom
Paterson called Nadia, were all he possessed in the world. No
other boy in Burma possessed such things. No other boy ever
could.

Paterson's bungalow stood with its back to the river, facing
the plain of rice-fields, parched sulphur yellow now in the dry
season, and far beyond them the low violet horseshoe of
mountains. At the back of it grew a small plantation of pineapples and a group of papaia trees and a belt of wild bananas.
Drooping brilliant leaves waved dustily against dry bamboos

5

that screened off the corrugated iron roofing of the rice mill and the long cane basha where Paterson distributed payments to his Burmese workers in kind, mostly rice, every Sunday. Now, at the beginning of the hot season, in March, the entire bungalow was like a house of flame. It was consumed and almost hidden by masses of salmon and crimson bougainvillaea that flowed down the roof and dripped over the white verandah like suspended brilliant fire.

In front and to the sides of the house lay the compound, a quadrangle of dust where no grass grew and where small fiery jungle fowl sometimes came out to dust themselves in the evening and after the heat of the day. The previous manager, Davidson, had made a garden there: a circle of mown grass, with fringes of heliotrope and gerbera daisy, mauve and pink and orange, beside long lines of sweet pea, and martial scarlet and orange cannas in a central bed. Boys had watered the grass in the evenings and jungle fowl had scratched on it like little arrogant gilded scarlet toys. But Paterson did not seem to care for gardens and nothing now remained of it except, in the centre, a jacaranda tree that Mrs Davidson had planted. It had begun to blossom now with drops of bright blue flower among masses of tender pinnate leaves, and its fresh brilliance had the effect of making the dust seem dead. And purely out of habit the boy lifted his free hand to touch the branches as he passed. He missed them by two inches.

The smile faded for a moment from his face and then came back, immensely cheerful, as he went into the house. In the kitchen he filled the kettle for tea and began quickly to prepare a tray. It was a quarter to five. Paterson must be woken at five. Paterson would take the tea without milk, with two slices of green lime and a lump of sugar and as many aspirins as the day, or the night before, demanded. One aspirin was mere ritual; two were not serious; but after three the boy was never sure. Standing by Paterson's bed, folding the mosquito net, smiling, very cheerful, he would wait for Paterson to throw the cup at his head.

After that the day was very simple. He would lay out Pater-

6

son's ducks, his shirt, and his shoes. Paterson would go down
to the early shift at the rice mill. The boy would clean the
dining-room and lay breakfast; Paterson would return and lie
back in the long cane chair so that the boy could kneel silently
and smilingly before him and take off his shoes. Above all
Paterson would do most captivating things with the pre-selec-
tive buttons of the radio set. To the boy these things were
wonderful. In a second he could hear the strange far voices,
the music, the news of war that came from London and Rangoon. And as he stood dutifully and smiling by Paterson's
table, serving bacon and eggs, the iced papaia that Paterson
loved, the tea with lime, the small sweet green bananas and the
toast and marmalade, he could conceive of only one thing that
could delight him more. It was that Paterson should allow him
to wait at table in his shirt. This shirt was a discarded evening
shirt of Paterson's that covered the boy like a surplice. It had
about it a sort of comic holiness. And when it came out, on
great and important occasions, the boy felt the wearing of it to
be something more than an event. It seemed to make him
grow.

If he desired anything more than this it was to hear voices in
the rejected radio set that Paterson had thrown away and was
now his own. Every evening, in his own hut of bamboo and
palm-frond across the compound, he laboriously took the set
to pieces in the light of a paper-shaded candle and then laboriously put it together again. Every evening he listened and
waited. Nothing had so far happened to break the silence and
bring the voices and the music to him as they were brought to
Paterson, but he did not doubt that, in time, if he were patient,
something would.

The bungalow was two-storeyed, opening on to sleeping
verandahs back and front. The nights were still cool enough
for Paterson to sleep inside. On the upper back verandah slept
the boy's sister, and as he went upstairs with the tea at a
minute to five he stood on the top of the stairs for a moment
and listened and waited. She did not seem to be moving and he
went on. In both the cool and the hot weather and through the

7

short hot rains she always slept there, alone or with Paterson.
Ever since the day the boy had first brought her to the house
Paterson had called her Nadia, partly because it was a name he
liked, partly because he could not bother with Burmese names,
beautiful though they were. In the same way he called the boy
Tuesday: because that too was simpler and because Tuesday
was the day he had walked in, dead-beat and smiling, from the
country somewhere east of Shwebo.

'Patson sir,' the boy whispered. 'Patson, Patson sir.'

He stood at the side of Paterson's bed, looking down on
Paterson embalmed under the white mosquito net.

'Patson sir,' he said. 'Patson sir. Tea.'

He called once or twice more before he set down the tray by
the bedside and began to fold back the mosquito net, flinging it
soundlessly over the top of the frame.

'Patson sir. Tea,' he said. 'Tea.'

When Paterson stirred at the fifth or sixth call he sat straight
upright, as if something had hit him. It was the moment for
which the boy was always ready and yet in a way, from one
morning to another, never really sure. And now he stood
transfixed and smiling, again like a small, handsome, cream-
faced monkey, waiting for Paterson's first act of the day.

It astonished him terrifically when it came. Paterson pushed
back the single sheet and blanket which covered him and got
straight out of bed. The boy could remember nothing of the
kind ever happening before. He did not move. With the unbroken and unsurprised smile on his face, he watched Paterson
walk three times across the bedroom.

Sometimes Paterson, huge and dark, seemed to the boy no
less than ten feet tall. And now as he strode across to the
window, to stare briefly out at the sun, already brassy and clear
above the north-eastern cloud of hills, and back again to pour
out his own tea, he seemed unbelievably gigantic because the
boy was unprepared for what was going to happen next. He
had just time to notice that Paterson had not even touched the
aspirins when Paterson astonished him again.

He came over to the boy and ran one hand through his hair.

The enormous hand seemed for a moment as if it would pluck the cream-black skull from the little shoulders and throw it jovially away. For a second the boy's heart began beating very fast and his smile widened to the edges of terror.

'Tuesday!' Paterson said.

'Yes, sir. Yes, Patson sir.'

'Tuesday, things are happening. Understand that?'

'Yes, sir.' He smiled and did not understand.

'The war is getting bad, Tuesday. Things are happening.'

'Yes, sir. Yes, Patson.'

'I want you to go over to Betteson sir with a chit. See?'

'Yes, sir. Getting breakfast now.'

The boy made a very swift, sliding movement over to the door before Paterson could stop him.

'Don't worry about breakfast!' Paterson said. 'Over to Betteson sir now.'

'Yes, sir,' the boy said. 'No breakfast?'

'Let Nadia get it. Come up in five minutes for the chit to Betteson. Understand?'

'Yes, sir. Yes, Patson.'

'All right. And brush your hair!'

As Paterson pushed the boy away with his terrifyingly friendly hand the black hair stood upright as if for a moment it had really risen in fear. With a movement of his hands in which there was the tiniest fraction of disbelief he brushed it down. For a second he believed that Paterson was joking.

Then he saw another astonishing thing. Paterson was dressing. He had not taken the aspirins; the tea stood untouched on the table where the boy had placed it. The tall athletic body of Paterson pushed itself into the corner wardrobe and remained there for a moment, half-submerged before reappearing with a pair of clean duck trousers.

He waved them at the boy.

'Get on, for Christ's sake! The whole damn war is coming down on top of us!'

And then the boy knew that Paterson was not joking. Always until now he had gauged the temper of Paterson by the number

of aspirins Paterson took. It had not occurred to him that
there could be a kind of temper that arose from the taking of
no aspirins at all. For a moment it almost baffled him. Yet the
smile did not go from his face. It remained, in the second
before he dived out of the room, as serene and broad as ever,
supremely trustful, the brown eyes flattened outward as if
Paterson were really joking after all.

Downstairs he laid out by the long chair in the dining-room
Paterson's white shoes for the day, loosening the laces so that
Paterson had nothing to do but slip them on.

It slightly hurt his pride that Paterson preferred Nadia to get
breakfast. In the kitchen he cut slices of iced papaia and laid
the orange quarter-moons of fruit, frosty with juice, in a glass
dish, dusting them lightly with sugar. It was Paterson's fav-
ourite fruit; he knew how Paterson liked it. Nadia might lay
the table and even fry the eggs and bacon; she might even pour
the tea, but the cutting and sugaring of a papaia was for him
alone to do. It contained all the essence of his devotion to the
huge, inconsequential man upstairs.

He had not time to do more than cover the sugary fruit with
muslin before Paterson shouted again. He slipped out of the
kitchen as if something were chasing him, only to meet Paterson at the foot of the stairs, fully dressed, with the note to
Betteson in his hand.

The boy began to tremble at the unexpected sight of Paterson
already dressed. The entire morning ritual of things was now
shattered. He saw that only something of incredible and gigantic seriousness could cause Paterson to get up so swiftly, without tea, without help, without aspirin, and without a single
moment of at least jocular violence against him.

Yet the smile once again did not go from his face. It remained as blissfully enormous as ever. It directed itself to
Paterson as if in joyful surrender, as if there was nothing
human or inhumanly possible that Paterson could demand and
that the boy would not do.

'Get over to Betteson like hell and come straight back.'

'Yes, Patson sir.'

He took the note from Paterson as he might have taken a piece of chocolate, smiling greatly.

'You understand, like hell?'

'Like hell, Patson sir!'

'And come straight back.'

'Yes, Patson sir, straight back.'

'Bring Betteson sir with you and make porridge.'

'Porridge for Betteson sir like hell!'

Almost as if it were the boy who was joking now, Paterson let out with his right hand a playful lead at the boy's left ear, but the brown-cream elbow came up and took the blow with neat swiftness and Paterson grinned, delighted. It was something he himself had taught.

'Make a fighter of you yet. Go on, you little bastard, get on.'

'Yes, Patson sir, bastard.' The boy grinned immensely.

'Bad word!' Paterson roared. 'Bad! Very bad!'

'Yes, Patson! Sir!'

The boy began running at once, going out of the back of the bungalow as Paterson turned, still grinning, and went out of the front. Paterson too walked swiftly, striding out across the bare compound where the circle of grass had once grown and where the tender flowers of the jacaranda tree, blue as hyacinths, still more bud than flower, made the only colour against the white dust that came right up to the steps of the verandah like a stretch of deserted shore.

As he walked across the open compound and out to the dust road leading down to the mill the girl Nadia leaned against the balcony of the upstairs verandah to watch him go. The brown eyes watching him with tenderness seemed quite impassive; against the morning sunlight they were delicately held in a dream. And unlike the boy she knew what was wrong with Paterson. In the night she had waited for Paterson to come to her; but nothing had happened; and later she understood why. For a few moments in the middle of the night she had stood by Paterson's door, listening to the radio he kept by his bedside. From Rangoon the news came first in English that she could hardly understand, and then in the educated Burmese that was only a little less foreign to her. She understood only that the voices were desperate voices and that they spoke of something catastrophic. She understood that the war which until that moment had seemed very far away had now begun to come very near to her. She knew that it might involve not only herself and Tuesday, who did not matter, but Paterson, who mattered very much.

Standing on the verandah, quite naked, just as she had got up from the bed, watching Paterson hurrying along the dust track towards the mill, she picked up her purple-red skirt and folded it over her body. She was very slim, and it gave her something of the appearance of a flower with swinging petals. And as she stood there, the skirt brilliant over her legs, her creamy-brown breasts still uncovered in the already warm sun, she saw Paterson turn and look back. For a second it was as if he had seen her. And in that second she too began smiling. It was a smile rather more grave and more tender and because of something fearful in it more devoted even than that of the boy. And it remained there, transfixed and slightly disturbed, while she reached down to the bed and began to put on her little cream-white jacket that was half like a bodice and half like a blouse.

A moment later she saw that Paterson was running too.

2

It was a little after six o'clock when Mrs Betteson, dressed in a faded red kimono the loose sleeves of which were tied up above her elbows with pink lengths of tape brought home by Betteson from the offices of the steamship company, saw Paterson's boy Tuesday running down the road. She was already busy in the front garden of the Betteson bungalow, fanatically attacking with a pair of shears long orange-tinted trailers of bignonia that seemed, even so early in the hot weather, to grow inches a day. She had something of the creased and floppy look of an unironed garment. She wore heavy gold-rimmed spectacles that hooked back over her ears and gave her eyes a startlingly fixed protuberant gleam.

Everyone in the town knew that Mrs Betteson was batty. And as the boy saw her there in the garden, fanatically and smilingly clipping the flowers, he remembered it too. He stopped running. The smile faded from his face and it did not come back until he opened the little gate of bamboo and began to walk up the garden path. Even then it was not the smile he gave to Paterson; and it was not the smile, at once defensive and polite, he would eventually give to Betteson. It had in it an odd stoniness, transfixed and lightless, made up of misgiving and wonder. He had seen Mrs Betteson before.

On a day six or seven months before he had brought another note to Betteson, and Mrs Betteson had taken him into the kitchen because Betteson was not there. Those whitish, protuberant, almost albino-like eyes, magnified by her glasses, had waved about in their sockets like sterile flowers, and all that hot afternoon she had kept him in the kitchen until Betteson returned, giving him fruit drinks and sad, sugared little cakes, moist and sickly with heat, fussing over him with damp and sweaty affection. Ever since he had been half-frightened of those startling flower-like eyes. 'Lucky Mr Paterson to have a boy like you. We never had a boy like you. Where did he get you from, where did you come from? Lucky Mr Paterson. Isn't he?' And as she talked to him, mostly in a language he did not understand, he felt more and more sick with the too-sweet, ill-cooked cakes until at last sickness became a terror that she would keep him there.

'Joe! Mr Paterson's boy! Tuesday.'

Waving her scissors, she shrieked the news to Betteson, who presently came out from the bungalow, fierily corpulent, bald head leathery red from the brows downward and then blood-lessly white in the upper half, where his old-fashioned topee had kept off the sun.

The boy, smiling, waiting for the Bettesons to come to him, stood in the centre of the garden path.

'It's that nice boy of Paterson's, Joe! That nice boy.'

'What do you want?' Betteson said.

The boy did not speak. He simply held out the note from Paterson, smiling all the time.

'Chit from Paterson, eh?' Betteson turned the note over and over in his hands, to make sure the boy had not read it. You could never tell.

'What's the matter, Joe? What is it?'

'Nothing that concerns your nose. Keep it out!'

'What a nice boy he is, isn't he, Joe?'

Mrs Betteson stood smiling at the boy through glinting spectacles, with greedy sterile eyes, as if once again she wanted to keep him there, and he was glad when Betteson shouted at him to get out.

'Answer please?' he said.

'What nice English,' Mrs Betteson said.

'Get my hat!' Betteson said. 'Instead of gawping there!'

Mrs Betteson fluttered scrappily into the house, a vague dream in the kimono.

'Answer please?'

The boy smiled, waiting.

'Get back before I knock that damn grin off your face!' Betteson said. 'I'll be over! No need to wait for me.'

'Yes, sir.' The boy smiled only a fraction less broadly, less certainly, than before. He thought for a moment of saying something about the porridge he would make for breakfast. Then he saw Mrs Betteson reappear from the house, shears in one hand and Betteson's old biscuit-coloured topee in the other, while Betteson stood on the path and swore at her savagely.

Afraid of both of them, he began to run up the street. At the corner he waited for a moment for Betteson to appear from the gate of the house. Beyond the tamarind trees that lined the street the gilded roofs of several pagodas, delicate upper pinacles white as sugar, were catching already the glittering brassy light of sun. The eyes of the Buddhas were staring with immobile emptiness across the plain and for a moment there was a sense of something oddly uneasy in the street where no one but himself had stirred. He had lived long enough with Paterson to know that sending chits to Betteson of all people before breakfast was a strange thing. It could only mean that something far stranger was happening. What it was he didn't know; but in time, at the proper moment, and when it was right, Paterson would tell him. He had faith in Paterson.

As he stood waiting for Betteson to come out of the house, uneasy about going home until he saw him appear, he looked up once more at the Buddhas staring out to the plain. The great dark and hollow eyes were something like the sterile eyes of Mrs Betteson. Across the white pagoda the morning shadows of high palms fell like thin black fingers and from the monastery on the far side of the town came the sound of bells.

In the monastery were thousands of Buddhas. Everywhere they lined the high cool walls and the making of them never ended. Unceasingly they were made by boys who sat in the dust of the courtyard and put into image moulds wet dabs of grey plaster; the two halves of the mould were slapped together over the plaster and then the image, like a grey cake, was turned out, to be laid in the sun and baked to whiteness. In time there would be millions of Buddhas so made by small boys to whom it was no more than a game in the dust. But he was not like other boys. He was not concerned with the making of a million Buddhas. He was not concerned with being a novice in a monastery. He knew very well that Buddha was great and eternal and all-seeing and all-understanding and that he could exercise over him, for ever, now and always, the great protection. But so too would Paterson. And whereas Buddha was simply an image, huge as he saw him now in the street behind the palms and in every conceivable size in the cool tomb-like niches of the monastery, both great and small and yet always dead, Paterson was living flesh. Buddha could never die and nor, he was sure, could Paterson. From Paterson could come a nearer and even greater protection than Buddha could give. It would protect him from people like Betteson who swore at him and from people like Mrs Betteson who wanted to keep him. And it would give him, in time, the greater understanding.

A few moments later he saw Betteson come out of the garden of the bungalow, and he turned and began to run.

Twenty minutes later, in Paterson's dining-room, Betteson sat eating his porridge with large spoonfuls of salt. You needed it in the climate anyway. And he had been in the climate long enough to know.

At the other end of the table Paterson scooped with a thin spoon at his sugared papaia, only now and then looking up from its frosty coolness at the grey mess that Betteson was slopping in. Betteson in turn looked at him with envy. He had worked for thirty years in the dust, the heat, the discomfort, and the mosquitoes of the steamship offices only to find himself, at the moment of retirement, caught in a trap. War had trapped him into a lengthened service in rather the same cheating way that life had trapped him with Mrs Betteson. But then he had never been lucky. He had never had the wonderful luck of people like Paterson, fresh out from England and yet preferred for managerial posts over the heads of better men. He had no luck like that. Portman had none of it either.

Portman was under-manager of the rice mill and although it was hard on a man with great experience in Indian mills not to be given an expected post he at least had some compensations. Mrs Portman was a lovely woman of thirty with long fine legs and the nicest figure in the town. Betteson had watched her often at the Swimming Club. She swam and sun-bathed in a silk two-piece costume of pure white, and sometimes the minutest fraction of her pale breasts, untouched by sun, became visible like the rim of a saucer between her sun-brown body and the silk cups above. Paterson was not a member of the club. This omission deprived him, in Betteson's eyes and the eyes of everyone else including especially the Portmans, of some standing. When Paterson wanted to swim he took a towel and swam in the river naked and his Burmese boy stood on the bank with his bath-robe and waited to rub him down. 'I like to swim in water, not people,' was a remark of Paterson's that for a long time went round the club.

The Portmans certainly did not like Paterson, and they had reason, but Betteson was not so sure. In a small town it raised tricky issues to go as far as openly disliking a man. The whole of Betteson's life had suffered from the complication of raising tricky issues. The problems of going back to England before the outbreak of war might have been solved except that very tricky issues had been raised and in the end the Bettesons had not gone.

Betteson spooned the last of the porridge into his mouth and licked the spoon and looked up to see if the boy was still in the room. You could never trust a boy not to spread all over the town any little thing he heard, and he was a little annoyed to see him still standing by Paterson's chair. Paterson was sprinkling more sugar on a second half of papaia.

'My passion,' Paterson said. 'Papaia with snowfalls of sugar on it. Hope you don't mind waiting?'

'Carry on, old man,' Betteson said. 'Carry on.'

The boy stood waiting behind Paterson's chair and the sight of him reminded Betteson of another tricky issue. That too of

course rankled with the Portmans: the business of the Burmese girl living in the house. It was no affair of Betteson's but
in some mills that would not have been tolerated and was only
tolerated now, he thought, because of war.

War had complicated, sharpened, and disrupted everything.
For some time the whole town had been in a state of nerves.
Since December the war had become nearer and nearer, im-
pinging sharply on the well-made European quarter, with its
pleasant white and red bungalows, drenched with bougainvillaea, set out on a plan of palm-fringed shady squares. It was
no longer an affair exclusively of Europe, far away. It was
beginning to drift relentlessly and unpleasantly in, as the sulphur sandy dust drifted in all summer from the plain, hot as
furnace breath, under a sky of harshly glittering light, to parch
up in the neat European gardens and compounds the last
blades of their fondly tended grass. Already most of the Europeans, with the children, had gone. The jalousies were nailed
up at most of the windows and already the mass of bougainvillaea flower, spreading with prolific branches in the rising
heat, was beginning to fall down and cover them with ten-
tacles of salmon and purple and rose. Of the Europeans that
had made up the pleasant parochial life of the Swimming Club,
the Burma Club, the English tea-rooms, and the English Church
only Paterson, the Bettesons, and the assistant-manager
Portman and his wife, Mrs McNairn and her daughter,
and Major Brain, secretary of the Swimming Club, remained.
Dr Fielding and some nurses remained over at the hospital, but
the nurses were mostly half-whites and in any case Fielding
had already made it clear where his duty lay and no one
doubted that the nurses would remain too. Caldwell, the district officer, was over at the hospital too, a wreck after gastro-
enteritis picked up at some village celebrations up river at the
moment when everyone needed him most. They would probably fly him out from Mandalay.

'I spoke to Fielding on the telephone last night.' Paterson
had finished his papaia and the boy, taking the plates, had left
the room.

'I thought it funny you sent for me.'

'Funny?' Paterson said. 'We'll all be out of here by dawn tomorrow. Rangoon was practically gone.'

'Good God! What do we do?'

Betteson was alarmed and yet it was pleasant to think of himself and Paterson in co-operation.

'It's what you do. Caldwell will be flown out. The rest of us go by road together. I want everyone over here by twelve o'clock. I'll give them lunch. I'll tell them what Caldwell plans. The rest of the day they get ready.'

'Who do you mean, everybody?' Betteson said.

The boy came back into the room with a dish of bacon and eggs and held it in front of Betteson, who stopped speaking. The eggs were very small and Betteson took three.

'You and your wife,' Paterson said, 'of course. The Portmans. Mrs McNairn and Connie. And I suppose Major Brain. The rest have gone.'

The boy went out of the room again and Betteson leaned forward, sucking in a half egg before he spoke again.

'I can tell you now Mrs McNairn will never come.'

'She'll come.'

'Not to your house, Paterson old man.'

'I think so.'

'It'll raise pretty tricky issues.'

At Betteson's elbow the boy quietly refilled his cup with tea, put milk in it, and then held the sugar basin so that Betteson could help himself.

'No sugar,' Betteson said, and he watched over his shoulder to see the boy depart.

Paterson cut slowly away at an egg. It suddenly seemed specially delicious to him because, in the act of cutting it, it occurred to him that it might be the last he would ever eat there. In this preoccupied way he seemed not to be listening.

'I said it would raise pretty tricky issues,' Betteson said.

'Well aware of it.'

'What if she says no?'

'Ask her if she'd rather die of rape or cholera.'

'I think that's stretching it a bit,' Betteson said.

Paterson did not speak. That, thought Betteson, was one of the troubles with Paterson. A bit ironical. He didn't, of course, mean it about rape and cholera. That was simply his ironical exaggeration, his way of trying to get round Mrs McNairn.

The boy gave Betteson a slice of bread from a flat cane basket. Betteson broke the crust and mopped it in the juice of bacon fat and egg.

'This thing wants thinking out,' he said. 'It wants looking at from all sides.'

'It's all been thought out. Caldwell has thought it out. I've thought it out. I've been thinking and looking at it for months!'

That was another thing about Paterson: the clear, sure, rather snappy temperament that went straight for things. It offended some people greatly.

'All right, all right,' Betteson said. 'How do we set about it?'

'By road,' Paterson said. 'In two cars.'

Betteson, thinking of Mrs Betteson, who was like a child when it came to travelling, did not speak.

'Portman has his car. There'll be four in that. I thought the Portmans, Mrs McNairn, and Connie.'

'Yes, I see. Yes.'

'And then there's mine. The Buick. You and Mrs Betteson in that, with Major Brain and me. Six altogether.'

Betteson's office training was at once offended by Paterson's arithmetic and he looked sharply down the table.

'You mean six in yours? Two and two make four. Not six.'

'Six,' Paterson said. 'With the boy there and his sister.'

'Now wait a minute, old man.' Betteson had become suddenly so excited, in a deferential way, that he was not eating his third egg. 'That raises tricky issues!'

'For Christ's sake who said it wouldn't?' Paterson said. 'The whole issue is tricky. The Japanese are coming. They're probably on the Lower Irrawaddy now!'

'Good God,' Betteson said. 'They might come up by river.'

Paterson got up from the table, buttoning his jacket. As he walked across the room it was clear even to Betteson that there was nothing more to say.

'See you at twelve,' Paterson said.

'Where are you going?' Betteson said. 'What are you going to do?'

Paterson opened the light screen door that led out to the lower verandah and then let it swing from his hands.

'I'm going to blow up the rice mill!' he shouted.

At the table Betteson, gazing at the hollowed-out papaia rinds and his cooling eggs, did not speak, and behind him the boy, for the first time that morning, did not smile.

3

As Connie McNairn sat beside her mother in the bicycle rick-shaw taking them over to Paterson's bungalow at a quarter-past twelve, she wondered what was going on in Paterson's mind. She sat with her brownish-grey eyes fixed on the petunia purple of the rickshaw-boy's waist-cloth and on the naked rosy-brown back down which smooth rivulets of pale sweat were pouring in the noon sun. From behind, and with the waist-cloth that was so like a girl's skirt, the boy looked extraordin-arily like a woman menially and desperately dragging herself and her mother along the hot streets between the rows of tamarind and palm.

She could not conceive what was going on in Paterson's mind to make him invite her and her mother over to lunch on an invitation brought by Betteson. They were late already; but that, as she knew, was exactly her mother's way. It was exceed-ingly bad to be early; it lowered you in people's eyes. Her mother sat upright in the rickshaw with something of the ap-pearance of a moulting hawk : a woman of nearly sixty whose face had the arid shantung-yellow texture that came of thirty years' service under the Burma sun. She wore a dress of dull brown silk that, from the acid of much sweat, had gone com-pletely to pieces under the arms. It had been reprieved with parallelograms of lighter colour that would have shown badly if Mrs McNairn had ever lifted her arms more than waist high. In her determination to do no such thing she sat with her arms clenched in her lap, grasping the ivory handle of her white parasol. It was the parasol, with its hooked handle curving out from her clenched hands and knees, rather than anything in her angular beaky face, that gave the appearance of a faded bird of prey.

The reason neither she nor Connie had left Burma with the rest of the Europeans was Mr McNairn. Just as the Bettesons gave out their ill-luck as the cruel coincidence of war, so Mrs McNairn gave out Mr McNairn as the basis of whatever humiliation, including the affair of Paterson, that could ever happen to them.

'This would never have happened if your father had been alive.'

The girl had nothing to say to a remark she had heard a thousand times before, and she set her eyes even harder on the brown and purple figure of the sweating boy.

'Your Mr Paterson would have been tearing over to see us. Not us to see him.'

'I thought it sounded very serious,' the girl said. 'After all, we've been told to be ready.'

'It'll be a change for Mister Paterson to take anything seriously.'

Mrs McNairn folded her hands more tightly over the beaked handle of the parasol. The only colour on their bloodless flesh was the cluster of rubies that lay like a large bright raspberry on her left hand. Rubies were the emblem of Mr McNairn, who had been engaged for thirty years in buying them wholesale for a firm in Calcutta. Here, in Central Burma, McNairn had lived, worked, and died, with something of the same anonymous devotion as Betteson had worked at the offices of the shipping company. It would not have been very different if the Scot had worked in his native Dundee or if Betteson had remained in London, adding up someone else's accounts there.

But Mrs McNairn did not take this view. She conceived it to have been McNairn's lot to devote to the Crown and to the extension of the British way of life qualities that she thought had been terribly underestimated. She thought McNairn ought to have been a district officer, perhaps even a senior district officer; he ought not to have been in trade. She was fond of saying to Connie, 'Your father was a great man. He never got his just deserts.' In preservation of this myth she would not leave Burma, and McNairn was buried in the well-watered

23

dust of the English cemetery, under the shade of pipal trees, in the quarter beyond the Swimming Club, and every Sunday Mrs McNairn laid on the grave circular wreaths of hibiscus or frangipani that in an hour were blistered dead by sun. 'This is our place,' she said.

Now the rickshaw-boy was standing on the pedals of his bicycle, working hard, sweating deeply, to beat the last short incline out of the residential quarter towards the mill. It would have been better to have taken a taxi, the girl thought. It was already half-past twelve.

'I hate being late for things,' she said.

'Personally I should have thought the later the better. After all—'

The girl sat grimly concentrated on the back of the boy, now liquid rose and gold with sweat as he pedalled up the hill. There was no need for her mother to finish what she had begun to say. Thousands of unfinished sentences had piled up mountainously on the affair of herself and Paterson. She felt suddenly wretched, depressed by the sweating rickshaw-boy, agitated into wishing more than ever they had taken a taxi.

In her agitation, she was unaware of sitting forward, on the edge of the seat, and it was her mother who brought her to herself again.

'You're going to work yourself into a state, aren't you?'

'I hate this rickshaw business. I hate it when they sweat.'

'You were born in Burma,' Mrs McNairn said. 'You were practically brought up here, except for the seven years in England. Of course they sweat. It's a hot morning. Anyway they're all bone lazy.'

The girl knew all that and did not speak again. She knew too that it was not the rickshaw-boy who upset her, with his sweat and the illusion of being a slaving girl, but Paterson and herself and the greater illusions all that entailed.

In a dream, not listening and not even looking at the rickshaw-boy any more, she remembered how, in London, at the steamship agency, she had quite by accident met Paterson on a day before the war. Two people overhearing each other inquir-

ing for passages to the same remote river town on the Irrawaddy could only laugh in surprise at each other before they
began speaking. It was a happy beginning; she was nineteen
and her schooling in England was over; Paterson was twenty-
three and had to her the appearance of a conqueror. She remembered Burma: the little town, the port, the steamers coming up from Rangoon, the hibiscus and the heat, the dust and
the exquisite white pagodas, the glaring dazzling plain with its
tender distant mountains, the delicate sad monastic bells and
the jacaranda trees. It was part of the ecstasy to describe it all
to Paterson.

At that moment her mother began waving at someone coming out of the gardens of the English Club.

'It's Miss Ross!' she said, and for the first time her hands
sprang up, like rusty-yellow springs from between her knees,
revealing the lighter patches of silk underneath the arms.

'Miss Ross! Miss Ross!'

The rickshaw pulled up under the street trees, and across the
sunshine Miss Ross, in a suit of white linen that made her look
very like a nurse, came forward to Connie and Mrs McNairn.

'Miss Ross, are you coming too?'

'Coming? Where on earth to?'

Miss Ross had come to Burma as an Anglican missionary
and had remained to embrace Buddhism. Her thoughtful pale
face, elderly and delicate, had the contentment that arises from
frailty; she was like the final leaf, sapless but strong, that will
not be blown from the bare tree.

'To Mr Paterson's. We're all going. I thought you knew.'

'No: I don't know.'

'There's some awful rumour of our all being packed up and
sent away.'

'Yes: I heard of it.'

'Then we shall see you there.'

'No,' Miss Ross said. 'I shall be over at the hospital.'

'But you ought to come,' Mrs McNairn said. 'You ought to
know what's happening. What will happen if the Japanese
come?'

J.T.—2   25

'They'll probably rape me,' Miss Ross said and then smiled and began to walk away.

Mrs McNairn was offended and could not speak, and in the silence that followed as they drove on, past the last of the made-up streets and out to the narrow road where bullock tracks began to run parallel, like dusty yellow cuttings, on either side, the girl gave herself up to a few more thoughts of Paterson.

He had come out to Burma, after all, about four months before she had arrived. She had written her mother several letters about it. What she had said in them was true and yet, in a sense, it was not true. What she had said of her feelings for Paterson was true. It was when she spoke of what she believed were his feelings for her that she became guilty of a sort of ecstasy of lies. It did not matter that she had believed in them; the trouble was that her mother had believed in them too.

That explained all the ghastly business of Paterson coming to meet her at Rangoon. She remembered something terribly rebellious in his face. He knew he had been caught up in a manipulated situation. He had seen it as something contrived by her mother. He had seen himself being cornered as the fresh, eligible newcomer, rich with managerial post, large bungalow, and infinite chances of rising in the world. All the time he had not had the slightest idea that she herself had caused it by the lying ecstasy of the letters. He had come to Rangoon simply out of decency and because he was sorry for her, and in a few moments all the charm of it was dead. She knew suddenly that all her lying had had the opposite effect of what she had longed for it to have. She knew that Paterson was not in love with her, though her mother believed he was, and in a few days she felt as if she were coming back not to the places she knew so well, to the friendly flowering little town of bright pagodas and the evening sweetness of margosa and frangipani and the bright golden daylight, but to a strange land, glittering under intense harshness of light, oppressed by sulphur dust blowing in from the outer plain, with a life riddled as if by maggots with gossip and disembowelled of all the expected beauty by respectable leeches.

It was as she sat thinking this that at last the rickshaw drew into Paterson's compound. She came out of her reflections just as her mother, provoked for the second time into showing the parched armpits of her dress, lifted her hands and snipped back the catch of her parasol and said:

'There goes that disgusting girl. She's here.'

From the plantation of pineapples, out of the bright sun into the broken shade of the papaia-trees, Connie looked up to see the girl Nadia walking into the back of the bungalow. She was carrying on her head a flat round basket of cane filled with papaia, green-skinned oranges and small bananas of parrot green, as if she had been gathering the fruit for lunch. She held the basket with both hands, so that the little yellow bodice was pulled up from her skirt, showing her naked cream back that had something of the same tender silkiness as a young banana frond. The swing of her body broke at intervals the division of her skirt, so that one naked leg, pale and silky as her back, split out of the purple fabric like a shining seed.

Mrs McNairn was so angry that she forgot to put up the parasol and simply waved it at the sweating rickshaw-boy. 'Don't tell me how much it is! I know!'

At the same moment two figures in white appeared across the compound. And to them too Mrs McNairn waved the parasol, so that the rickshaw-boy instinctively ducked again.

'Thank God the Portmans are here!'

4

As Portman followed his wife and the McNairns into Paterson's sitting-room, where the Bettesons were already drinking long tumblers of iced gin, he looked instinctively up at the windows, to see if Paterson had yet hung any curtains there. He saw his wife look up too and then, as she saw the windows still empty except for the thin green cane blinds and as she caught his glance at them, she looked away. Her face, narrow and brown and very smooth like the rest of her body and cool even in that heat and aloof with its slender ears lightly pinned into the neck with earrings of rather too large pearl, looked suddenly annoyed. And Portman could not tell if the annoyance was directed against the windows or against him.

He went across the room and stood by the window, looking out. He did not drink at midday and he had been the entire morning with Paterson at the mill, so that he had nothing to say. At the mill the charges were laid; the whole place was ready to go up at a touch. It had all been very difficult. Half the Burmese workers had started to run already and the other half would be gone by midnight, when the charges were blown. All morning the tension had grown under the hot sun, so that he felt the place might easily blow up of its own accord.

Dust rose across the compound in a little puff of sulphur cloud that was like a minute explosion set off by a spark of sun. It travelled on a breath of wind across the space in front of the house, disturbed for a moment the blue buds and the tender pinnate leaves of the jacaranda tree and then moved away, light as an egret, flying away and vanishing with a rustle in the dry bamboos of the road.

The dust only served to remind Portman what a disgrace the compound was. No garden, no curtains, no sense of the proprieties – all this, of course, was our friend Paterson all over. If it was possible to do anything in perfect defiance of all the rules you could trust Paterson to do it. The Burmese girl, for instance – well, thank God they were getting out; so that there would be an end of that. Then the affair of Miss McNairn. That was grim. And then the more ordinary, accepted things. Vacations, leaves, for instance. Whereas everyone else behaved sensibly and you might say hygienically by going up to Mamu for two weeks in the cool of the hills Paterson took the Burmese girl and her brother and went trekking off to the Chin Hills or Northern Shan in order to study the flora and fauna or some such nonsense. Or even living with head-hunters.

He found it hard to accept the man. He sometimes thought Miss McNairn was well out of it. He was quite sure of one thing: Paterson would not have lasted long in India. In his bitterest moments of disappointment at seeing Paterson in the post he coveted so much, Portman could console himself that he had left behind him in Calcutta an enviable and decent reputation. He was still a member of the Bengal Club. That was something Paterson had still to achieve. Here in this small one-eyed Burma town Paterson got away with a great deal; but there were, after all, other things.

He did not mind so much for himself; but it was after all very hard on Celia. They had always wanted to have children; had always intended to; but now all that was over. It was not possible to have children on Portman's salary. It was simply out of the question. What made it more damnable was that they were of course the right sort of people to have them. But that, he sometimes thought, was the trouble with the world. The wrong people were breeding like flies, whereas the right people were economically forced into sterility. Here was Paterson in this great barn of a house, the best bungalow on that side of the town, with not a decent blade of grass or a decent curtain to bless it, half the rooms not occupied, half the fences down, the whole ménage a disgrace to a man in his position – when Portman and his wife might have made it worthy and respectable and have raised a decent English family there.

On the other hand he had to be fair. The man was a worker; he had a diabolical kind of efficiency – even when it came to blowing up things. He might spend a lot of time playing football with Burmese boys down on the waste land by the river, but you saw the results in the mill. The people liked him; the rice yield had gone up. He had even started to improve the roads on the company's land. In a year or two there would have been an end of the bogging down of trucks and bullock carts in the mud of the rains and the sulphury gorges of dust that had for so long been part of the muddled tradition of doing things. You had to give it to Paterson there.

Even so, Portman could not like him. Nor did he altogether like this scheme of his for getting out.

All morning he had had the idea of taking the car and driving to Mandalay and getting a plane there. In five or six hours he and Celia could have been in Calcutta. The only thing that stopped him was the thought that Mandalay, after Rangoon, would be the next point of Japanese strategy. You might get stuck there. And Portman, unfortunately, did not share Miss Ross's sardonic resigned sense of charity about invaders.

He turned at last from staring at the dust of the compound, still and windless now in the hot noon, brilliantly crystalline and tiring in the sun. The morning had been most exhausting and he was very hungry. He could smell the fragrance of cooking and he turned just in time to hear the voice of Paterson's boy announcing lunch and to see him standing by the door.

At the sight of Tuesday he did not know whether to laugh or to be more enragedly angry than he remembered being for a long time. What he saw seemed to epitomize for him all of Paterson's tactless and unconventional temperament.

By the door, hugely and splendidly smiling, Tuesday was wearing the whitest of Paterson's shirts. It hung down over his entire brown-cream body like the surplice of a choir-boy, giving him a laughing radiance that almost sang.

As she went first into the dining-room Mrs Portman noticed two extraordinary things. Both offended and excited her. On the lunch table, with its cloth of cream Chinese silk decorated with half-moons of orange pink hibiscus and flame flower, there were glasses for champagne. The second thing was the sight of the Burmese girl sliding out by the other door.

Instinctively Mrs Portman looked to see if she was pregnant. And in those few seconds she was almost sure that she was.

At the head of the table Paterson stood for a moment, with Tuesday behind his chair. Beside Paterson's enormous bulk the boy looked something like a smiling toy dropped there by parachute.

Paterson arranged the guests. 'Mrs Portman here on my right. Betteson here, next to you, Connie.'

Tuesday moved up and down the table, deftly holding chairs. Paterson stood up the whole time, a slight frown on his face. With three men and four women it was rather difficult to arrange. It came out so that Mrs Betteson, who was wearing a sort of crocheted white silk shawl over her shoulders, sat facing him at the far end.

Paterson waited for everyone to sit down and then said:

'I thought we might just as well have one decent meal before we go. It'll probably be the last.'

Portman glanced at his wife as if to say 'Typical', but she was not looking at him. Betteson, crumbling thin toast with pistol-shot cracks all over the table-cloth said:

'I say, I think that's stretching it a bit.'

Mrs McNairn looked hard at the hibiscus flowers, determined not to speak unless it was forced on her, and was startled to hear Connie say:

'How long will it take? Three days?'

'I should say a bit longer,' Paterson said.

Connie did not speak again and felt rather glad; it meant that for three days and perhaps much longer she would be nearer to Paterson than she had ever been since England.

Mrs Betteson let off a series of giggles that were like suppressed jumping crackers and said:

'Joe, look at that boy. Mr Paterson, that boy of yours is a lamb. Joe, look at him.'

31

Tuesday was serving the soup, quietly, almost with reverence. In a few moments there would fall on him the exciting and wonderful honour, the immeasurable joy, of letting off the champagne corks.

'Mr Paterson, I think he's a godsend. Did he make this soup? I think he's a godsend.'

'Yes: he made it.'

'Did he? I think it's wonderful. I think he's a godsend.'

Betteson looked at her as if she were a slug that he wished to press to pulp between his large fingers.

'I think he's a godsend. He's the girl's brother, isn't he?'

Betteson had to stop it and said loudly, leaning across Mrs Portman:

'Did you do anything about the petrol?'

'All fixed,' Paterson said. 'The two cars can carry thirty-two gallons between them. We'll load another forty on.'

Mrs Portman thought the Bettesons, particularly Betteson himself, were quite classless. Betteson was the kind of man to be associated with an odour of onions. She turned from looking at him to look at Paterson and unexpectedly found herself transfixed.

'I suppose in a day or two we could rely on picking up a train?'

'Did you ever look at the map?' Paterson said.

Portman, furious, did not speak. He knew exactly how the one-track narrow gauge railway ran north through the plain and exactly where it stubbed itself out against the northern hills. But that was no reason for saying so in that offensive way.

For a moment the room was silent, the spoons quiet on the plates, and there was no sound in the still hot noon air except the voice of Nadia singing somewhere beyond the screen doors a few sad-sweet bars of some monotonous Burmese song.

In that moment Tuesday let off with a great bang the first of the champagne corks and the tension was relieved by Mrs McNairn jumping and saying, in spite of herself:

'Dear, I thought it was a gun-shot!'

'It's only that lamb of a boy,' Mrs Betteson said.

And now that she had begun talking, Mrs McNairn could not stop.

'When do we have to start?'

'Soon after midnight,' Paterson said.

'Isn't that rather leaving it a bit?'

'I don't think you'll find there's much time. You've got your packing. We've got files to burn. All the charges to blow.'

'Isn't anyone else coming? There's Miss Ross.'

'I don't think Miss Ross will come.'

'I saw her this morning. What about Dr Fielding and that girl?'

'I shall see Fielding this afternoon. I'm going over to ask him for cholera serum.'

Everyone looked up violently from the fish that the boy had served.

'Cholera serum?'

'I don't think he'll have any all the same.'

'That's a bit alarmist, isn't it?' Betteson said.

'We're going to take a hundred gallons of water in the trailer behind the Buick,' Paterson said. 'But you never know.'

'I still think it might be a decent long shot to go down to Mandalay,' Portman said.

'Try if you like. We had all that out this morning.'

Paterson looked round the table, resting his eyes finally on the childish, tender, faded face of Mrs Betteson, who looked as if she did not understand what was going on and did not care much.

'Well, here's to us, anyway,' Paterson said. He picked up his glass. The talk of cholera serum had shocked them all.

Everyone sipped at the cold glasses, pearly with film, so that the wine had something of the same diffused golden light as the sunshine seeping through the shutter bars.

'Drop o' good, this,' Betteson said.

'Very lucky to get it,' Portman said. 'These days.'

'A manager has his duties,' Paterson said, and Portman looked hard at Mrs Portman in unspoken answer.

Really, he thought, the lunch was damn good. The soup was first-class and you couldn't tell the river-fish from beckti, which Portman thought was rather nicer, in India at any rate, than sole. When the chicken came it wasn't hard and crisp as his own boy always served it, but melting and white, and nothing could have been more English than the touch of clove, like a breath of home, in the creamy bread sauce.

Not that he was going to say so. That, besides unnecessarily flattering Paterson, could only arouse new and sharper resentment in Celia. Perhaps more rows had been caused between them by ill-cooked chicken than by anything else except Paterson himself. After all one practically lived on it in Burma and yet, for some reason, it was never right. That was one of those simple things Celia could never make the servant understand.

In any case he was glad to see she was not looking, but was leaning across to speak to Miss McNairn.

'What are you going to take, Connie? Things, I mean.'

'Take as little as possible,' Paterson said. 'Warm clothes if you can. The nights may be a bit cold and we can always strip by day. Just a variation of the Swimming Club.'

Mrs Portman smiled narrowly and Paterson drank quickly after speaking, partly because he did not want to talk with Connie, partly because he was annoyed by the thought that a woman like Mrs Portman had to ask a stupid question about clothes in a climate she had known so well for so many years.

The champagne, in spite of its coolness, began to heat him a little. He felt the flush of it under his eyes as he looked down the table and he suddenly felt a little more benevolent, a little warmer in heart, towards the six people he saw eating there. For a moment he poised himself on the edge of the idea of getting drunk. But that, as Portman would say, would only undermine confidence; it would only raise, in Betteson's words, more tricky issues. Yet, as he sat there, drinking a little faster when Tuesday opened the second bottle of champagne, he liked more and more the sensation of kindliness that the wine inspired and the warmth it infused, like golden-pink haze, into his eyes. It occurred to him that Betteson, whom he loathed perhaps more than Portman, and Mrs McNairn, less stupid but more destructive than Mrs Portman, and poor silly Mrs Betteson, who was perhaps less of a fool than everyone thought, were really after all not so bad. For all of them he had only respect, touched by a little affection for Connie. Yet for a single moment before he ate the last creamy slices of chicken that Tuesday had cooked so well he regarded them with a deeper generosity, a more benign detachment, than he thought any of them were worth. It was certain he would never see them like this again.

Tuesday took rather more time with the ice than he would have liked, and Paterson himself got up from the table and poured more wine.

'No!' Mrs McNairn said. 'No!' and covered her glass. 'And I don't think Connie should.'

'It will help Connie find a mind of her own,' he said. 'Anyway, there are two more bottles.'

That, of course, was typical, Portman thought. He sat upright, rather gentlemanly and aloof, while Paterson filled his glass. He was going to give no opportunity for any kind of remark to him.

So he was harshly shocked to hear Paterson suddenly say, rather as if he were addressing simply him:

'We'd better outline the plan. So that you all know where you are and what you are and where we go and so on.'

'Well: I hope we all go together,' Mrs McNairn said.

'We may well do.'

There was a short silence as Tuesday brought in the ices, greenish-pink with shavings of water-melon and pistachio on top; and no one, not even Paterson, showed any signs of breaking it as the boy, floating like a ghost, passed up and down the table, serving quietly. To Portman it occurred that Paterson was waiting for the boy to go, but instead he began to make servings of the second bottle of champagne.

Mrs Portman found herself once again transfixed by Paterson. He was trying to get them all drunk, she thought, and the notion filled her with some of the pleasant golden dizziness of the wine. It would be very pleasant to get drunk with Paterson, in a pleasant way, in a pleasant place, so that she could get to know him better.

'There's no way out of the country north except by road,' Paterson said.

'Granted,' Betteson said.

'Or air,' Portman said.

'We have two cars. Mine and Mr Portman's. Mine has a trailer.'

Mrs Betteson was gazing at Tuesday, who was standing in the corner, smiling with the proud air of a surpliced chorister. There was something ethereal about that everlasting smile, as if no circumstance could ever defeat it, and Mrs Betteson, thrilled by it, tried to signal to Joe.

Betteson was looking hard at Paterson, who sat with his glass straight in front of him, cupped in both hands. There was going to be a hell of a row, Betteson thought.

'I think we can fit a trailer to Mr Portman's car too. If we can we'll take petrol in one and food and water in the other.'

Something cunning about that, Betteson thought.

'I thought Mr and Mrs Portman and Mrs McNairn and Connie could go in Mr Portman's car.'

At the familiarity of Connie being called by her Christian name Mrs McNairn felt herself prickle into sudden heat; but that was the sort of outrage you might expect from Paterson. To be familiar and cruel at the same time: that was Paterson all over.

'That would leave Mr and Mrs Betteson and myself with Major Brain.'

'By the way,' Mrs Portman said, 'where is the major?'

'He sent word he'd gone over to the hospital. It seems there's a chance Miss Allison may come.'

So that's it, Mrs McNairn thought. Collusion between Major Brain and that hospital nurse and Paterson. She saw in it the threat of fresh humiliation. Major Brain was a charming character and Connie had spent a great deal of time at the swimming pool. Still: there it was. They were all in the same boat, humiliating or maddening as it might be.

'How many does that make altogether?' Betteson said.

'If Miss Allison comes,' Paterson said, 'that's eleven.'

'Eleven?'

Even the effect of Mrs Portman's voice did not disturb Mrs Betteson, who was still gazing at that lamb of a boy.

'Eleven?' Portman said. 'I don't get that.'

Betteson dipped the remains of an ice-wafer into his champagne, and watched the wine soaking up.

'I make it nine,' Mrs McNairn said.

'You forget Tuesday,' Paterson said, 'and his sister.'

'Well, good God,' Portman said.

His voice was so low that it was drowned a moment later by the quibbling flutter of everyone trying to speak at once. No one succeeded in making himself heard except Paterson, who said:

'Don't worry. The Buick will take seven.'

'I don't think you quite get the point,' Portman said. He paused very stiffly. 'Once you start taking two of these people you can take a dozen. After all, we might as well take our boy.'

'Take him by all means.'

'How many sisters has he got?' Betteson said, and laughed a little, thinking it rather good, but no one joined him at all.

Mrs McNairn was stupefied. There was absolutely nothing she could say.

And in a moment everyone was silent too.

'Perhaps we might go into the other room for coffee?' Paterson said.

That was pretty cowardly, Mrs McNairn thought. And then as they filed out for coffee, out of the winey, diffused light of the dining-room into the northerly shadow of the other room, where Portman glanced once again at the curtainless windows and mentally fitted them with the cool flowered silk from the Army and Navy Stores in Calcutta, Mrs Betteson said loudly:

'Did someone say that lamb of a boy was coming too? What fun.'

Portman went over to his habitual place by the window, where Mrs Portman joined him.

'It's absolutely monstrous.'

'I know. But what can you say?'

She thought for a moment of saying something about the girl having a baby, but suddenly the triviality of it all vexed her. She was sharply aware of a new impatience and was glad when Tuesday, smiling, brought the coffee-tray, waited for them to help themselves and then slid away.

'Nonsensical get-up that boy has too.'

She did not speak. She wondered instead how often Paterson slept with the girl and then Portman said:

'The whole damn ménage must come. That's what infuriates me.'

'I'm going over to speak to Mrs McNairn,' she said. Then in the moment of her moving across the room Paterson said:

'Everyone got coffee? Please sit down.'

In a second everyone was silent. She felt conspicuous and awkward and Paterson, waiting for her to sit down, seemed to be smiling at her. He seemed to have adopted an attitude of kindly tolerance about them all.

'May I ask a question?' Betteson said. 'I mean, old man, quite frankly?'

Paterson gently spooned a lump of sugar into his coffee and watched it until it became the colour of pale brandy. And as he nodded Portman thought that this was it. He felt rather warmed, at last, to old man Betteson. Has was, of course, very much of a rough diamond. He had no class at all. Yet the old boy had the guts for this kind of thing.

'What is it?' Paterson said.

'You think it right to take these extra passengers?'

'Yes.'

'Well, I don't.'

'You know what you can do about it,' Paterson said.

'Well, that's what I was going to say,' Portman said. He felt stimulated by Betteson's remarks to a frankness of his own. 'There's no reason why we shouldn't split up and go separately, in the two cars, is there? There's no reason why we should go together if some feel it better not to?'

'There's every reason.'

'For instance, what?'

'We have the advantage of the two cars if anything goes wrong. We have more manpower. And in the end we can abandon one car and go on in the other.'

'I think that's a bit alarmist,' Betteson said.

'I don't see how that justifies your two extra people,' Portman said. 'Rather otherwise.'

'They can cook,' Paterson said.

'Oh! well, of course—'

'We may be three weeks on this thing. You don't know. Nothing like doing it in comfort. The boy can cook and so can the girl. And the boy knows the country.'

'You didn't explain that.'

'Well, of course, if they're coming like that,' Mrs Portman said, 'that's rather different.'

Looking straight at Paterson, she smiled.

'What do we sleep in?' Mrs McNairn said. 'Do you want me to bring sheets and things?' It was as if the whole notion of doing the thing in comfort had suddenly made her practical.

'Tents,' Paterson said. 'And I had the clerk type out lists of stuff for each of you to bring. Stick to the list and pack the stuff lightly. Don't bring sacks of souvenirs.'

There you were again, Portman thought. You couldn't help in some way admiring the man. So bloody outrageous in some ways, the way he treated people, and yet so efficient. He seemed to have thought of everything. And in a way of course it wasn't a bad thing about the boy and his sister. A few chips here and there would see you right. And there again you had to give it to Paterson. The boy could cook magnificently and whatever else you thought you had to admit that the girl, like so many of them, was beautiful. Perhaps it would result in a little extra comfort after all.

'The car's here now,' Paterson said. 'One of the drivers from the mill will take you back.'

'That's us, I suppose,' Betteson said.

'It can take you and Connie too, Mrs McNairn.'

'Thank you, but we could have taken a rickshaw.'

'Better take the car. He can wait for you to pack and then bring back your things. Then we can stow everything properly here.'

A moment later, as they all went out of the sitting-room to the verandah, beyond which the yellow-white dust of Paterson's untidy compound glittered harshly in the high light of midday and was softened only by the blue umbrella of the jacaranda tree. Mrs Portman looked back for the last time at the windows in which she would never now hang the curtains that she and Portman had so often thought of getting from Calcutta, and Mrs Betteson, so childishly and pleasantly tipsy from the heat and the champagne that Betteson felt he wanted to hit her, said in a loud and excited voice:

'I think it wonderful that lamb of a boy is coming with us, Joe, don't you? I think he's a godsend.'

Alone in the sitting-room the boy smilingly collected up the coffee cups, proud in Paterson's shirt, and from somewhere far beyond the mill, beyond the haze of the river and beyond the low fingers of dry bamboo that stretched southward on all that side of the plain, came the sound of the first explosions, no more than uneasy murmurs in the heat-charged air, like repeated thunder.

Outside, Mrs Portman felt the heat of the day, after the champagne, prickle up with unpleasant stickiness all over her body. She longed suddenly for the flower-fringed pool of the club. The Bettesons and the McNairns were already in the car and she was just in time as she called:

'Is there room for me? I think after all I'll come as far as the club for a swim. It's the last time.'

5

As Mrs Portman went into the Swimming Club there was no sound except the hissing of the fountain spraying from its scooped concrete shell at the shallow end. There was no one in the public rooms of the club itself or on the terraces or in the changing rooms except a Burmese woman attendant idly guarding the empty lockers of the women's room. When Mrs Portman arrived the attendant automatically got up and ran to fetch her costume, and as she did so the sound of her straw shoes went shuffling through the empty deserted corridors like the echoing hiss of water.

Undressing, standing for a moment or two naked on the concrete floor, Mrs Portman felt some of the irritation, the heat and the clamminess of Paterson's luncheon party drop away. She stood for a few moments idly drying the dampness of sweat from her body and looked down at the long butter-brown figure with its triangular spans of white where the sun had not burned. She had always wanted the sun to tan these places. She had always wanted the whole of her body to take on the same dark pure tone.

Alone, with no one in the club except the attendant, with Major Brain unlikely to come back from the hospital, she thought for a moment of going out and swimming as she was. And she wondered for a moment what Portman would have said to that simple and preposterous idea, and a needle of irritation pulled itself through her mind. It was the same sharp stab that had driven through her with thin vexation when Portman, with that affronted and miserable look, had drawn her attention to the windows that had no curtains.

For a second or two longer she held to the idea of swimming

as she was. It became part of an idea to shock her husband.
There were still enough white people in the town to make the
story of Mrs Portman swimming naked at the club have the
effect of revolutionary scandal. It would jolt him terribly. She
stood looking down at the long body, the breasts like peeled
white fruit against the golden dark husk of burned skin, and
she thought of the excitement it would give and the excitement
it would cause. Nothing else she could think of could bring
down so ferociously and completely the image of Portman
standing on his dignity, envying Paterson's managership and
his curtains, talking of his great experience in India or re-
expanding his dreams of the dignity and the curry of the Bengal Club.

She had been tired for a long time of all that; but suddenly
the shock of departure, the climax of all the life in the little
town, seemed to have sharpened it all. It filled her with angry
regret. She felt all at once that all her life there, the pretence of
wanting children, the pretence that the salary would not stand
it, the pretence of wanting curtains in a house that was not her
own, the pretence of standing on the high rung of a ladder –
all of it seemed suddenly to have been a hideous and monu-
mental bore.

A moment later she began to put on her costume. The sensation of shocking Portman suddenly did not seem worth the
risk of cheapening herself. She felt that there were simpler and
pleasanter ways of doing it than by publicizing the body she
liked so much and she began to think, for a moment, of Paterson. There was something infuriating and odd and attractive
about him. Like Portman she did not know what to make of
him and she wondered, as she had wondered so often, why he
was not a member of the club. It was too late to do anything
about it now.

When she walked out of the changing room it was for a
moment like walking into a world of burning glass. The pink
concrete of the pool edge scalded her naked feet as she ran.
The sky had the glittering hazy brilliance of full afternoon and
the brief dry wind that came across the water rustled crisply in

the papery leaves of the scarlet zinnias withering already on the terraces.

She stood for a second balancing on the blistering edge of concrete at the deep end of the pool and then shut her eyes and dived. The water that looked blue-green and very cold against the sun had none of the shock of coolness that she wanted as her body hit the water. It was as if instead she had gone down into a tepid and relaxing bath. There was no exhilaration in it and she swam slowly to the shallow end. The water bubbling in from the fountain shell was slightly cooler as she stood for a few minutes underneath it, arms outstretched, letting the water run down over her breasts and shoulders.

After a few moments she lay on the water, floating face upwards, eyes shut, letting the motion of the little currents from the fountain turn her round and round. She thought once again of Paterson and the luncheon party. It was practically all over, she thought. The whole thing was practically finished and no experience of Paterson remained, either to disturb or colour or beautify or excite it. Except for an odd dinner party, first at their own bungalow and then, only once, at his, they had hardly ever met. She had hardly ever talked to him. Other men, fresh to the town, were seized upon by the European colony as creatures bringing the stimulus of new blood to a tired stable. They were wanted for dances, parties, for dinners and bridge and tennis, swimming at the club, tea under the fragile arbours of vine and jasmine at the English tea-rooms. All the life of the little town drew the substance of its excitement from new arrivals, the new character that dropped like a stone, with no one knew what ultimate disturbances, into the flat known surface. Exciting to see a new man from England arrive: the speculation, the dissection of type, the jealous manipulation, the gradual division into factions for and against and then the final scandal or the final flop.

She heard the straw shoes of the Burmese attendant rustling through the corridor of the changing rooms, waking once again all the emptiness of the deserted pool, but it affected her only enough to make her think, once more, that it was her last afternoon. By another day they would be a hundred miles, she thought, up country. In two or three days they would be in India. In a week they would split up. She would never see Paterson again. Odd to think how different it might have been, she thought. Fascinating to wonder what might have happened.

In the entrance hall of the club the voice of the attendant talked in high tones. There was just the slightest chance, Mrs Portman thought, that it might not be too late. Would the journey be pleasant? She thought it probably would. As the road went up into the hills it would be cooler and the cars would push ahead of whatever traffic there was. In four or five days you could get to know people terribly well.

She heard once again the feet of the woman attendant running, and then her voice, closer along the edge of the pool. She looked across and saw her hurrying along the terraces of flowers and then, about twenty feet behind her, Paterson.

Excited and surprised and yet not moving, she floated rigidly on the water, feeling the sun burn her face and thighs and navel between the edges of the wet white costume. And then Paterson was speaking.

'Mrs Portman, I've come to take you back.'

'That's awfully nice, but I'm not ready to come back.'

'I think you'd better get your things on,' he said.

She floated in the same flattened way, talking upwards.

'You're not allowed in here,' she said. 'You're not a member.'

'I've come from the hospital,' he said. 'The rickshaw-boys are off the street. There aren't any taxis. I promised Portman I'd call for you and take you back.'

'I've only just come in.'

'I'll wait in the car.'

'I'll probably be hours. Your champagne made me very hot. It's a fatal thing.'

'This is probably a fatal day.'

'I suppose that was funny?'

'It was very funny.'

'Then will you stop being funny and fetch my towel from the deep end. It's on a chair. Then I can get out.'

He did not speak and she heard him walking along the hard edge of the pool. Listening, she raised her body slightly as it floated, her long brown legs close together and her brown navel holding, like a thimble, a deep drop of water. When Paterson came back she looked up at him for the first time and said:

'You're really not supposed to come in here. You could be thrown out.'

'This is the day when we are all being thrown out.'

'I always thought it a pity you weren't a member of the club.'

'Yes?' he said.

'Anyway I make you a member now,' she said. 'My guest. I'll get out and we'll have some tea.'

'I think we'd better go back.'

'That was an invitation and you threw it back in my face.'

'I don't think I did.'

'It sounded awfully like that but I forgive you.'

She smiled but he did not say anything and in another moment she had floated in to the centre steps by the pool. She turned sleekly over and then stood up and began to climb out, stretching up her hands for the towel. He held the towel out for her and she said:

'I like to dry in the sun.'

'I'll wait in the car.'

'There isn't that desperate hurry, is there? Now really? I'm absolutely parched and we're going to have tea.'

He did not speak and down on the lower terrace, where steps led down to the dressing-rooms, the Burmese woman stood watching them, and suddenly Mrs Portman called:

'Bring tea. For two. Quickly.'

She began to dry her shoulders with the towel, feeling the heat of the sun burn them at the same time. She dried the middle of her body and then her legs and Paterson stood watching her, not troubling to sit down.

'It's my last swim and you're not being very kind about it,' she said.

'Should I be kind?'

'I don't suppose so.'

'What then?'

'We could be friends and we needn't be so grim.'

She spread her towel on the grass of the terrace, between the pool and the scarlet beds of zinnias, and lay down flat on her back, to dry in the sun. For some moments she did not speak. He sat down at last on one of the cane arm-chairs under the green and blue umbrellas that lined the pool and then she said:

'Don't be so glum. Talk to me while the tea comes. Tell me about this journey. Is it going to be fun?'

'Well—'

'Am I going to see more of you than I've seen here? Or are we all going to go on in the same way and be grim and things like that? People always quarrel on expeditions, don't they?'

'I don't know and it isn't an expedition.'

'Well, whatever it is.'

She did not know for a moment whether to be furious or amused and then she heard the feet of the attendant shuffling along the terrace with the tray for tea and she said:

'How long will it take? The journey, I mean?'

'If you do as you're told, six or seven days.'

'Does that mean me?'

'It means you.'

'And what does doing as I'm told mean?'

The attendant came with the tray of tea, setting it down on the table under the umbrella. As she went away there was a sudden short explosion from beyond the forest fringe along the river and she let out a cry and began running, frightened. Slopping her shoes on the terrace, then losing one shoe and turning to pick it up, she stared for a moment, terrified, at Paterson and Mrs Portman, so that Mrs Portman forgot she had asked a question and said:

'Everyone seems to be getting a little jumpy.'

He did not answer and it occurred to her suddenly that the attendant was running away. The whole place seemed oddly deserted. Over the fringe of trees the smoke of the explosion, dark yellow against the sun, flowered for a moment and then dispersed. She stood up, watching it, idly fingering her dry body across the waist, luxuriously pressing the warm clean brown flesh with her hands. In another moment she was aware of Paterson watching her and she was amused suddenly to remember how she had thought of swimming without her costume and the thought struck her, half-excitedly, that in an hour the sun would begin to go down. It was very pleasant in the evenings by the pool, in the hot tropical darkness, on the grass, under the scented trees, watching the light and the stars in the deserted shell-like water.

'Milk or lime?' she said.

'Lime,' he said. 'Please.'

Something made her stand up, legs gently pressed against the table, as she poured tea. He sat looking flatly at her body and she wondered suddenly what went on, in that large bungalow, between himself and the Burmese girl. She felt excited by faint jealousy and wondered if it were true, after all, that the girl was going to have a baby, or if it were just a fancy on her part or just a mistake. And suddenly, fascinated by it all, she hated all the idea of leaving, the disintegration of the life of the little town, the end of the pleasant parties, the pleasant intrigues, the pleasant affairs in the dusk by the pool while Portman was still working at the mill. And above all she hated the notion that she had missed something with Paterson. It would have been exceedingly nice, she thought, to have played with a person one was supposed to detest, to have brought the impossible Mr Paterson down a peg, to have found in him, for fun, some of the things she missed in Portman, too correct to excite or succeed.

'Why don't you sit down?' he said.

'My costume's wet in an important place and I hate sitting on it.'

He took his tea, stirred it and did not say anything in answer.

'I'll lie on the grass again and get dry.'

She took her cup and set it on the grass and lay down, face

downwards, her face close to the cup, so that she could put her lips to it and drink where she lay.

'It's awful to be going. This was an amusing place. You should have belonged.'

'I suppose so.'

'I remember the first day you came here. I expected somone older.'

'I'm sorry you were disappointed.'

'I was disappointed. Naturally we all thought you'd belong to the club and then you didn't belong and then of course it's never so nice.'

'I found it nice enough,' he said.

'Yes, but in all sorts of ways it could have been nicer. And now everyone's going and we've got this hideous journey and all the nice things are finished. It is going to be hideous, isn't it? It's not true what you said?'

'I said it would be all right if you did as you were told.'

'I'll try,' she said.

She leaned her mouth forward and held it against the warm edge of her cup. As she sipped the tea, cat-like, quite silently, she felt the sun luxuriously burning the skin of her back and drying, at last, the fabric of her costume.

'It's odd about swimming,' she said. 'You go in to get wet and then you come out to get dry and then no sooner are you dry than you want to go in again and get wet.'

'There's no time to go in again if that's what you're thinking.'

'Oh! there isn't that hurry, is there? Why don't you drink your tea and then swim too? I could get you a costume.'

'I've got to take you back and then still make one more visit to the hospital and then get the cars packed. There isn't time.'

She rolled over on her back so that her body was flat and rigid, the breasts firm and tight as seeds in the white cups of the costume, and sighed deeply.

'Oh! that hospital. Is Fielding coming?'

'No.'

'Is that nursing girl coming – what's her name – Allison?'

'She can't make up her mind.'

'That's because she's in love with Fielding.'

'Is it? I didn't know.'

'Oh! these girls. These half-whites. The intrigues that go on.'

A group of palms at the far end of the club gardens moved brittle fronds in the sudden breeze of air coming up from the river and the sound for a moment was like the sound of the attendant running with her straw shoes.

Mrs Portman sat up as she heard it but no one was coming and once again she felt the strange deserted brilliance of the empty pool. And as she did so she thought once again of the sun going down, the hot fragrant darkness under the hibiscus trees, the intensely vivid stars, the luxuriant and voluptuous feeling of cool grass on skin warmed all day by sun, the sense of mystery brought about by the scent of jasmine and the smoke of evening fires. And suddenly she was overcome by nostalgia for it all and said:

'I really hate to be going. All of it breaking up. India isn't like this.' The sudden movement of sitting up had pulled the bust of her costume upward so that the lower white edges of her breasts were visible like the soft rims of saucers, as Bette-son had so often seen them too. She was aware of it and she was aware also of Paterson looking at it but she did not move.

'Time to go,' he said.

'Oh! must you? Won't you really swim?'

He shook his head and drank the last of his tea. She listened once more for the sound of the woman attendant running but there was no sound and she lay down again, deliberately stretching out on her back, looking up at him with her mouth parted, and saying at last:

'Five more minutes. Please. It's the last time. I've had an awful lot of fun here and it's the last time.'

He did not speak.

'Have some more tea,' she said. 'Or a drink. I could get the woman to bring you a drink. We could both have one. We could bid the place farewell.'

'Farewell it is,' he said.

Before she could speak again he got up and saying, 'I'll wait for you in the car,' began to walk slowly away along the terrace.

And for some curious reason, as she walked back along the hot concrete between the oblongs of grass and scarlet flowers, she did not feel frustrated and she did not mind. In the dressing-room she took off her costume slowly and stood for a few minutes quite naked, as she had done when she had first come in, gently powdering her brown skin and then rubbing it evenly and smoothly with her fingers. The feeling of her own hands on her own body was as luxurious as the first feeling of sun after water or water after sun and when she dressed again her clothes seemed to bind her and she could feel her blood running tightly. But it would have been better, she thought, if we could have stayed till darkness. There was a feeling in warm darkness by water that never came by day. There was a feeling of cool grass on your body that you got from nothing else on earth. There was a feeling of two bodies lying together in the humid darkness that you could never forget.

She went out of the club in a mood of tender excitement, thinking of it, telling herself once more how the journey perhaps after all would be fun and how terribly well you could get to know people in a few days or even a single day.

It was only when Paterson had driven the car half-way to the bungalow that she remembered her costume that she had left from long habit in the dressing-room.

'We just must go back. It's my only real one. I treasure it and it was expensive anyway. It would be simply awful to lose it and we must go back.'

'I'll send the boy,' he said.

She opened her mouth to protest but from over by the river came a series of new explosions, close and thunderous in the hot air, that smothered all she had to say.

When Major Brain bicycled over from the Swimming Club to Paterson's bungalow, just before midnight, the explosions

50

were still going on. All over the town, lighting up with shadowy starts of pinkish-orange the theatrical palms, the exquisite pagodas of white and gold, and sometimes the bright tributaries of salmon and purple bougainvillaea that covered almost all the brick-brown roofs of English bungalows, there flowered hundreds of little fires. In the deep upper darkness they seemed to be reflected infinitely in stars.

It was no night for leaving Burma, the major thought. And bicycling without a light through the half-deserted streets of the European quarter, he felt very alone after the strenuous day at the hospital as orderly in the male wards; and he thought grimly also that he was not like those plutocrats Portman and Paterson, who rode everywhere in cars. He thought of himself still as an army man, retired, blessed with an army pension that gave him no room for the pleasures of travelling in luxury. He was a plain man who had remained unmarried, not for the reason that the Portmans purported to have remained childless, because on his sort of salary he could not afford it, but because he did not like women. Curious, he sometimes thought, that he should have drifted into a job like the secretaryship of a tropical swimming club, where from early morning till dusk he saw practically nothing but women: European women exposing their white bodies in the sun until they were browner than the bodies of the Burmese and half-Burmese girls they so pretended to despise.

The only woman he really admired was Miss Ross. He had talked to her that very day at the hospital, where for some weeks she had been giving Fielding her part-time services. Fielding was an excellent fellow; but nothing he or the major could do or say would persuade Miss Ross that she would be better out of the country. She had been quite firm and serene. He felt that her life had become rather like the suit she wore: smooth and pure and white; and also in many ways miraculous. Of all the women he knew in Burma she alone had managed to keep clean; not physically, sexually, or merely socially clean, but clean in spirit and clean, wonderfully clean, in heart. And she had got all this not, as one would have hoped, from

Christian faith, but from Buddhism. Her life had become serenely filled with an immense tolerance, a great practical habit of service and meditation. It had affected the major very much. She was, like everyone else, a member of the Swimming Club but she always bathed early, regularly at six o'clock, before the waters, as she put it, became defiled. And often Brain was there, to talk to her in the first exquisite morning coolness, with the dew undried on the fresh-unfolded hibiscus flowers, to hear her talk drily and volubly on Burma, the English, and her faith, in a voice still so English that it was like a mockery of all that Englishness, back home, that Brain had not seen or experienced for thirty years. It had almost persuaded him to come to Buddhism himself, except that any such step would automatically have lost him the job at the Swimming Club.

Nevertheless, as he bicycled out in the fiery darkness to Paterson's bungalow, hearing the explosions and thinking of Miss Ross, he was very uneasy. There was no serum at the hospital. That was one thing he had to tell Paterson. Another was that Caldwell had gone. Another was that neither Fielding nor Miss Ross would leave the country. Another was that Miss Allison, the young Anglo-Burmese nurse whom Mrs McNairn had called 'that girl', could not make up her mind. Her life hung suspended in the critical hour between East and West, and in indecision she had cried hysterically in Fielding's office that afternoon. This meant that Paterson and himself were to watch out for her at the last moment, by the hospital gardens, as they drove out of the town. They must make room for her in case she came.

And then suddenly, while he was still half a mile from the bungalow, the entire rice mill blew up. Out of the darkness, with the roar of the explosion, came a hungry sort of wind that sucked back and blew the major off his bicycle.

He stood panting, at once trembling and fascinated, pressing himself against the handlebars. All about him the little fires, half-hidden by trees, seemed suddenly to be extinguished by the new fire. It rose like an orange cloud, so that he could see the bungalow quite clearly, silhouetted against it. And then above it he saw also the leaping cloud of smoke, blacker than the sky in the shadows, mountainously growing until it suffocated the stars.

And in that moment all his life in Burma seemed to become extinguished too. Somewhere among the shadowy mass of palms and palm-fences, huts and houses, and from the intersecting dusty streets full of the sweetness of evening-scented trees, he could suddenly hear the rising cry of voices and the sound of feet, in thundery whispers, running away.

'And by God,' he thought in misery and bitterness, 'that's all I'm doing. I'm running away too.'

For the rest of the way he did not ride the bicycle again but pushed it slowly forward, under the obliterated stars in the face of the fire.

The moment Paterson saw Major Brain slowly pushing his bicycle into the compound, rather like a man who had lost himself and did not know where he was going, he was sharply annoyed. Already the illusion of kindliness had gone. He had begun to hate the Bettesons, the Portmans, and Mrs McNairn with vicious gloom; the smell of the fire at the rice mill worried him like the unpleasant odour of a dog.

And then when he saw the grey, nebulous, tired figure of the major actually pushing the bicycle into the compound, hours late and not even riding, he felt he had suddenly had enough.

'Major! Where have you been?'

'At the hospital. There's no serum,' Brain said.

'Never mind about the serum. Where are your things?'

'This is all I have.' The major had a small army haversack and a water-bottle slung over either shoulder. 'This and the bicycle.'

'What do you mean, the bicycle?'

'Isn't there room for it?'

'For heaven's sake, man,' Paterson said.

'I'm sorry.'

'Put it in the house and leave it there.'

'I'm taking it with me,' the major said.

'You're what?'

'I'm taking it with me.'

'Riding it?'

'I thought it could go on the back of one of the cars.'

Paterson could not speak. The two trailers, lightly made of bamboo by boys at the mill had taken some hours to pack with petrol and water. The boots and grids of both cars were filled with boxes of food; tents and bedding were lashed on top; and inside were suit-cases of personal things. Already, he thought, they had too much.

And now here was Brain with his bicycle. Not a camera or a telescope or a radio or even a fat bronze Buddha such as Betteson had insisted on bringing and that Paterson had found and thrown out. But a bicycle: the most hideously, impossibly unpackable thing in the world.

'It won't take up much room,' the major said.

'Oh! no.'

'I've no luggage. I can sit anywhere.'

'I don't care!' Paterson said. 'Put the damn thing in the house.'

The major hesitated. It seemed to him for a moment that this was the solution of his personal problem. Because of the bicycle his indecision, made more wretched by the choice of Fielding and Miss Ross, could be ended now, once and for all.

'If I can't take the bicycle it's no use my coming either.'

Once again Paterson could not speak. Here they were about to start on a journey in which only life and food and water and fuel and luck were precious, and all Brain could do was to haggle over a bicycle.

'It might come in useful,' Brain said.

'In that country? Up there? Have you ever been up there?'

'You never know,' Brain said.

'There just isn't room! We may have Miss Ross and Miss Allison.'

'Miss Ross is not coming.'

Some people were coming; some were not coming; some had bicycles. Paterson felt impotent under the weight of a mass of idiotic triviality.

'Is Miss Allison coming?'

'It's not sure. If she's coming she'll be at the hospital gardens as we pass.'

'Considerate of her.'

Over at the mill the entire corrugated iron roof of the main building fell in at that moment with a roar like a single slab of hot metal thrown into a cauldron of water. In the orange fountain of sparks that illuminated all the compound, Paterson turned to see the face of the major motionlessly staring, infinitely saddened as he clutched at the bicycle he would not lose. It seemed to typify for a moment all the other faces, too brightly lit up, ghoulishly staring as if caught for a flash-light photograph, like a crowd of refugees, gaping and disinherited, clustering about the cars in the compound.

And he felt suddenly that he understood the major. A fraction of the tolerance he had known in the morning came back.

'All right: strap the damn thing on the petrol trailer.'

The major, oblivious of greater calamities, pushed the bicycle slowly away. It brought Paterson's anger rushing back.

'And hurry, for God's sake. We're ready to go!'

In the centre of the compound the jacaranda tree, in the orange light of a million sparks, seemed to blossom among its tender leaves like a tree of smouldering bluish-purple, itself a gentle fire. Over by the Buick he found Tuesday staring at it in a dream. And for a moment Paterson stood looking at it too. Behind it the fire of the burning mill was so vast that it seemed as if it might rush forward and suddenly consume, in a second or two, all the little umbrella of glowing flower.

'Ready, Tuesday?'

The boy smiled magnificently. Under one arm he was clutching the radio set. He had no other possessions except the football jersey, the shirt and, even in the moment of calamitous departure, the defeatless smile.

'Ready, Patson sir.'

55

'Nadia ready?'

For a moment the smile went from the boy's face. As if for a second the fire had gone out and left it dead, he stood staring beyond the jacaranda tree without a word.

'I said is Nadia ready? Where is she?'

'In house, Patson sir.'

'Is she ready? Fetch her.'

'Nadia not coming, sir,' he said.

Once again for a moment the boy did not smile.

'Not coming,' he said.

Paterson did not speak again. He walked slowly past him, past the Bettesons and Mrs McNairn and Mrs Portman, who stood watching Major Brain and Portman strapping the major's bicycle on to the trailer of Portman's car. He did not speak to them but walked slowly up the steps of the verandah into the house.

Inside, the rooms were in darkness except for the light of the fire. The power station had gone up at eight o'clock. Through the curtainless windows the light came with flickering brightness, as far as the foot of the stairs.

He remembered then that he had hardly seen the girl at all that day; he had hardly spoken to her from the moment he had woken, faced with all the calamity of the day, until the moment he had set off the fuse to blow the mill.

And somehow he knew that it was because of that that she was not coming with the rest of them. He knew that he had hurt her by what must have seemed neglect and preoccupation. He stood at the foot of the stairs gently calling her name into the dark house and knowing somehow too, that she would not answer.

She did not answer. He did not call again but walked slowly upstairs, feeling his way out of the half-light into the darkness and then into the upper light of the landing beyond. He went straight along the landing and into his own room and then out of it, quietly, through the gauze doors, to the balcony outside.

'Nadia,' he said. 'Where are you?'

He walked quietly along the balcony. Now in the light of the fire he could see her lying on the bed, and in a moment he knelt down beside her and put his hands against her face.

'Nadia,' he said. 'Little one.'

She did not speak.

'Time to go.'

As she turned her face he saw it fixed and immobile, black eyes staring straight up at the roof above her. She lay with her body rigid, arms like two golden pieces of bone clenched against the edges of the purple skirt, where her thigh shone like a long arrowhead in the light.

'Little one,' he said.

He leaned down and pressed his mouth in the upper hollow of her thigh, where the skirt fell away. In the same moment he felt the last of the day's irritation, its fatigue and its impatience, go out of him. It fell away as the skirt fell away from her body; as something artificial, not part of him; as a covering falling away to leave only the true clean self, simple and tender as her own body, below.

In a moment she stretched down her two hands and held them against his face, pressing his face at the same time harder and harder into the shape of her thigh. And as he lay there it occurred to him suddenly that it was an act of farewell. She was really not coming; she was really saying goodbye there, without a word, in the light of the fire. And the agony of it made him leap up again and put his hands on her face.

'Nadia. We're going. It's time.'

'No.'

'It's time. Where are your things?'

For the first time she turned her face towards him. Where she had turned away, pressing her face on the bed, the flower she wore in her black hair had flattened itself out like a scarlet saucer.

A moment later she began to smile. He knew then that she was smiling because of his question: because she had no things, because she had less in the world even than the boy, with his broken radio set and the faded football shirt. All that she had in the world, like the boy, was himself. And for a moment he saw her against the Europeans who stood waiting in the compound below, hands clutching possessions, minds possessively desiring the things they could not have: the Bettesons, with their luck and their Buddha, the major with his bicycle, the Portmans with their ambitions and their curtains, Mrs Portman with her delightful body, the McNairns who wanted himself. He saw them clearly and was not angry. The tenderness he felt for her and which now rushed up through his body warmly seemed to cut him off from the current of all outside emotion and leave him happy.

Once she had smiled he knew that everything would be right again. She sat up on the bed and he smoothed her hair with his hands. And then suddenly he could not bear the thought of her coming without a possession of even the simplest kind; and he made her get up from the bed, so that he could fold up the blanket for her.

'It may be cold at night,' he said.

'Shall I sleep with you?'

'Yes.'

'How?'

'Under this blanket.'

'Always with you?'

'Yes.'

'Then I shan't be cold,' she said. She put her mouth against his face, rubbing it softly. She took the blanket from him, folding it up. She carried it in her arms with some of the air of intense and cautious pride that the boy had in the radio set and the shirt. As they went downstairs he saw her smiling in the light of the fire.

Ten minutes later the two cars drove out of the compound. There was some final argument and difficulty about the seating. The possibility of Miss Allison still having to come rather upset things, and Mrs Betteson kept saying loudly:

'Let that lamb of a boy sit on my knee! I don't mind a scrap!'

Finally the Portmans, Mrs McNairn and Connie and Major Brain rode in the Portmans' car. Mrs McNairn had begun to cry and Portman felt glad that he was not Major Brain, pressed in with her snivelling at the back. The Bettesons rode in the back of Paterson's car, leaving room for Miss Allison if she came. An Anglo-Burmese girl would be less of an embarrassment to the Bettesons than to the Portmans and Mrs McNairn. This left Paterson on the front seat with Nadia and the boy: the girl with the blanket still folded in her arms, the boy with the radio set on his knees and the smile even larger on his face as he pressed forward to see the road in the light of the headlamps and the fire.

The two cars pulled up at the gardens of the hospital, on the north edge of the town. It had been very slow driving out there. Out of the town, northward, people were trooping in long procession: on foot, on bicycles, in bullock-carts that no longer kept to the bullock tracks, in low rolling buffalo-carts, in rickshaws that danced like fireflies, in cars, in open-window trucks and buses.

At the hospital gardens Major Brain got out of the car and walked along the road to look for Miss Allison, the nurse. It was some time before he fought his way back with her to the car. Paterson, leaning out of his driver's window, saw her blown out of the shouting crowd of refugees like a pale cream feather. She had the long slender legs of the half-caste; the pained distant eyes, deep smoky-amber underneath, as if from bruising; and the melancholy air of delicate pride.

'In the back with Mr and Mrs Betteson,' he said. 'Glad we found you.'

She smiled sleepily without opening her lips and got into the back of the car with the Bettesons, and Major Brain shut the door.

'Room for a little 'un,' Betteson said, and moved over against the window so that she could sit between himself and Mrs Betteson, who said once again, 'That lamb of a boy could easily have sat on my knee. I wouldn't mind!'

As the girl sat down and the car moved away, into the stream of faces that turned towards the light of it like so many gold-white flower heads blown that way by a single wind, Betteson took something out of his jacket pocket nearest the nurse. Secretly he put it into his other pocket and sat clutching it with his hand.

It was the bronze Buddha Paterson had angrily thrown across the compound as something that was not wanted. Betteson could not help thinking that there had never been a moment when he had wanted it so much as now.

It was the thing to bring them luck.

6

Waking in the morning, the boy had nothing to fix his direction but the northern hills. They lay like bars of warped steel, gently undulating, purple-blue, under the burning salmon rim of sky. Between them and the two cars, driven off the road and parked on dry rice-stubble, the tents not pitched, lay the plain, emptily huge and yellow except for the intersections of scrub and track between cropless rice-fields. Above scattered water-holes squares of palms sprouted like painted brushes, and over the wide dust wandered a few white egrets, like tired bird-moths that had settled in the night and could not find their way.

Once he had fixed the northern hills the boy had nothing to worry about. He knew the country very well; he had been far beyond it several times with Paterson. The exodus for him was no more than another journey. He knew that in the south cataclysmic things might be happening; he knew of the Japanese; he knew that the turn of war had become very bad because Paterson said so. But the centre of his life, Paterson, was not affected. Paterson was with him. He did not care about other people. Paterson had to be cared for, guided, succoured, obeyed, and protected through whatever circumstances the journey might bring. That was very simple.

When he got up from under the car, where he had dozed for the last two hours of the night, he was surprised to see Mrs Betteson already awake and out of the car. She stood watching the sun come up over the hills and when she saw the boy she waved her hands ecstatically.

'Ah! There you are! Isn't it nice, isn't it wonderful? Like picnicking.'

The boy nodded and smiled. It no longer worried him very much that Mrs Betteson was mad; she was just another person. There was nothing strange to him in the way she constantly giggled and waved her hands. Plenty of people, he thought, were like that.

'What are you doing? What are you going to do?'

'Get fire,' he said. 'Breakfast.'

'Marvellous. Can I help? Can I do something?'

'Please,' he said.

As she wandered away across the dust, vaguely gathering wisps of rice-straw and fronds of bamboo that winds had blown down from the road, two hundred yards away, she occasionally stopped, like a lost gleaner, and stared at the traffic coming down the road. She had heard the noise of it all night. Bullocks and buffaloes, bicycles and rickshaws, hand-carts and barrows, people walking; women with children on their backs and bedding on their heads; men running elastically in the dust, balancing baskets like scales. Sometimes a motor car, driving on its horn. The road seemed to be covered with a stream of brown and purple flies creeping north-eastward to the sun.

When she got back to the cars the fire was already burning and the boy already had the kettle on its wire sling.

Paterson was awake and the Burmese girl was dragging a foodbox across the dust.

'I was saying to your boy it was like picnicking, Mr Paterson. Good morning!'

'Good morning. Sleep all right?'

'Not a wink! I like my bed. Is there something I can do?'

'Call the others,' he said.

Still clutching the gleanings of rice-straw and bamboo she walked over to the Portmans' car, but Major Brain was already up, and like a true soldier was shaving with an egg-cup of water and a steel mirror behind the car, and in another moment she saw that the Portmans and Mrs McNairn and Connie were getting out of the car too.

'I'm supposed to call you!' she said and giggled.

By the time she got back to the Buick the only people who had not stirred were Betteson himself and the nurse. Mrs Betteson peered into the back of the car. Betteson was sprawling across the seat and one of his hands was lying across the naked arm of the girl. Mrs Betteson stood staring for a moment or two before she tapped the window. The girl was still in her nurse's uniform. Exhausted, she had gone to sleep long before the cars had stopped, and now it seemed as if nothing would wake her. But it was not this or even Betteson's hand lying across the girl's too slender dusky-cream arm that affected Mrs Betteson. What she had not realized was that Miss Allison was half-caste, and the discovery took a little of the dithering morning joy out of her face as she tapped the window.

Waking and seeing her face outside, peering in at him with that gaunt curiosity he knew so well and hated so much, Betteson felt immediately that she was spying on him.

He gave a furious grunt and got out of the car, swinging the door angrily back so that it hit her. Nothing of this surprised Mrs Betteson and it did not wake the nurse.

'I'll bung your eyes in one of these days,' Betteson said. 'I'll bung 'em in, I tell you! And then perhaps you'll see something you ain't lookin' for!'

'I only wanted to wake you,' she said.

'Well, I don't want waking! I can wake myself, can't I?'

'Yes, Joe.'

'Well, for Christ's sake don't stand there!'

She walked vaguely away with the dry husks of straw and bamboo still in her hands. In the car the nurse did not wake and over by the Portmans' car, where Portman was doing the thing he loathed most in the world, shaving in cold water, Mrs Portman stood looking at the Bettesons and said:

'If that's the sort of delightful domestic scene that's going on, I shall wish we'd come alone.'

'And you won't be the only one wishing that,' Mrs McNairn said. 'I wished it from the first.'

'I think we're safer together,' the major said.

'I can't think why you say safer,' Portman said. 'I worked it out on the map and I should say we'll make Kohima in three days. Or somewhere that way.'

'Somewhere that way,' the major said.

'Well, let's hope it's no longer,' Mrs Portman said. 'One of my pet aversions is living in suitcases.'

'Where's Connie?' Mrs McNairn said.

'Probably gone to pick daisies,' Mrs Portman said. 'That's another of my pet loves.'

'It'll be a bit more civilized when we get the tents up,' Portman said.

'I see Connie over with Paterson,' the major said. 'Cutting bread.'

Mrs McNairn had not time to recover her astonishment or her feeling of affronted annoyance before Paterson called that breakfast was ready. Connie was already pouring tea into a number of large white cups and Paterson was taking them from her and handing them round.

Then in another instant Mrs McNairn's abrupt annoyance had gone. It was replaced by the first touch of anything like a pleasant feeling she had experienced since Paterson had sent that extraordinary message by Betteson. She had cried most of the night before and she hadn't slept. Now, when she saw Connie and Paterson engaged in the simple business of buttering slices of bread and pouring cups of tea, she felt startlingly touched. It suddenly occurred to her that she ought to be nicer to Paterson; that this dreadful trip might, after all, turn out to have something good in it; that it might reveal in Paterson, as exceptional circumstances did in men, the beginnings of a little decency.

But I am not, she thought, falling over myself. I shall not concede anything. I shall come to it gradually. And I shall see to it that Connie comes to it gradually. She's not going to give herself away.

As she walked over to the fire the boy met her with a cup of tea in the saucer of which was a slice of bread and butter.

'What sort of milk is it?' she said. 'Cow milk or buffalo?'

'Cow milk, yes,' the boy said.

'That's all right,' she said.

The milk of buffaloes was something she could not bear. She had something of the same physical-spiritual aversion to it that the Hindu has for the eating of pig. It made her sick. And mentally she said a little prayer over the good, hot, English-tasting tea and the bread on which the butter was already melting a little in the rising warmth of day.

And then as she reached the fire there was a burst of laughter. She looked up to see that Mrs Betteson had never put her bunch of rice-straw and bamboo-husk on the fire. She was standing absently holding it in one hand, with her tea in the other. Now and then she held the straw half-way to her mouth, dreamily as if she were going to eat it. And now the burst of laughter was because she had actually taken a straw in her mouth and was chewing it slowly, with that infantile vacuous smile.

Betteson was furious; but to everyone else, standing there in the sun that had already begun to burn up the purple ridges of the northern hills and leave them smouldering in the late smokiness of sunrise that was really the beginning of heat-haze, it seemed like a moment of wonderfully good humour for the beginning of the day.

Only Nadia and the boy, sitting apart on the running-board of Paterson's car, did not seem to see anything very amusing in Mrs Betteson's absent-minded childish error; or in the laughing faces.

'Absolutely the damn funniest thing I ever saw,' Portman said. 'The cream of it was she didn't know.'

He had put on a pair of dark sun-glasses and was staring forward at the road, following Paterson's car at a distance of about three hundred yards, as far as possible out of dust range.

'We ought not to laugh at the old thing,' Mrs Portman said.

'There's a story that she put her best straw hat under the toast grill and the toast on her head,' Portman said. 'One Sunday.'

'The town was full of stories about her when I first came,'
Mrs McNairn said. 'Thirty years ago.'

'She'll keep us from getting bored anyway,' Mrs Portman
said.

'Oh! by the way, Major,' Portman said. 'To change the subject. While I think about it. What about the boy?'

'The boy?' the major said.

'I thought if we clubbed round.'

The major did not speak. For some reason he was uneasy
and could not get Miss Ross out of his mind. Nor did he quite
know what Portman was talking about.

'I thought perhaps ten chips apiece would do it. Wonderful
what it does. What do you feel?'

Sitting by the window, staring at the bullock tracks that lay
on either side of the road, deep gorges of dust through which
the ponderous lumbering carts, the iron-grey buffaloes, the sad
grey oxen and the streams of men and women were ploughing
sombrely in a yellow cloud under the trees, Connie McNairn
was not listening to the talk going on between the Portmans,
her mother, and the major. She had not been very amused at
the joke of Mrs Betteson eating the straw. She had been thinking at that very moment, much as she was now, of Paterson. It
had seemed a very wonderful thing to be standing there, in the
open air, at the beginning of a journey of which no one could
know the consequences, pouring out tea, and cutting bread
and butter. It had seemed extraordinarily miraculous to be doing these simple things.

Now, as she sat looking out of the window, she found the
thought of Paterson stimulating once again the recollection of
the time she had come back from England. She remembered
how the boat had called at Calcutta and how she had spent the
day with some Scottish friends of her father's, in one of the
jute mills up the river, somewhere off the road to Barrackpore.

She remembered the rancid dark odours of the bazaars as
she drove out there; the women kneeling beside the hovels by
the roadside, making eternal cakes of cow-dung and plastering
them on the walls to dry; the women crawling on railway

tracks, grovelling like hungry scraggy fowls for cinders; the dark, stoical, bruised faces; the stench of vulture-infested cows ripe in the great heat; the dust and flies on fruit and lips and eyes and dogs and all the trees by the roadside; and the bullock-tracks in the suburbs of the city, the oxen and buffaloes laboriously struggling, dusty and wretched, under the great trees of scarlet flame-flower, on just such journeys, into just such unknown distances.

That had been the first blow at her remembered romantic notions of what the East was like; and Paterson was the second. Now because of them she felt ready for what she saw. She had not the long ingrained experience of Burma, of the little English community, parochial as a cathedral town at home, that coloured all her mother's attitude. Her mother could hardly have known less of the East, certainly less of the road now clotted across all its width with the nearest thing the girl had seen to the rancid running crowds of Calcutta, if she had stayed at home in Winchester. The girl herself did not know much more; but she felt she was trying to know. And she was beginning also to be a little frightened as she sat there: frightened and horrified, horrified and fascinated, fascinated and repelled, by what she saw. Something about the stream of black and brown and purple beetles, ploughing through the dust, had in it the beginnings of a hungry terror.

Violent bumpings and jerkings at the back of the car shook her out of her recollections at last, to hear Mrs Portman say:

'Is this the only road? This is frightful.'

'How far do you calculate we have of this?' Mrs McNairn said.

'I did the map very carefully with calipers yesterday,' Portman said. 'I should say six or seven hundred miles. Awfully hard though to judge the contours.'

Yes, the major thought, it was awfully hard to judge the contours.

Portman blinked a little and felt his eyes, even behind the dark glasses, strained and tired. Already the sun, glittering sharply back from the crystalline surfaces of track and fields, struck in past the edges of the spectacles, as with the light of reflected glass. The car, which had begun by doing about fifteen miles an hour, was now sometimes down to ten; it was running quite hot whenever he was down in gear.

Still, he thought, even at ten miles an hour they could do a hundred a day, and like that a week would see them through. That would be very good going on roads like this. He would mark their progress on a map each day.

When they camped at noon, they were all a little cramped and tired, and Miss Allison, the nurse, was still asleep and no one woke her. Apart from this nothing unusual had happened except that Mrs Betteson, living out her dream, still carried in one hand the remains of her gleanings of bamboo and straw.

And to Mrs Portman it was still terrifically funny.

7

By evening the two cars had worked ahead of the stream of refugees. Only the bullock tracks were dotted with the dusty purple-brown procession of people and beasts, the dust rising like sulphur smoke, hanging low above the parallel lines of trees like part of the heat haze. Northwards the mountains did not seem, in fifty miles, to have come any nearer. They seemed rather to have grown more and more fragile, infinitely pallid against the steely glare of sun, only gaining colour, the tenderest dusky rose, as evening came. Far across the yellow plain they seemed like unattainable clouds.

The problem of sleeping was much the same as the problem of seating, except that it was complicated by the sexes and Miss Allison, who was Anglo-Burmese. She was still asleep at five o'clock, when the cars pulled off the road and parked on the border dust of a clearing of bamboo.

There were three tents, and it seemed to Paterson that it would present the least of complications if Mrs McNairn, Mrs Portman and Connie slept in one; Portman, Major Brain and Betteson in the other; and Miss Allison, Mrs Betteson and Nadia in the third. Tuesday and himself would sleep in the car.

He explained this while Portman, Major Brain, Betteson and himself were putting up the tents in the evening sun.

'Now, wait a minute, old man,' Betteson said. 'That raises some tricky issues.'

'I've been working it out all day, and I think it's the best we can do.'

'Not for me it ain't,' Betteson said. 'I've lived in this bloody country for thirty years and my wife's never slept with natives and half-caste bitches yet, and she's not going to start now.'

'I think that a bit thick, Betteson,' Portman said. 'After all—'

'After all what?' Betteson said. 'Why doesn't your wife try it, eh?'

Portman did not speak. He wanted to say that after all Mrs Betteson was batty; that she was hardly a woman to notice these things, walking about as she did with straw in her hands.

'Go on, let her try it,' Betteson said.

Paterson walked tolerantly round the entire circumference of the tent, tightening each guy-rope. He had known that something of this was bound to happen and he wanted to keep it, by his own tolerance, a little thing.

When he got back to the mouth of the tent he was surprised to see Connie there, with Mrs McNairn. Betteson had begun shouting something about his wife being as good as the rest of them.

'If there's any difficulty I'll sleep in the tent with Miss Allison,' Connie said.

'You'll do no such thing, you'll certainly do no such thing!' Mrs McNairn said.

'It's very simple.'

'It's not very simple!'

'Why isn't it simple?' the girl said. 'Three girls in one tent. That's very simple.'

'On the contrary nothing could be more difficult.'

'How is it difficult?'

'Never mind how it's difficult or why it's difficult.'

'If you're going to talk about being difficult I think it's all very difficult for Mr Paterson.'

'It's one of those monstrous things and I don't want to talk about it.'

'Please let me,' the girl said. 'I'd rather do that than sleep with the rest of you.'

'Thank you,' Mrs Portman said.

'Well, I tell you flat my wife won't do it!' Betteson said.

Except for Mrs Betteson herself, who was with the boy at the evening fire, they all stood about the tent, arguing. Only Major Brain had walked away. Mrs McNairn, Mrs Portman, and Portman himself all wanted to say the same thing. They wanted to say that Mrs Betteson was batty anyhow and did not know colour from white any more than she knew straw from bread; so what could it matter anyway? But Betteson, furious, kept raising his voice in defence of her, as if she were something he doted on.

'I think Connie should know her own mind,' Paterson said.

'Oh! you do, do you?'

'It could all be so simple,' the girl said.

'She made up her own mind once,' Mrs McNairn said, 'and what did you do?'

'My wife and I'll bunk up in the car,' Portman said.

'That only shelves the issue!' Betteson shouted.

'And what did you do? You treated her like dirt, that's what you did. And you've gone on treating her like dirt. And now you want to treat her like dirt again – worse than dirt –'

'This is a bit much,' Portman said.

Mrs Portman, fascinated by the utter calmness of Paterson, had nothing to say. Once again she felt transfixed and faintly excited.

'The girl shall not be humiliated,' Mrs McNairn said.

'Earear,' Betteson said.

'Nobody is going to humiliate her,' Paterson said. 'Certainly not Nadia and Miss Allison.'

'Nor you, I suppose. You're not in England now, Mr Paterson, where you can get away with anything and these things don't matter. You're in Burma where these things do matter.'

Over by the fire the sound of Mrs Betteson laughing idiotically seemed to strike a curious light note of mockery that made Paterson smile.

'Nor am I here to be laughed at!'

Suddenly Connie began crying and Mrs Portman put her arm about her and began to lead her away. Mrs McNairn made a high acrobatic sort of gesture of protest, violently raising her arms, so that Portman could see the sweaty paler parallelograms of silk under her armpits. Betteson stood there like an enraged pig, yellow with sweat, head down, as if in anger he wanted to rush at something and smash his skull.

The whole thing was a bit much, Portman thought, and simply came from people not playing the game.

'There's nothing in you!' Mrs McNairn shouted. 'There's not a decent thread of anything in you. There never was.'

Portman began to walk away. Paterson shouted after him:

'Portman! give Major Brain a hand with the other tent! It'll be dark in half an hour.'

'All right, all right,' Portman said. 'Keep calm.'

Paterson too began to walk away.

'You're afraid to listen to me because you know what I say is right and because you're afraid to listen to me!'

Mrs McNairn began weeping too. Then at the same moment Mrs Betteson, over by the fire, once again began laughing the gay idiotic laugh that had made Paterson smile. This time he did not smile and it was Betteson who walked away.

'You make me wish to God we could go on alone!' Mrs McNairn shouted. 'By ourselves! Without you!'

Once more the faded parallelograms that were never to be revealed became revealed, ugly and sweaty, as she lifted her arms, and over by the fire Mrs Betteson, enjoying herself enormously with something, let out a new giggling scream of joy.

Betteson, astounded, angry and pig-like still, watched her for another moment or two before he moved. She was squatting down on her haunches by the fire. On the other side of the fire the boy was standing with the kettle in his hands. From the fire she had taken a little length of smouldering bamboo and now she was smoking it, saying at the same time, over and over again, that she loved playing with fire. She had never smoked in her life before, and now as she drew the smoke in through her faded lips the grey pupils of her eyes seemed to bubble up and down in the wide distended whites as if they were really boiling with joy.

In another moment Betteson knocked the smoking cigar of

bamboo out of her mouth with a blow that flattened her back-ward off her haunches.

'Don't act so damn wet!' he shouted.

And on the other side of the fire the boy stood with the kettle in his hands. Speechless and not smiling and not moving, he felt in that moment that he rather liked Mrs Betteson after all.

Later in the dark evening the major walked up through the clearing of bamboo to where the ground rose, free of scrub, above the road. It was very dark and the entire sky, even down to the iron corrugations of mountain beyond the plain, had cleared to a great purity in the night air. There were no houses, and here not even the steely fringes of palms, to cut into the expanse of stars. They were scattered above him like green and yellow seed, with that intense brightness of which in all his years in Burma he had never tired.

The squabble about the tents had been solved, and back in the camp he could see the hurricane lamps shining orange through the pale sepia canvasses. These lamps, with a light or two that crept like a glow-worm along the bullock-tracks below, were all that broke the lower darkness of the plain.

And after all the squabble about who should sleep with whom had turned out to be very simple. Miss Allison had solved it all by not waking. Paterson himself had covered her with blankets in the back of the car and the boy was to sleep in the front seat, in case she woke and wondered where she was. The men were to sleep as arranged and Connie and Nadia were to sleep together. In the end Mrs McNairn had given in partly because from weeping she could not argue any more and partly from a sense of martyrdom. It had given her a chance after all of showing herself to be capable of something in the higher decencies, a little above Mister Paterson.

It was after eleven o'clock when the major reached the rise of ground. He could not sleep and yet, except for an occasional thought of Miss Ross, back there at the hospital, he was quite happy. Something about the hurricane lamps shining through the sepia-orange canvasses of the tents seemed to him extraordinarily eternal. Like the sky of the East, like the shining sowing of stars, like the smell of dust in the darkness faintly scented by invisible flowers from the trees by the road, it was a changeless thing. If you looked back, through the wars, this was the thing about war that had not changed: the hurricane lamp hung by the tent-pole, the orange glow, the dying fire outside, the infinite sense of tranquillity that the creeping shadows on tent walls gave.

And as he walked back to the camp, watching the stars and the settling shadows moving under the orange cubes of light, he was troubled only by a small sense of desertion, in that he was not only leaving Burma, but Miss Ross, who stood for so much that was most beautiful and most permanent in the country.

This feeling continued to gnaw at him a little as he came back to the tent and he counteracted it by going to contemplate his bicycle. It was still strapped to the back of Paterson's car, and he stood for some minutes looking at it in the quiet glow of light, rather as another man might have taken a final look at his horse. He was very glad Paterson had allowed him to bring it; he did not dislike Paterson and he was relieved that that simple problem had been solved.

As he contemplated the bicycle for a few moments longer the light in Miss McNairn's tent went out, and then as he moved away Portman and his wife came up from the lower clearing of bamboo.

'Very quiet,' Portman said.

'Wonderful.'

'I was just saying you'd think the war was a million miles away. So peaceful. Hardly think we were part of it.'

'No,' the major said, 'just so,' and as he walked away, saying good night, the fragment of his uneasiness about Miss Ross and the fact that he himself seemed to be getting a smaller and not larger part of the war began to itch again in his mind.

The Portmans said good night and stood for a moment before separating. Somewhere on the other side of the Buick Paterson was lying half under the car, covered with blankets.

Portman spoke in a whisper and took the arm of Mrs Portman and moved her away.

'Well, that's what I shall do. The slightest friction and I shall put the cards on the table and we'll go on separately. After all, in India I'll join up and Paterson can go to hell.'

'All right. Good night now.'

'It's a question of everyone playing the game. If he doesn't we don't.'

'Yes. Good night now,' she said.

'Good night.'

'I don't think I shall undress,' she said. 'The whole thing's a bit crummy.'

In the tent beyond Mrs Portman's Connie lay staring up in the darkness. She had undressed and had put on her pyjamas and had brushed her hair. She did not want to sleep. She wanted to get up and find Paterson and explain about the things her mother had said. She wanted to tell him that there was no truth in those things; that to her there had never been any humiliation, any sense of social wrong, any effrontery. She knew where Paterson was sleeping; by the Buick, half under the car. It needed courage to get up in the darkness and go to Paterson and wake him if necessary and say those things. But sooner or later they had to be said. This journey was not like life back in the town, with the mill, the Swimming Club, the English Club, and all those things. Everything was breaking down; it was very different now.

She waited for a few moments longer, listening for a movement from the girl in the other bed. It was utterly still and there was no sound from outside except briefly, from deeply across the plain, the sound of jackals crying with their echoing human wail. She waited for a second or two longer and then in the moment before she lifted herself up on her elbow Nadia got up and went outside. In the light that still came from the men's tent Connie saw the golden Burmese skin shining in the lamplight with the same silky tender sheen as a banana leaf would shine in the sun.

Under the Buick Paterson moved over, to let the girl come

in with him. She did not speak and he lay for some moments
holding her and then running his hands down her body, in
deep tender sweeps over her breasts and thighs. If the girl and
the boy conceived it as their duty, without ever saying so, to
protect him and go with him as far and wherever he wanted,
he in turn, without ever saying so, felt the same of them.

'I wanted to sleep with you,' she said.

'Yes,' he said.

'Can it be like this? Every night?'

'Yes. It can be like this.'

'For how long?'

'We have a long way to go.'

She did not speak and he held her quietly and calmly in the
darkness, his hands under her breasts, his head slightly upwards from hers as he listened to the voices of the jackals,
beginning again now, thinly haunting the darkness of the plain,
so remarkably like the wailing, squalling voices of the women
who had quarrelled that afternoon.

8

On the third day the mountains seemed to move forward, shaped at last. They appeared above the plain like giant crusts, mouldy with grey-green mosses, clear of haze. Out of the vaporous fragility given by great heat in the glitter of the sun, through the powder of microscopic dust, forest folded endlessly into forest over rising escarpments of rock, and the rock had the savagery of iron contorted harshly by sun. All of it was slung across the north horizon like a barrier in which there was no visible break that could have been a road.

By the middle of the afternoon of that day Paterson was worried by the running of the car. He drove all afternoon with his head forward, listening. Sometimes the engine coughed shortly and it was as if he were pressing the accelerator against nothing but wool; and then as the car coughed again the throat of the exhaust cleared itself with the sound of pistol fire.

When Paterson pulled up at last over the crest of the short rise the car had come up badly, without punch, and the Portmans' came up behind quite fast, Portman pulling up beyond Paterson before he realized quite what had happened.

He leaned out of his driving window and called back:

'Anything serious? Shall we hang on?'

'Don't know. Probably muck in the petrol. We'll camp, anyhow.'

Portman, switching off the engine of his car, felt suddenly and sharply annoyed. Everything had been going very well. They had pushed ahead of the main batch of refugees, and now they ran across them only as sporadic clusters of purple beetles crawling on the bullock tracks or the central road. They had overtaken long ago the first mad rush of rickshaws and bicycles and gharries and communal ancient buses and even the cars that had started from Shwebo. One of these cars had been driven by a Dutchman, who had called out from campground as they passed that the Japanese were already in Yamethin.

As Portman got out of the car Mrs Portman said: 'I think it's ridiculous camping at three o'clock. We lose hours. We'll get caught up in that mass of stuff again.'

'It's probably nothing,' Portman said.

'Well, I don't see why we should stop even if he does.'

The feeling had grown with her that the cars were no longer together; that they had separate destinies; and suddenly the effect of being for the first time in front of Paterson's car increased it. She felt as if it were a kind of triumph over Paterson, who dictated routes and times and stopping places and hours of rest and departure as if, she thought, the rest of them were children to be bullied and drilled. That side of Paterson's behaviour had become part of an intense picture. Like his behaviour at the club, it was an attraction that would not let her rest. It was constantly with her like the glassy irritation of glittering crystal dust, the heat of the afternoons, the awful shattering road that kicked her stomach like a mule and left her bruised and strained and miserable so that she could not sleep at nights.

Portman walked back to Paterson's car, and suddenly the road was split by repeated back-fires that reverberated from the rocks ahead like rifle fire. Mrs McNairn gave a little involuntary shriek and half-shouted:

'As if there were any need for that! I ask you!'

Paterson had the bonnet of the car open and was pushing the carburettor arm up and down, creating fierce revolutions. The exhaust fired its shattering gun-shot against the hills. Tuesday, holding the tool-kit ready for Paterson in case of need, had on his face a vast and joyful smile. The exhaust seemed to bring him the joy of a gunner playing with limitless artillery.

Something about that smile increased Portman's annoyance by another degree.

'What is it?' he said. The exhaust shot out its cracking back-fire so that Paterson could not hear. The heat from the engine roared out and met in one stifling breath the heat of the after-noon.

'What's up?' he shouted.

The engine died, leaving Portman shouting in the silence, comically.

Paterson laughed and the smile on the boy's face quivered with new delight. It seemed very rich to have the fun of Port-man and the artillery of back-fires at the same time.

Portman felt that he could have knocked him down.

'Well, what's up? What is it?' Portman said.

'Carburettor job. Probably a matter of cleaning jets, that's all. Can't tell till I get it down.'

'Do we have to stop? Must we?'

'It has to be done.'

'Yes, but I mean now.'

'I'm not tackling the hills on a dud carburettor. Even if I could.'

'It seems a ghastly waste of daylight time. We'll have the clots catch up on us.'

'It's their country,' Paterson said. 'They have a right to get out of it. We're all running anyway like hell.'

Portman stood impotent, unable for a moment to speak in the face of Paterson, too-calm, and the boy, too-smiling, and all the frustration the incident roused in him; and then Mrs Portman called back from the car:

'What's all the argument, darling?'

Paterson said: 'You'd better trickle down the hill and camp at the bottom. You may find water. I'll see what part of the job I can do here. If I can't finish it I can always coast down.'

'Well, I suppose we have to!'

Portman went back to the car. The Portmans with Mrs McNairn and Connie rode on down the hill. Betteson and Major Brain came to offer help to Paterson. Betteson had been sitting all afternoon pleasantly squashed against Miss Allison, who wore no stockings. Her legs had the delicate beauty of long peeled sticks that had grown golden cream in the sun and her slim neck, flowing down between the lapels of her nurse's tunic, had the same delicate colour before it faded into her small breasts.

'I'll manage with Tuesday,' Paterson said. 'You'd better carry the other tent down.'

'Good idea to carry it on my bicycle,' the major said.

Paterson, head under the bonnet of the car, was not really listening and he did not look up to see Major Brain wheeling the tent down the hill on his bicycle, or Betteson walking ahead of him with the nurse.

It was some time later when he looked up to see that Mrs Betteson was still there. She had come out of the car and was sitting on the running-board. Under Betteson's biscuit-brown topee, which she wore because Betteson had long ago bullied her into terror of the sun, she had something of the appearance of a caricatured missionary. Her eyes, from which all colour had faded in the bleaching white light of full afternoon, had a kind of prayerful caution as they looked up over the hills.

'There doesn't seem to be a road there at all.'

'One,' Paterson said.

'What happens if –' She left the rest of the sentence unspoken: partly from habit, partly because she felt her unspoken fears to be foolish things. For many years she had been ceaselessly told that she talked like that. Everything she said was the blabbing of a fool; Betteson was always saying so; but she had never really had the strength to put sanity into the things she said and did, or to protest against the idea that she was a fool, since the time of losing her first and only baby thirty years ago in the hospital at Mandalay. She had never felt quite right in herself since then.

What she really wanted to ask was what happened if you lost the road? Was there another one? Or supposing a bridge was down? Or supposing something blocked it? Could you get round?

Nadia came out of the car and stood by the bonnet, watching Paterson and the boy working on the carburettor.

And seeing her, Mrs Betteson forgot the question and the fears it brought about the hills. In the evenings, when she and Mrs Portman and Mrs McNairn were alone in the tent, the talk sooner or later was about the girl. It was obvious she was going to have a baby, Mrs Portman said. You had only to look at her to know.

Mrs Betteson stood for a moment gazing at the girl's full round breasts, and the body curving gently at the belly of the skirt; and then the words were out, in her foolish way, before she could stop them:

'I had a baby once. A long time ago.'

Nadia stood smiling: not with the habitual smile of service and joy, as the boy did, but with the politest smile of friendliness because she did not understand a word. With Paterson she spoke her own language. The boy was passionate in a desire to amplify his English with new words, even to bad words that Paterson did not teach or tolerate. She did not want to learn. It was as if it gave her greater secrecy with Paterson.

When Mrs Betteson had repeated what she had said the girl smiled again in answer. Mrs Betteson said: 'Doesn't she speak English? I thought she did, I thought she understood,' but Paterson, too busy with the carburettor, was even then not listening.

It was only when the girl spoke in Burmese that he pulled his head sharply up from the carburettor.

'I'm very busy, Mrs Betteson. What are you trying to say?'

'I thought she spoke English, I thought she understood. I was saying I had a baby once too.'

It flashed suddenly on Paterson what she was trying to say. Involuntarily he swung round with the spanner uplifted. In a moment the habitual terror of Betteson became for her a new terror of Paterson, whom she saw standing there as Betteson did, as if he would hit her.

'Have I said something silly?'

'Who says this? Who says it?' he said.

'Isn't it true? Have I said something wrong?'

'Who says it?' he shouted.

She stood there for a second staring at him with eyes that were distantly and bloodlessly pallid. They looked deathly. And sorry for her suddenly, he recovered himself.

'Mrs Betteson,' he said quietly. 'Who says this?'

'They say so.'

'They? Who's they?'

'Mrs Portman.'

He stood there for another moment impotently. Across the iron crustations of rock on the hills there seemed to bounce backwards, hitting the retina of his eyes with painful light, an awful flash of sun. He felt the pain melt through his body into anger.

And then he recovered himself again.

'You'd better go down with the others, Mrs Betteson. You'd better get some tea and rest.'

'Have I said something silly?'

'It doesn't matter.'

Half-blinded, the sweat pouring down over his brows into his eyes so that dust silted stingingly down into the pupils, he banged the spanner against the carburettor in grotesque efforts to loosen the nut that held the pipe. It resisted him until he began suddenly to swear against the entire soulless mechanics of the thing that had let him down.

And hearing it, as if it were directed against her, Mrs Betteson broke into a terrified shuffling run down the hill, raising dust like a runaway playful train.

When Major Brain came back up the hill with a message, bicycling slowly, the heat seemed to advance solidly against him, as if to knock him down. Even so, the necessity of carrying down the tent on the bicycle seemed to him a wonderful piece of sheer luck. It had given him more pleasure than anything else on the journey to bike the half-mile up the hill. In a wonderful way, even in that staggering heat, it had refreshed him.

Under the roadside palms Paterson seemed to be sorrounded by the crazy débris of several kits of tools. The sweat on his face had the bleared, green-brown oiliness of a stokehold engineer. And by his side the boy and Nadia, holding tools in their hands, stood with some of the scared anxiety of assistant of an operation gone wrong.

'Portman wondered –'

'Wondered what, for Christ's sake?'

'Well, he wondered how long you'd be.'

'And what the hell is he doing?'

'They're having tea.'

'Wonderful!' He reached out a frantic left hand towards the boy, yelling for a screw-driver. 'Nice of you to have brought some!'

The major, embarrassed, felt shaken. Gripping the handlebars of his bicycle he said he was sorry.

'I'm sorry I shouted. Not your fault,' Paterson said.

'That's all right. It's very hot. The whole thing is very trying. What shall I tell Portman?'

'What does it matter to Portman? It's not his car. The job has to be done.'

'I rather think they want to push on.'

'What makes you think that?'

'They haven't pitched tents.'

'Well tell them they can't go on! Tell them I cracked the damn pipe. Tell them not to be such damn fools!'

'How long will you be?'

'Tell them we'll be off by morning – perhaps!'

The major felt there was no more to say; he was very much with Paterson. It was very trying. Even as he stood there the heat kicked savagely down, seeming to bruise the top of his head. He personally would be glad to rest. And he felt rather mean about the tea as he lashed his bicycle on the back of the car and then walked away down the hill.

At four o'clock the Dutchman came over the crest of the hill in a cloud of yellow dust that was like a prolonged explosion, the dust cloud splitting up through the narrow gap of trees overhanging the road and forcing its way clear to the sun, belching outwards in sulphur fog over the bullock tracks, drowning the straggling Burmese in a solid spray of powder.

As the car passed Paterson, travelling too fast, the dust hit the side of the Buick and the raised bonnet, forcing its way under the chassis. It clouded up past the engine block and spewed full into the face of Paterson as he bent over there.

The Dutchman shouted something as he passed and then slowed down. He leaned out of his driver's window, hand against his mouth, as if about to speak again.

Then he saw Paterson. Through the creamy-sulphur fog he seemed to leap out from the bonnet. He carried the spanner. He swung it so fiercely that even in the fog of dust it seemed to leave his hand and come straight at the Dutchman's head. Instinctively the Dutchman ducked down and in the same moment put his foot hard on the accelerator and went on down the hill.

'Plenty of time!' Paterson yelled. 'They won't catch you!'

The Dutchman, hearing the words bellow through the thicker dust, saw Paterson once again madly waving the spanner. He concluded at once that Paterson had heard what he said. He did not agree with the answer, and it surprised him utterly that the man could be such a fool in the face of what was happening. The man was mad.

At the bottom of the hill he saw Portman: the car pulled off the road into terraced rice stubble, the tents not pitched, the four women sitting on the dust in the shade.

Portman was coming up from the water-hole with a green canvas bucket of washing water. The Dutchman leaned out of the window as he pulled up the car.

'Is that madman at the top of the hill one of your party?'

'The fellow doing the repairs? Yes.'

'The sooner he does that repair the better.'

'What's up?' Portman said. All over him dust was settling like sulphurous smoke, gathering heat from the air, covering him with gritty sweat. 'Where have you come from?'

'It's not where I've come from, my friend. It's where I'm going. Damn quick.'

Portman put down the bucket. The Dutchman began speaking in a lower voice.

'They're already trying to turn on the British. They butchered fifty on the railway station at Shwebo.'

'Who's they?'

'The Burmese. The fifth column.'

'I didn't know there was a fifth column.'

'You never do, do you?' the Dutchman said. 'That's why it's a fifth column.'

Portman felt himself go white and sick, the sickness part of the dust-choked heat, his fear breaking out of him in prickled sweat.

'I always knew there was a fifth column here. I always told the British so. They're treacherous people, these nice pleasant Burmans. We're just finding out.'

'Where did you hear this?'

'I tell you something else too. Only don't tell your ladies. Cholera. That's started.'

Suddenly Portman remembered what Paterson had said about cholera serum, and how, at the last moment, Miss Allison had failed to bring any with her.

'Of course the fifth column is half dacoit. But it's the same thing. One cuts your head off just like another.'

'Yes.'

'And I tell you something else. The whole of Burma is coming up this road about thirty miles behind you. They're all running. In one bloody great horde.'

'I thought that.'

'You don't want to think it, my friend. You want to get out.'

'Yes,' Portman said.

'Can I be of some help?' the Dutchman said. He was alone in the big American car. 'You know your way?'

'I think so.'

'You don't want to think! You want to get out. Quick.' He nodded back down the road. 'Before you're smothered.'

He smiled for a moment before letting in the clutch. Portman smiled too, not knowing why. Then as the car started forward down the hill he picked up the bucket of water and stood for a moment or two watching the ploughed-up column of dust come thickly between himself and the car. With the dust there once again whipped into his face all the dry concentration of heat, like a solid flame; and with the heat the new sweat of anxiety, the awful sick half-coldness of fear.

As Miss Allison began to walk up the hill, partly to ask Paterson how the repair was going, partly because she was tired of trying to get out of Mrs Betteson what Paterson had said to make her hysterical earlier in the afternoon, she was surprised to see Paterson coming down the hill, coasting the car.

The boy Tuesday was riding on one running-board and the girl on the other. The boy was smiling broadly and the breeze blew against the skirt of the girl, flattening it away from her bare legs. And with the boy's pink and brown football shirt and the girl's skirt of yellow and purple, the stripes running about her body like hoops, the cream blouse fluttering with the light transparence of wings, they had something of the look of two bright and powdery moths, clinging with dusky antennae to the car, innocent and happy.

As the car went past they called something to Miss Allison in Burmese, but she did not answer. She never spoke Burmese.

Walking back down the hill she was suddenly oppressed once again by the feeling of loneliness that had been with her ever since she had woken up in the car and had wondered, on the second day of the journey, where she was. She did not speak Burmese; she was not English; she was not of one world or the other. For a month now she had been on night duty at the hospital and that too produced in her a comparable sensation – a sensation of isolation, almost physical twilight, in a way indicative of all her life, all she was and all she stood for – neither of night nor day, one blood nor another.

It was a long spell of night duty at the hospital that had

made her very tired, putting her into that long exhausted sleep when she was quite oblivious of Betteson holding her arm, pressing himself close to her, for most of that second day. She had felt herself silently isolated on waking. She had not heard the argument as to whether it was fit that Mrs Betteson or Connie should sleep with her; but it made no difference; the echo of it was there. She did not belong to the boy and his sister, she did not belong to Paterson and the rest. Major Brain and Paterson had been very nice to her; she put them, in decency, side by side with Dr Fielding, at the hospital. But that did not destroy her feeling of inferiority; it hardly even lessened it. In some ways indeed it merely aggravated it, as if they were giving her that decency as a special dispensation against her Eurasian status. Not that it was a status – it was something infinitely less than that. It did not even come into the range of the colour problem, of whether black was fit for white, white finer than black, or whether the ways of one should be open to the other. She belonged only to the half-colour problem – the problem that was not much more than a sniff in the air, the problem of disinheritance of blood – the problem of the damned.

And now as she reached the bottom of the hill and walked over to where Portman's car was parked beyond the line of teak trees, on the ridge of rice stubble, she saw Paterson and Portman talking by Paterson's car.

It struck her sometimes that her father must have been very like Paterson; and her mother very like the girl whom she heard creep out of the tent at night to sleep with him under the car. Time and situation were a little different – but that, or something like it, was how her mother and father had behaved twenty years before on the sea-coast of the Arakan. Nobody in those days thought very much of a Burmese girl marrying an English trader or a planter or even an administrating officer. It was a very natural thing; sooner or later the man's fiancée turned up and the coloured girl went back to her people. Nobody thought much of that. Nobody thought much of the consequences either.

But she, here in the moment of Burma being split from top to bottom by the invasion and exodus of war, was one of the consequences. And because of it she was troubled rather as Major Brain was troubled – by whether she had any part in this journey, by whether she ought to stay behind, impersonal and succouring, with the people to whom she only half-belonged, or whether she ought to go on, escaping from them, with the English to whom she wanted to belong. Ever since she had woken up she had been troubled by that – more and more troubled until sometimes now she was sick with conscience and isolation.

Then as she went past Paterson and Portman she heard Portman say:

'He was quite definite about it, I tell you. Cholera has started, he said.'

The word did not surprise her. She knew if the exodus got out of hand cholera must follow; malaria and dysentry and even typhus almost certainly too. The heat was growing in violence every day and all across that dry plain, blistered white by sun, there was very little water except in the irrigation ditches and the water-holes. It did not take very long for cholera to begin.

She had enough sense to know at once why Portman and Paterson were talking alone. She had seen Portman talking to the Dutchman. The thought of cholera did not frighten her; but she knew suddenly that it was something that it was better the other women should not hear.

A moment later she was startled to hear Mrs Portman go past her, saying:

'There's nothing like getting it from the horse's mouth. I'm going to ask him what he said.'

Under the tree Mrs Betteson was still crying, in silly flutters of dying hysteria. A lot of unnecessary fuss had been made of it, Miss Allison thought, and as Mrs Portman went by she said:

'I think I should drop the whole thing if I were you.'

'You would what?'

'I think I should drop it all if I were you.'

'You don't happen to be me.'

'I know. But hysteria patients are like that. They keep on because they enjoy attention.'

'I don't care about hysteria! It's the truth I'm after.'

'All right. Have it your way.'

'And don't talk to me in that offensive way!' Mrs Portman said. 'I've had enough to put up with already!'

Mrs Portman walked straight over to Paterson and her husband. She felt intensely offended and infuriated by what the girl had said. It was typical of the whole Eurasian set-up. Too many of them were throwing their weight about as if they had social and educational equality. Too many of them were teachers and nurses, stuffed with half-baked psychology. Too many of them were growing far more superior and far more maddening than the Burmans themselves.

'Mr Paterson, I suppose you know we've had Mrs Betteson prostrate here all afternoon.'

'No,' Paterson said. 'I'm sorry. I didn't know.'

'Ever since you bullied her up there about something or other.'

'I don't remember bullying her.'

'She says you bullied her.'

Portman said: 'Look, dear. Mrs Betteson isn't that important.'

'You haven't had her on your hands all afternoon. It's not enough for her to be half-batty. She has to be hysterical too.'

Paterson began walking away. The carburettor would certainly not be finished that night and it was time to get the tents pitched.

'And you needn't think you can get out of it by walking away, Mr Paterson.'

'We have to make camp,' Paterson said. 'If you'd made camp, instead of fussing, Mrs Betteson would have been all right now.'

'We didn't make camp because of your wretched carburettor.'

'Well, we'll make it now.'

'Isn't the carburettor finished?'

'No.'

'When is it going to be finished?'

'I hope by tomorrow afternoon.'

'You hope! I think that's monstrous.'

Portman looked very worried and said:

'That rather alters things, Paterson, doesn't it? I mean –'

'You mean what?' Mrs Portman said.

'Oh! it's all right.'

'How does it alter things?'

'Nothing,' Portman said.

'You're keeping something from me. First you upset this mad woman and now this.'

'It isn't anything,' Portman said. 'Anything to matter.'

'Then if it isn't anything why talk about it and why don't you tell me?'

Paterson shouted across the clearing:

'Major Brain! Could you and Betteson start pitching, please! I'll be coming in a second.'

Portman felt relieved that camp was going to be made at last; and then Mrs Portman said:

'Things are trying enough without your being on his side.'

'I'm not on his side.'

'Then why don't you treat me with confidence! What were you hatching up?'

Paterson heard and, tired and very hot, his hands sticky with oil and his face caked with sweat intermixed with the dust the Dutchman had fired at him, he came back.

'Your husband has heard a rumour that cholera has broken out. I don't think it's true.'

'Why don't you think it's true?' she said. 'You talked about cholera serum.'

'That was an obvious precaution.'

'You wouldn't have wanted to take precautions if you didn't think there was a chance of it.'

Portman said: 'It's probably not true. It's probably malaria.'

'Of course that's a picnic too,' she said.

'Anyway, I wouldn't worry,' Paterson said. 'We have decent water and we can chlorinate it. All we have to do is stick together and take proper care.'

'It's all very well to talk about sticking together when you're going to delay us a day.'

'That can't be helped,' he said. 'There's nothing we can do about that.'

'I'm not so sure,' she said.

Paterson walked over to where Major Brain and Betteson, with Tuesday and Nadia, were putting up the tents. Already one tent was up, and the girl was brushing the floor with branches of palm frond, smoothing the dust flatly so as not to raise it. He stood looking down for a moment into the open tent, smiling. He was determined not to start a row; even the things Mrs Portman had said about the girl were not going to make him start a row. He felt convinced that the security of the party depended, largely, on decent cohesion, on giving and taking, on the smothering of the little differences. He did not believe the story about cholera. Malaria, yes; dysentery most likely. He bent down into the browny-orange shade of the tent, where the girl was kneeling, the fan of palm frond spread before her knees, which were pressed together, her hands fan-like too on the dust she had smoothed. She did not speak; but the way she looked up, eyes almost purple-brown and tender in the shadiness of the tent canvas, suddenly dispersed all the sharpest of his irritation, the edginess of his fatigue and sweat, his tenuous anger against Mrs Portman. For a moment he bent lower and held her hand with his two hands, feeling the smooth oil of the purple-black hair, spreading his hand downwards over her ears, tenderly, the flanks of hair empty and silky as ebony in his fingers.

'There's no flower in your hair,' he said.

'I will find one.'

'A red one.'

'I will find one,' she said.

Smiling, feeling that to see her without the flower in her hair was to see her only half-dressed, he was suddenly perturbed by the voice of Portman, outside the tent, behind him, in a half whisper:

'Can I have a word with you?'

Paterson drew back from the tent and Portman walked a little distance away.

'You see the point is this. It isn't only the cholera.'

'What else is it?'

'It seems there's a fifth column.'

'I'm not surprised.'

'They butchered fifty British in Shwebo yesterday.'

'There weren't fifty British in Shwebo to butcher.'

'These were on a train.'

'Who said this?'

Portman told how the Dutchman had stopped to tell the story, and Paterson remembered him.

'It's just the usual retreat story,' he said. 'They run to a pattern. Rape, cholera, murder, fire –'

'I can't help feeling this one isn't quite like that.'

'They're always like that.'

'The fact is my wife is awfully worried,' Portman said.

'Then tell her not to worry. The thing is to be patient and stick together and not worry.'

'She rather wants to push on.'

'That's idiotic.'

'I'm rather with her there, I'm afraid.'

Paterson did not speak.

'Speaking frankly,' Portman said, 'would it be all the same to you if we split and went on?'

'It would be all the same but it would be bloody silly.'

'Of course, I knew you'd say that.'

'If it's bloody silly I always say so.'

'The Dutchman said the whole of Burma was coming up behind us in one terrific great horde.'

'I shouldn't be surprised. They're bound to run.'

'Yes, but God knows we don't want to get caught in that.'

'If we're caught, we're caught. We've only got to die once. Don't be so bloody windy, man.'

'I'm not windy!' Portman said. 'I'm not windy!'

'Then go and tell your wife to stop being windy. We'll be off by tomorrow afternoon.'

For Paterson there was no more to say. He did not doubt that the situation, complicated as it already might be by disorganized refugees, perhaps still further complicated by malaria and dysentery and almost certainly by typhoid even if cholera were held back, might grow very difficult. It might even grow very dangerous; even terrible. Everybody was running; soon the stench, in that fierce March sun, would rise in the bullock tracks, and there would be no organization to stop the pillage of the water-holes. The pi-dogs and the vultures would begin to feed. But they themselves had good water; they could chlorinate it and boil it and take every care. He felt convinced they were well organized. Everybody was fit and the journey, except for the business of the carburettor and his own anger at the whole incident back on the hill, had gone quite well. The hills might be tough, but he knew the road, if you could call it a road, for about a hundred and twenty miles north-westward, roughly in the direction of the Naga country, but beyond that he did not know it and there were few who did. He could only guess what lay there. Soon the scraped-out terraces of blistered rice-field would give way to the wretched fields where nothing grew but the thinnest sesamum and millet, where in harvest the flocks of raiding paroquets were like hordes of banana-green locusts, ravaging the seed. It had always been a country of continual exodus up there: a wandering from place to place by lean cattle, lean men, sore-eyed children, women with the faces of teak-wood, an endless search for the hills' less bitter places. And soon all that would go, to be replaced by the folded parallels of forested rock, basaltic, bitter, waterless, like hills of iron veined with minutest cracks of sand scorched to whiteness by the long dry season, mockingly like rivers between the great sunless towers of forest and bamboo.

He alone of the party, except perhaps Nadia and the boy, knew what might possibly lie there, beyond the first friendly-looking terraces of rice, the recurrent villages still neat with huts of palm-thatch, the vines of betel and the shade of pipal and margosa, sweet in the evenings, over undisturbed compounds. It was not the things that lay behind him that troubled him, as they did Portman; but the things that lay in front of him. If he feared anything at all it was that the road might die up there, somewhere in the high jungle, between the foothills where they now were and the far tea country of Assam.

When he walked away from Portman, back to the tent where Nadia had been sweeping the floor, the girl had gone. The imprint of her knees, between the fan-like twistings of palm, was still clear in the dust of the floor, like a double hollowed shell.

As he turned away Mrs Portman advanced with Mrs McNairn.

'I hear you oppose the idea of our going on separately.'

'Nothing of the kind. We'll be away by tomorrow anyway.'

'Yes, but *when* tomorrow?' Anger had again made her excited and transfixed.

'I hope to get the pipe welded somehow back at the last village tomorrow morning.'

'But that's miles back.'

'About four,' he said. 'I can go on the major's bicycle.'

Mrs Portman alone had spoken; now Mrs McNairn said:

'I think you ought to know the Portmans, the Bettesons, Connie, and myself are all agreed we should go on.'

'You'd be very crowded,' he said.

'That Dutchman had an empty car. We ought to catch him up quite easily.'

Mrs Portman said: 'I don't see how you can stand there and oppose it. After all, we're free agents.'

'Quite,' he said.

'We're six English people. Whereas –'

'Whereas what?' he said.

'You're quite incapable of seeing reason,' Mrs McNairn said. 'You always were.'

'Whereas what?' he said.

Mrs Portman gave a deep breath and looked away to where, beyond the third tent, Tuesday was gently fanning the first curls of flame in the evening fire.

'Whereas we're just two whites, a half-white and a brown boy,' he said, 'and a girl that isn't going to have a baby.'

Mrs Portman looked terribly shocked and could not speak. He remained quite calm, so that even Mrs McNairn's flat stare of habitual hatred did not shake him.

For some seconds longer he stood there looking at the two silent women, aloof and affronted and even a little disappointed because they had failed to arouse him to expected anger, and then he let out:

'For Christ's sake go! Don't let me stop you! Go for Christ's sake and don't talk about it any longer!'

He turned away without another word, leaving them standing there by the tent, the face of Mrs Portman deadly white, the stuffed, hawk-like eyes of Mrs McNairn caught in an expression of hungry alarm as if he had thrown out some terrible ultimatum.

A moment later he saw the girl walking in from the forest fringe. She had in her hair the big scarlet flower he had so much wanted and in her hands little branches of frangipani and forest rose and flowery creeper – the flowers that she gathered every evening for the table in the tent of the Englishwomen, to make them feel more at home.

9

In her tent, Mrs Portman undressed, hesitated for a moment about the susceptibilities of Mrs McNairn, clasping her umbrella as she lay on the bed, and then turned her back on her and took off the last of her things. She stood for a second or two feeling the slight wind of evening blowing on her body through the tent aperture and then put on her dressing-gown. It was a gown of pure straw-coloured silk that folded over and tied with a sash of the same colour and she knotted it with a single tie.

When she went outside a few moments later there was a light in the tent where Major Brain, Betteson, and her husband were sleeping but there was no light by Paterson's car. The car stood forty or fifty feet from the tent and she walked towards it slowly, playing with the sash of her gown with her fingers, loosening it and tying it tighter and then loosening it again. When she reached Paterson's car she stood by the near front wing and for the first time stopped playing with the sash of her gown and rested her hands on the car instead.

'Mr Paterson.'

She stood for a moment waiting and then she spoke again, calling in a whisper.

'Mr Paterson.'

Paterson came out behind the far side of the car, still dressed, drying his hands on a towel.

'It's me,' she said. 'I hope I haven't disturbed you?'

He came and stood by the opposite wing of the car, still slowly drying his hands. She did not seem to know what to do with her own hands and began once again nervously playing with the sash.

'Something the matter?' he said.

'I came to apologize.'

'I can't think what about.'

She laughed very slightly. 'About that ridiculous business this afternoon.'

'Ridiculous business?'

'About Mrs Betteson and all that. It was my fault and I'm awfully sorry. All that argument about going on.'

'There needn't have been any argument,' he said.

'I know,' she said. 'That's what makes it so awfully silly. But whenever you and I get together it seems we start arguing.'

'I wasn't aware of that.'

'Well, at the pool,' she said. 'I suppose it was really my fault but you were awfully naughty really. You got me arguing and then I left my bathing costume.'

He had been working late on the car and now as he finished drying his hands he put them on the bonnet of the car, face downwards, suddenly tired. He did not speak again and after a moment or two she moved over to where he was standing, tying and untying the sash of her gown with the fingers of both hands as she went.

'I had to say I was sorry about the whole stupid thing,' she said. She gave the sash a sudden jerk, nervously, so that it tightened across her waist. She stood with her legs pressed against the wing of the car and the silk of the gown seemed to take on a sort of ripened shining tautness over the curve of her breasts and legs.

'It wasn't necessary,' he said.

'It was just one of those silly things,' she said. 'They start out of nothing and before you know where you are it's a shambles.'

'Yes.'

'I didn't awfully want to have any part of it, but then the wife really ought to argue as the husband does, I suppose, and that's why I came.'

He did not speak. Her hands picked nervously at the sash, which fell loose before she suddenly tightened it up again.

'I felt I couldn't sleep until I'd straightened it out.'

She was speaking all the time in a low voice, rather deeply. She had a habit of staring at the ground and then suddenly, in an intimate and disarming way, looking up.

'About this business of going on,' she said. 'Tell me.'

'There isn't anything to tell.'

He picked up the towel and although his hands were dry began automatically to wipe them again. He was staring in a tired way towards the tents, which stood like small orange-glowing houses against the dark trees, and it occurred to her suddenly that he was wondering about her husband. She moved several paces nearer to him, her hands not playing with the sash of the gown, so that its knot fell for a moment completely away. And then she said:

'I know Alec wants to go on, but then he's always an awful fuss-pot and you've only to say and I can argue him out of it.'

'You must do what you think best.'

She laughed and said: 'No: I want to do what you think is best.'

Her hands moved down to the sash as if to keep it from falling completely away but she did not grasp it and after a moment she felt the sides of the gown sliding gently apart; and then at the last moment she held them with the tips of her fingers, so that they were just together.

Then she said a surprising thing:

'Well, I mustn't stay here. Arguing back and forth. I'm getting chilly. I've nothing on my feet.'

The remark surprised him at once into looking down. She saw him in the faint light of the tent lamp glance quickly down at her feet, bare in the dust, and then at her fingers, holding like a single pin the edges of the gown just below her waist. She felt herself begin trembling and she thought 'I've only to open my fingers and everything will be different. Just two fingers. Not yet. In a moment. Then all that stupid business about going on alone will be settled. Because there will be no reason to go on,' and she felt her fingers slipping away. The silk of the gown slid through them softly and she felt for a moment the air begin to creep coolly on her legs and breast, reminding her of the feeling of grass on her skin after the luxury of water. The deep plum-purple of night sky, greenly and vividly wonderful with stars down to the far edges of hills, attracted her into throwing back her head and looking up. Her body was very brown between the pale lapels of yellow silk and she felt Paterson look up too. In that moment she put her hands up to her throat, feeling the sun-smoothed skin, and she let the gown slip away.

'Wonderful night. Wonderful to be talking to you for once and not arguing.'

He did not answer.

'I don't want to go on alone. I'd rather be with you. I know how right you are and that's what I meant just now.'

She spoke with her throat arched back, so that her body curved slightly back over the bonnet of the car, the gown falling completely away. She remained like that for half a minute longer, waiting for Paterson to speak, but he did not speak and at last she brought herself slowly upright.

She discovered then that he was not looking at her. He was looking once again at the orange-lighted tents and she, almost without thinking, still unperturbed and speaking with great softness, said:

'There isn't any need to worry. No one will come.'

He was leaning forward on the bonnet of the car, resting his face on his hands, watching for a movement in the lamplight, and after a moment, so that she could be closer to him, she twisted her body and leaned across it too. She felt the metal of the bonnet press warmly against her skin and she said:

'The car's still warm with the sun. Can you feel it? Feel it with your hands.'

She reached out to take his hand, wanting terribly to press it down on the still warm smooth steel, and then in the moment of reaching out and of saying, 'That's settled then, isn't it? We shall stay with you? I always felt it was right ever since that afternoon at the pool. I never meant it to be otherwise but you know how it is,' she saw his head jerk sharply up and over by the tents she saw the orange tent patterns broken by moving shadow.

Then in another moment she knew that it was not Portman who was moving there. All the sense of luxury and silence, of air cool on her body, of intimacy deepened by the need for whispers, shrivelled harshly as she saw the girl walk across the triangular shapes of light and move away from them towards the car. And suddenly her body between the open edges of the gown felt chilly and she whipped the sash across it, tying it savagely.

'If you'd have the decency to pay attention, one could arrange things. I came here to straighten things out but you simply don't care. Good night!' she said. 'I don't want to keep you!'

'Good night,' he said.

He did not move from his position of leaning across the bonnet of the car and as she hurried back across the dust between the car and the tents, tying the sash of her gown furiously as she went, her fingers trembling, she thought: 'And for that we shall go. He doesn't care a damn about us and he never did care and now for that we'll go the way we want to.'

She felt herself trembling violently, half-crying with dry, tearless anger as she folded her arms across her chilly body. 'No Mr Paterson,' she thought, 'is going to tell us what to do.'

10

When he bicycled back from the village just before noon on the following day, the pipe repaired after some difficulty because even there the exodus fever was beginning, aggravated by wild rumours that the Japanese had bombed Rangoon and left it nothing but a burning wilderness of ravaging vulture and pi-dog and crow gorging on streets of scorched and rotting flesh, he knew at once by the way Major Brain and Tuesday were waiting for him on the hilltop, the boy without a smile on his face, that the Portmans had gone.

'I feel in some way it's my fault,' the major said. 'I ought to have dissuaded them.'

'It's not your fault. It's nobody's fault but theirs.'

'One felt they were determined to go.' The major looked wretched. 'I superintended everything. They were six and they took rather more than half the water.'

Paterson did not speak. He thought of Mrs Portman and was relieved. He looked anxiously at the cans of water and petrol and saw with relief also that someone, possibly Major Brain, had had the sense to mark the water-cans with crosses of chalk. Nevertheless, in time the crosses would rub off and he decided to repack both water and food and to have the water, or as much of it as possible, inside the car. With one passenger less they could afford another twenty cubic feet of space inside, where the water would be away from the sun and the chance of evaporation and the contact of petrol. Major Brain could superintend these things while he himself assembled the pump and carburettor.

As they drove on about two o'clock that afternoon, the car running normally again and without roughness on the first gradient between the rising terrace of little rice-fields, the

major and Miss Allison quite comfortable in the back among
the rearranged water-cans and boxes of food, he felt an extraordinary sense of release at the thought of going on alone. He
did not cherish a single thought of resentment, still less anger,
against the Portmans and Mrs McNairn. When he thought of
them there was nothing positive in his mind.

Even the thickening of refugees on the road, now only a
track with sometimes enough space for one bullock cart to
pass another in dusty switchback hollows between deepening
rock-cuttings, did not trouble him greatly. Freed of the irrita-
tions of the Portmans, the responsibilities, the silly fretful
anxieties, he could take the road as he liked to take it, not
thinking forward or back, but living only in the present moment, about a dozen yards ahead of the bonnet of the car. His
speed was down to about ten miles an hour. Up the gradients
he crawled in second and sometimes even lower gear. The noise
of the engine and the horn continually brought round to stare
at him a double stream of faces, brown and pinkish-cream and
black and Indian red: the faces not only of Burmese but of
half-Burmese, of scraggy Indians running like starving saints,
clutching filthy dhotis, of Bengalis and Tamils, of odd mix-
tures of Indo-Burmese, of flat-faced infants wrapped like yellow cocoons on the backs of flat-faced mothers; the lean grey
faces of starving cattle, full of moon-eyed hunger, extraordinarily like soulful humans as they stood dumbly to let the car go
by. Sometimes the road ran up sharply and came out on a
narrow crest clear of trees except for a brief civilized line of
hill-acacias, thin-trunked in this rocky earth. And then the sun
came in, fiercely shattering in flickering parallels of shade and
light, running in hot bars of black and crystal that opened and
closed like shutters on the turning faces.

An hour further on a woman lay dead on the track and a
little farther on an Indian, a scarecrow of sun-wrinkled
leather, died even as the car went past. He stood for a second
weakly crucified by the sun, eyes darkly waxen, arms clutching
faintly back at hot glittering rock, fingers failing in bony despair.

As the carcase fell forward, grotesquely doubled, seeming to shrivel as it lay, Paterson stopped the car because Major Brain was shouting.

He kept the engine running while the major and Miss Allison got out and went back.

The Indian had no friends. All about him the faces that watched the major and the nurse as they pulled him out of the sun into the shade of the nearest tree watched imperviously. They did not belong to him. An Indian – Hindu, Moslem, Untouchable – it was not for them. A strange man, anonymous, foreign, a worker from another country.

'A Bengali, I think,' the major said as he and Miss Allison got back into the car.

'Exhaustion?'

'It seemed like it.'

'He would have died anyway. They're always the first to go.'

'I suppose so.'

Very upset, the major did not speak again for a long time.

All afternoon the sun burned down on the gullies, through the shadeless expanses of road and even the shade, with numbing savagery. The light became a fiercely impersonal thing. It shot down with the white pain of an electric bulb of high power held brutally in front of the face. It stabbed out the colours of rocks and trees, leaving them black; then bleached out the identities of the scrambling bodies that streamed between them. And as it left near-colour and humanity more lifeless it gradually disintegrated the colour and life of the closing hills. It showed them to be endless things. It ripped away from them the last grey tenderness given by the great distances of the plain and threw into relief the scarred incrustations of forest, unbroken and shadowless, that folded infinitely northward.

Later that afternoon there were three more bodies on the road. A bullock that had died had the vultures already on it, slipping and clawing and gorging on the ripe flesh like bald evil turkeys. The odour of the rotting body sprang out of the after-

noon, hot and foetid. The air was poisonously charged for half
a mile beyond it, and in the great heat the major could not get
it out of his nostrils.

And when they camped at five the major was still at the
point of vomiting up that ripe hotness of putrid flesh.

That night, since they had only one tent, the major slept in
the open air. And when Paterson came to say good night to
him he discovered that he had fixed up for himself a mosquito-
net, quite simply, by driving two bamboo supports into the
ground and tying two more overhead.

He lay underneath it, smoking his pipe, looking up at the
stars.

'I suppose you think it's damn silly. The net,' he said.

'No.'

'Purely a service habit. Can't get out of it. One gets malaria
all the same.'

It struck Paterson that the major, lonely perhaps in the neat
cage of netting, wanted to talk, and he sat down.

'Ever get malaria? You must have.'

'Once.'

'You'll get it again. One always does. I knew a private in
Madras had it nineteen times.'

Paterson sat watching the major pull at the pipe, creating
every few seconds a small red star under the netting.

'Madras can be bad. I was there for several years. I don't
really like India, you know.'

It seemed to Paterson that the major had an almost anxious
desire to talk of small things.

'Of course, Rangoon can be bad, just the same.'

'Yes.'

'It's a city I never cared for. It's not the real Burma. Last
time I was there some of the men had taken to European
dress. A few of the women too. That was bad.'

Once again Paterson did not answer, and over in the solitary
tent Miss Allison's light went out. He knew that there in the
same tent Nadia was lying awake, waiting to come to him, and

he got up from his sitting position, ready to go.

'Paterson.'

'Yes?'

'I shall be going back tomorrow, Paterson.'

The major spoke simply and firmly, without fuss. It did not occur to Paterson to utter a word, either of surprise or protest, in answer.

'I was never happy about coming.'

'No.'

'It was purely and simply why I brought the bicycle.'

There was a touch of coolness in the air that seemed to drift down from the higher hills like invisible misty breath, but the stars everywhere had great brilliance in the plum-dark sky. All the time the major stared straight up at them.

'It'll be a little difficult riding,' Paterson said.

'When I can't ride I shall walk, and the bicycle will be aw-fully useful to carry my stuff on.'

Somewhere in the hills the jackals had already begun to cry, wailing like lost women in the darkness.

'I haven't been able to bear the thought of Miss Ross and Fielding back there at the hospital.'

'No.'

'I suppose one's training is all against the thought of retreat. The idea of running away. That's the most miserable thing in the world.'

'I can see that.'

'Then I love this country. I love the people. Always have. Rather as you do.'

'How do you know that?'

'One sees it simply in the way you go about things.'

Over against Miss Allison's tent the flap of canvas moved and made a stir of noise in the thick darkness, and Paterson suddenly felt poised, not restless but tense, between the major and the girl who was stirring to come to him.

'The way you treat the people. Out in the East the average European becomes a savage. It does that to him.'

'I wouldn't say that.'

'But you love the people. And the country. It's not something that's been imposed on you. It really matters.'

Paterson felt touched and did not know what to say. The affection of which the major spoke, described to him for the first time by another person, became intensely alive.

'You see, one can't run out on things like that.'

Over by the tent the girl, hearing their voices, crouched down, and Paterson heard her body slide against the canvas, softly.

'Of course, one understands Portman and Betteson and those people. They're office chaps. They have no notion of service. One can see their point of view. They have values.'

'Portman's all right,' Paterson said.

'An affair like this is simply a godsend. It lets them out.'

Paterson listened again for the girl, but now there was no sound.

'But I'm not made like that. I can't do it. I've never been to England for thirty years, and I wouldn't know how to go on there if I did. This is my country.'

'When do you think of starting?'

'I shall see you off in the morning and then go.'

'We'll fit you up with the latest comforts,' Paterson said.

He stood up; there seemed no more to say. From against the tent there was no movement or sound, and for a few seconds more, before the jackals began crying again, the silence was limitless, tropically deep and breathless, all across the forested hills.

'Terrific number of stars,' the major said. 'Extraordinarily like fish, I always think, swimming round up there.'

Paterson laughed and the major looked up at him quickly.

'You don't think it's awfully bloody silly?'

'The fish? Not at all.'

'No. I didn't mean that. I meant the idea of going back.'

'Not a bit.'

'I'm awfully glad.'

There seemed nothing more to say and in a shy and embarrassed way the major held out his hand. Paterson took it and held it for a moment and the major smiled. They did not speak again and presently Paterson walked away from the little cage of mosquito netting, where the major lay looking up at the stars, and over to where, by the Buick, his own bed-roll was spread.

When, after a few moments, the girl came to him he could smell the fragrance of the thanaka powder she had dusted on her face and her body; it was very sweet and delicious and he could feel the flower in her hair. He lay for a moment or two looking up at the sky. He could see all the stars swimming above him, exactly as the major had seen them, and he felt he understood the major and his love for Burma and why he was going back. Then he began smiling at the recollection of the stars that were like fish, and then as the girl lay with her mouth against his face, he told her about the major and his fish-like stars and she too began laughing. They laughed together for a long time.

And under his mosquito-net Major Brain heard the laughter, envied Paterson and thought he understood.

Straining to make up time, Portman drove rather fast. Repeatedly the narrowing track switchbacked and now and then swung out in treeless arcs cut on a perimeter of rising rock, and a speed of twenty and even lower seemed like the seventy of an open road. Sometimes the car struck pockets of dust milled by wheels to the fineness of flour, and where wind had drifted the yellow flour over lumps of submerged rock the car, hitting the rock, leapt up as if dynamited and then down into the dust hollows, wheels churning madly for a second or two until Portman pulled it out again. It was only by taking these pockets fast, Portman discovered, that they could get through them at all. The dust seemed bottomless and once, at the start of the journey without Paterson, the car had become stuck and it was only by getting the women out and then cutting bamboo and laying it under the spinning wheels that they had ever succeeded in getting out again. Even so, there had been a two-hour delay while he and Betteson sweated.

And he was very anxious for that not to happen again. He thought they were well ahead of Paterson; and more important, well ahead of the refugees. He was pleased about that: pleased because he saw no reason not to believe the story the Dutchman had told. Cholera and butchery were the natural results of a shambles like this. Or if not cholera and butchery, then typhoid and treachery, malaria and dacoits – it was all the same in the end. He was taking no chances.

All the time he kept looking ahead for the Dutchman. Sometimes when they stopped they could see, finely imprinted on the shallower dust, the tyre marks of his car. He had an idea that if they could catch up with the Dutchman the Bettesons could ride with him. It would relieve the load and they were rather a bore. He had discovered, for instance, that Betteson carried the bronze Buddha. And when he had asked why and Betteson had said, 'My lucky charm', Portman had suddenly the feeling that Betteson was one of those helpless people for whom nothing ever goes right, a sort of Jonah, and he wished they hadn't come. That night he had told his wife about the Buddha and of what a Jonah he thought Betteson was. She thought the whole idea very comic. 'I can't think why we didn't call her Mrs Jonah before,' she said. 'It's the perfect name.'

Speed was down to under fifteen by noon of the third day. Sometimes for stretches of half a mile there were no refugees, and then they came in sudden bunches, ten or fifteen families, perhaps a whole hamlet, clotted together: the lumbering bullock cart piled high with bundles, the bundles piled high with children, the weedy grey cows straggling behind, a mass of thirty or forty people trailing out for a hundred yards. All the time the road was narrowing as it climbed. There was room to pass only if the carts pulled closely in. The country had a wild and blistered desolation about it that Portman hated: nothing but scalded rock, glittering and harsh as iron, above the road, and then long declivities of shale, explosively scattered, darkly glinting under impersonal fierce light, and then beyond them the fingers of hill bamboo, short and white-husked and dead-brittle from the long dry season, and beyond them the forest, woven on endless contours, not green or grey but glassy, crusted and veined with shadowy glitter, as if it were not really living but only a lake of leaf glass, sterile under the straight white sun.

Merely for something to say, he leaned slightly back in the driving seat and spoke to Betteson:

'By the by, I meant to ask you. Did you give the boy anything?'

'No.'

'I offered him twenty chips. Funny: he wouldn't take it.'

'Getting particular,' Betteson said. 'Next week they'll be sucking up to the Japs.'

'He won't say no to twenty chips in India,' Mrs Portman said.

'Good old India,' Portman said. 'The first thing I do in India is to go to the Club and order myself the longest coldest Tom Collins you ever saw.'

'On the contrary,' Mrs Portman said, 'we'll be at Vanini's almost before the car is in Chowringee. You know Vanini's, Mrs Betteson?'

'No.'

'It's Swiss. The most wonderful tea in the world.'

'It's painful,' Portman said. 'Don't let's talk about it.'

'And the cakes,' Mrs Portman said. 'Just like a piece of Switzerland.'

'Well, it won't be long now,' Portman said.

The car went slowly forward, penned in by forested hills. The road wound into them like a yellow river-bed, salt-fringed at the edges by blown dust, its distances killed colourless by sun.

Connie McNairn, not listening, thought of Paterson. The Portmans had never liked Burma; the Bettesons had never had any luck there. Major Brain and Paterson knew the country and loved it. But what, after all, did she know of Burma? She felt now that she knew less than she knew of Paterson. In a way they were two parallel experiences in romanticism. She had met Paterson by chance in England and back in Burma she had created the illusion, the monstrously idiotic illusion, that Paterson was ready to marry her. And now Burma and Paterson were vanishing together. They were both behind her and she would probably never see them again. They were her parallel disillusionment too.

And then suddenly Portman was shouting, raving at a new mass of traffic ahead. He was pushing the gears and trying to keep the car running, and his elbow was hard on the button of the horn.

Ahead was a stationary bullock cart and in a moment Portman had stopped too. It was the very thing he wanted to avoid.

'Get the damn thing out, you idiots! Get it out! Get on!'

The massed brown Mongolian faces that turned to look at the raving Englishman had the flat neutrality of plates. They did not smile. When the bullock cart moved forward they too moved forward, dumb, squinting, impanderable as the bullock and the cart.

'Pull it over!' Portman shouted. 'Pull it right over!'

He revved the engine madly and kept his elbow on the horn.

'That's the East all over!' he shouted. 'Bags of time for everything. Centuries to get out of the damn country.'

Betteson leaned out of the back window and shouted too, in Burmese.

'They're these hill-clots,' Portman said. 'They speak an entirely different lingo.'

'All Burma has one language. It's not India,' Connie said.

'Mr Betteson will make him understand,' Mrs McNairn said.

'They're like the deaf,' Portman said. 'They hear all right when they want to.'

Betteson leaned from the window and called again and slowly, after another minute, the bullock cart drew over.

'Wonderful,' Portman said. 'Marvellous. The clots understood.'

'They have one language,' Connie said. 'But it's not English.'

'Connie!' Mrs McNairn said. 'That's enough.'

'Thank you,' Portman said.

The car moved forward and then stuck. Portman held it for a moment, let it into reverse and then again into forward gear. It jumped and gripped and went ahead, too fast, straight at the bullock cart. Mrs McNairn let out a short scream. Portman, frantically troubled by his fear of being bogged again, pulled the car sharply over and suddenly there was nothing between him and the long, sun-scalded declivity of rock plunging downwards into the forest impenetrably lying below. He pulled the car back in time, and the twist of its wheels took it safely through the hollow of dust where the bullock cart had been bogged a moment before. He yelled for the cart to be pulled

over again, swearing out of the window. A Burmese woman
with a baby on her back swore back at him. He belched the fury
of the car-horn at her and she leapt as if shot. Suddenly the
baby puckered its flat Mongolian-eyed face and began to cry
and Mrs Portman said: 'Don't antagonize them. You never
know.' The sweat poured down Portman's face and down over
his neck and chest until he could feel it soaking like tepid
water through his shirt. Outside the window the woman with
the crying baby picked up a rock, and as Mrs McNairn
screamed again he remembered the Dutchman's story about
butchery and he was newly frightened because of it and then
angry with himself, more stupidly, simply because he was
afraid.

In fear he swung the car over again. This time Betteson
shouted: 'Theres' not room to get through, man!' and Portman remembered what a dreadful Jonah, with his stupid Buddha and his luck, Betteson was.

'I know what I'm doing!' he shouted. 'For Christ Jesus shut
up!'

And then once again there was nothing between him and the
declivity of rock below. The car seemed to be riding out on the
glittering air. There was nothing under it; the dust did not hold
it; and in front of him the Burmese were prancing about in all
directions. He saw a figure in a brilliant magenta waistcloth
spring up out of the dust like a flame just in front of the
bonnet of the car. Whether it was man or woman he never
knew. The figure was caught up by the car like a shred of
purple paper and for a single earthless second the car and the
figure were one. They rode skyward towards the glassy incrustations of forest extending infinitely beyond the rocks below.
In the stab of sunlight on the terrorized face Portman saw the
lips of it open as if in laughter. They simply bared the yellow
teeth in a scream. At the back of the car Mrs McNairn was
flaying about with her parasol and someone was wrenching at
the handle of the door. In front of him the bullocks were
locked together in a cumbrous stampede, lunging across the
road to give him, at the last moment, another foot of room. He

pulled the car into this space and miraculously the screaming
face, the flying crazy piece of human paper, bronze and purple
together, were flung free.

In another moment the car went over.

12

As the day went on and the column of refugees thickened up the road more than ever like overloaded stumbling beetles groping through sunlit fog, the act of the major appeared to the boy as an increasingly astounding thing. He clutched the radio set dreamily on his knees and, puzzling constantly, tried to understand it all.

He could understand Paterson; he could understand his sister; and he could understand the refugees. The refugees were as simple to understand as night following day. They were running away, as sensible people would, from an approaching enemy. He could even understand Mr Portman, in great haste to run in the opposite direction to the major. Perhaps he could understand Mr Portman best of all. Mr Portman had offered him money; and then afterwards had asked for six extra cans of petrol and two of oil.

'It's absolutely nothing to you,' Mr Portman said. 'Sling them in the back of the trailer. Twenty chips when you've done.' But it seemed to the boy that it meant much more than nothing. He did not take the money and he did not smile. Mr Portman did not like it and the boy did not like it either. But at the same time he understood; he could not fail to understand. Quite simply also he understood Mr Betteson, who looked sometimes as if he could knock his head off, and Mrs Betteson, who treated him with that funny, troublesome affection when she helped with the fires. He also understood Mrs McNairn, who was taking her umbrella to India, and her daughter Connie. Sometimes it seemed as if the black silk umbrella, which put Mrs McNairn into such a panic because she slept with it as a possible weapon every night and then could never find it again in the morning, was of more material importance than the girl. But then that was understandable too. The girl could look after herself; she was older by two or three years than his sister, who after all not only looked after herself but after Paterson too. Whereas the umbrella could not look after itself. With its silver-topped handle it was a valuable thing, and in two months, with the coming of the rains, it would be an essential thing. All these things were simple to understand.

But not the major. The major was not running forward, but back. Worse still, he was the only person in Burma running back. Everyone else in Burma was running forward. Not a young man, obviously not a man of high status because he rode only a bicycle, the major appeared to have behaved with vast incalculable folly. Yet at the same time it did not seem so simple as that. If it was plainly an act of such idiocy why hadn't Paterson tried to stop him from going backward as he had tried several times to stop Mr Portman from going forward? The boy had heard all the raging arguments about it. But Paterson had done no such thing. On the contrary he seemed to have encouraged the major. He had shaken hands with the major, cordially, sadly, and yet with a smile. And the major, holding the bicycle loaded now with the spare watercan Paterson had insisted on his taking, but otherwise carrying nothing for his comfort except a haversack of tinned milk and biscuits, had smiled too. The boy had pumped up the back tyre of his bicycle and Miss Allison, coming out for a moment from her drowsy, self-effacing quietness, had said: 'Oh! Major!' and had suddenly given him a note for Dr Fielding at the hospital. That was all. For a moment it seemed as if Miss Allison would cry, but she did not cry after all, and a moment later the major was pushing his bicycle into the oncoming crowd of beetles, smiling quietly and waving his hand, looking rather like a respectable beggar on a pilgrimage going the wrong way.

But if the behaviour of the major greatly perturbed the boy it shattered Miss Allison. She sat staring into the dust that overhung the road in a perpetual sulphur-grey cloud: the dust that as it fell on the naked backs of refugees turned the dark Indian skins to rose, and the smooth coffee silkiness of the Burmese to a creaminess as light as her own. This transforming fog of dust, perpetually rising and falling all along the road until it was part of the brilliant heat haze, was for her the transforming fog of war. It bewildered and clouded all her vision and thought. It scrambled all the events of the past three or four days, from meeting the major at the hospital gardens to seeing him going back that morning with the absurd-looking bicycle, into a meaningless mess. It killed all chance of her seeing things truly and clearly just as it murdered the distances under the savage glitter of sun. And it shut out Dr Fielding. Most of all it did that.

Fielding was not young; but a greyish-haired heavy man of fifty-nine or sixty who had served a little in the army, first in France and then remotely in places like Agra and Mizapur, and then had suddenly thrown it up. He had come to Burma non-medically, as he used to say, just looking round.

And somehow, from the first, it had got hold of him. It had fascinated him and would not let him go. That was twenty years ago. Now he was Chief District Medical Officer and the hospital, from being nothing much more than a converted godown, had grown a high cool white wing on either side of itself, and pushed away the half-jungle of waste land in which it stood and had become a place of shade-trees and watered grass where beds of cannas paraded like soldier-flowers, salmon and orange and scarlet, and purple tributaries of bougainvillaea overflowed all the new white walls.

That was Fielding: to take something that was half-nothing, half-something, and perform a transmutation. And since it was his genius to do it not only with buildings and places but most of all with people he had done it with herself. She too was a creature that was half-nothing, half-something; neither European nor Asiatic, neither white nor coloured, neither of one world nor another. She had been thrown up with no status at all. And at the hospital Fielding had given her one. She was one with a dozen others, all Eurasian, who had worked up through the usual things: probationership, bed-baths, back-rubbing, enemas, bed-making, bed-bottles, temperatures, confinements, ante-operational duty, night-duty fatigue, sickness, babies, death. She had gone to Fielding at sixteen, when the sight of blood and the thought of an enema had turned her thin hypersensitive stomach sick. Now she was twenty. Now the sight of blood was no more than the spilling of red ink; an enema no more than blowing a nose; and she was not afraid of death.

Fielding had done all that. Yet when it came to it she was still neither one thing nor another. She had neither the temper, the phlegm nor the fibre of the English; and the joy of what were really her own people, the flower-in-the-hair gaiety, was never part of her. Fielding could not change that. She knew what girls like herself so often became. Prostitutes in the brothels of Rangoon or the mistresses of Europeans in up-country bungalows. They drifted to Calcutta. Or they became shop-assistants: too proud, as she was, of being thought Burmese or of speaking Burmese; passionate in their fear of not being thought white. Still only half-something, half-nothing; despised by one side, not mixing with the other.

And so when Fielding had put to her and the others the question of staying at the hospital, facing the conquest and quite possibly the rape of the country, she was not good enough to remain. The forces of opposing blood had disrupted her completely. White women like Mrs Portman and Mrs McNairn and Mrs Betteson had simple choices; even the girl Paterson treated so tenderly had a choice more simple than hers. And even if the choice had been simple she had really neither the tenacity nor the strength to make it. She was really just a mess. She was really nothing more than a half-coagulated jelly of blood that quivered in the moment of testing and shook to pieces and melted away.

And eventually she had done that: melted away, started running. The fact that she was half in love with Fielding, and yet not quite in love, did not prevent that. Half in love, half adoring, she was not ready to lay down her life for him. She wanted to stay with Fielding and yet inside she was empty, nothing but a negative fluctuation, not even fully frightened. Something inside her that was the half-something had begun to disintegrate a little further until at last, wretchedly but half-gladly, she had decided to go with Major Brain.

Now it was Major Brain who had started it all up again: whirling into all her thoughts the dust of indecision, regret, conscience, treachery, fear.

It was fear that slowly clarified in her mind as the car climbed forward up the sun-scalded gorges in the heat of afternoon: fear most of all of being confronted with a decision like the major's, the decision of going back; but fear also of the wrongness of going on, of sitting helplessly in the back of Paterson's car, of being borne away on the shattering roads, running with all the rest. Unlike the major she was not sick at the sight of death, of flesh ripely rotting, of the vultures' cleansing and disgusting gorge. It was not death that would turn her back. She felt sick only of the half-death, the half-rottenness inside herself. She felt in certain moments that she wanted terribly, oh! so much to go back to Fielding, and yet the thought of Major Brain trekking back with the bicycle, alone, into the face of it all, across that burning bitter malarial plain, terrified her completely. She wanted once again to see the cannas blossoming against the white walls of the hospital, and Fielding holding a chart between his yellowish grey-haired fingers in the barred shade of a ward. But it was too late now. She ought to have gone back with the major; but it was too awful and too much.

The fog of thought in which she had been groping all day was suddenly shattered clear about four o'clock that afternoon.

In the front seat of the car the boy leapt up as if shot. The radio set he had been hugging on his knees jumped out of his arms like a living rabbit. It bounced clear out of his hands and he clutched it back with a shout.

A moment later the girl was shouting too.

'Patson sir! Patson sir!' the boy yelled. 'Patson sir! Miss Con!'

A hundred yards up the road Connie McNairn was waving her arms in slow signals, the sleeves of her blouse flapping up and down like injured wings.

Just before Paterson stopped the car Miss Allison jumped out and walked ahead up the road. She did not break into running. She was quite calm now, and she seemed quite tall as she reached up and took Connie McNairn's waving arms out of the sky.

Mrs Betteson had behaved with extraordinary sanity as the car went over.

She had had a vivid impression of Mrs McNairn madly flaying about with the parasol. In the front her husband and Mr Portman were shouting at each other. Any moment the rock which the Burmese woman had picked up would come through the window. For some moments she had seen quite clearly what would happen. And suddenly as the car went over, not fast, but in a great cumbrous terrifying roll, she snatched the parasol out of Mrs McNairn's hands and hooked it into the handle of the door. She pulled with a strong calm tug and the door flew back, taking the parasol with it. A second later she gave Connie McNairn a violent push and the girl was flying clear of the car. What seemed a long time later she went out herself. She went out into a barrage of rock and petrol cans, and over her head the trailer flew down the cliff in an arc of uncanny clearness, like a flying cart.

When Connie McNairn picked herself up she was about twenty feet down the face of the cliff. Great pressure of monsoon rain had brought down from the road a bank of sand that lay like a cushioned plateau on an underlip of rock before the perpendicular drop below. She lay there for a second or two on her stomach; and then she looked up to see the face of the cliff ringed with moons, half-hostile, half-terrified, of Burmese faces. In another few moments she could reach the long yellow arms that hung down from the cliff like creepers, and she hauled herself up.

In the moment of catastrophe she felt quite calm. She stood

on the cliff edge in frigid suspense, looking over. The Burmese were all about her, talking, shouting, gesticulating, staring down. Down the long yellow sand-face of cliff, the skin of sand, still moving with the quivering pulsation of hidden muscles, seemed like the sinister beginning of something, not the end: as if the whole face of cliff were slowly beginning to slide, break up and melt away. Far down below, beyond the point where sand and rock met salt-grey bamboo and hill-scrub, dust was rising slowly into the sun like the column of smoke from an explosion. Against the impersonal background of folding hill-forest it seemed pitifully small. For a moment or two the girl thought of it as fire; she expected every moment to hear the crack of a real explosion. The Burmese almost seemed to be expecting it too. In a massed line they pointed down, staring, and waiting, partly hushed, as the dust sailed upward and then, as if really the centre of a fire, burned orange in the sun. And then nothing happened. Down the cliff-face the rocks ceased falling and the dust, rising to treble the height of the bamboos, suddenly came to the end of its violence and fell away like vaporous pollen on the trees. There was no explosion except from the Burmese: a long final explosive 'Ah!' of wonder.

Far down the cliff, a foot or two away from where a new succession of rock-steps went steeply down the last hundred feet of gorge, something glinted. The girl saw it curled on the sepia shale like the discarded skin of a snake, shining in the sun.

It was Mrs McNairn's umbrella. More even than the long fatalistic sigh of wonder from the Burmese it brought home to the girl that the thing was over. The sun seemed to strike the silver handle of the parasol and glance painfully upwards and hit her. She felt very sick. She felt for a moment incapable of holding herself back from the long fainting fall over the edge. She was falling and dying. For a second or two the sun blackened her vision and then in the ghastly insupportable horror of it she became aware of the parasol slipping over the edge of rock in sliding sand, until it disappeared.

When she came to herself a second time she was sitting back on the road, in the shade of a rock. She felt very cold and bleak and two Burmese women were giving her water from a bottle. It was a square empty gin-bottle and on her cold lips the water felt almost tepid. It tasted of nothing but dust and the queer artificial flavour of her lipstick. She could feel her lips cracked and dead where the skin had contracted and the lipstick had dried.

She began almost at once to think of Paterson. And at the same moment she discovered that she was still clutching her handbag. In fear or horror she had wound the leather thong of the strap round and round her wrists. As she slowly unlocked the strap she felt for a moment inexpressibly rejoiced. She had the bag; she had fresh lipstick and there was Paterson. Because of these things the rest did not matter. She was seized with exactly the sort of fatalism that she had seen in the faces staring over the cliff and had heard in that final explosive exclamation, the long 'Ah!' of wonder that was the end. The rest were dead and it did not matter. Her mother was dead and it mattered even less.

Coming completely back to herself, thinking with ecstatic violent relief of Paterson, she took another drink of water. While she was drinking one of the younger women went away and came back, some minutes later, with fruit wrapped in a piece of pale-blue cotton: a few parrot-green bananas, some green-skinned oranges, and a small papaia. She laid them in the girl's lap and almost at the same moment the girl opened her handbag to look for her lipstick. It was as if she had been seized with the outrageous idea of paying for the fruit and water. The two women stood up. In distress the girl let out the few words of Burmese that she knew, but they were not adequate and the women, yellow faces passively unrelaxed, stared down.

There was nothing for her to do but wave the lipstick. Across the face of the younger woman went the faintest of smiles. The girl drew the lipstick across her lips and the women gesticulated with the bottle of water. The girl nodded, and crustily the older woman spoke and spat into the dust, the crimson betel-squirt like a shot of blood.

And suddenly in the middle of it all the girl once again felt very sick. Drawn upwards by waves of coldness, the life ran out of her face. She remembered holding to the handbag with bloodless desperation as one holds to the edges of the table when the anaesthetic first pours in. And then there was nothing. The sun blackened her vision again and she felt herself swim away. In a strange re-enaction she was falling once again from the car.

She came to herself lying in the bullock cart. She had been covered with a shawl of blue and cyclamen in some light half-transparent material that she had pulled instinctively over her face. She was in a world of blue-rose cloud. Savagely the sun came through the cloud, stabbing her eyeballs, hammering whitely at her consciousness. When she came fully to herself she did not move. She did not want to move. All she could do was to think once more, with inexpressible relief, of Paterson and her handbag. Underneath her the road rocked in slow ship-like rolls, pitching the cart. She could smell the dung-warm odour of bullocks, and she could feel the leather strap of her handbag across her wrists, and then above her face the savagery of sun.

No one came to her for most of that afternoon and she did not get up. She relaxed gradually into a state of stupefied calm. She moved only once, to roll half-over so that she could lie in the narrow shadow given by the side of the cart, and then she was still again, covered by the cloth; half-conscious in the world of blue-rose cloud. The thought that she was alone in the world for the first time shaped itself in that queer half-consciousness in the strangest way. Except for Paterson she was quite alone now and she was very glad. Sooner or later Paterson would catch up with her. For the first time since the meeting in England they would be together without the devastating intervention of her mother. They would go on to India together; they would be free; he would be desperately sorry for her. Out of pity and relief the death of her mother aroused there would come, sooner or later, a sort of affection. She was glad her mother was dead. She was glad the Portmans were dead. All of that world of stupid intrigue, of narrow jealousies, all the petty plotting gossip of that tiny microcosm back in the European quarter: all of it had suddenly been consumed in a flash. Nothing remained of it except her mother's parasol: the cast snake-skin of the old life, glittering and dead and shrivelling and worthless back there in the sun.

Once that afternoon the cloth was pulled back from her face. The younger woman had come to see if she needed water. For about a minute she sat upright and coming up out of the narrow shade of the cart, free for the first time of the covering of cloth, she could not see. She groped for the bottle and held it against her lips. Once again she felt the lipstick harsh as cracked enamel. And at the same time she remembered that she ought not to be drinking the water. But the sun beat about her face and she could smell the bullocks in the hot air and suddenly she needed the water eagerly, with ravenous thirst, and did not care what happened.

She asked for the bottle to be left with her; the woman understood and the girl kept it by her side when she lay down again under the cloth for the rest of the afternoon.

It was only when the cart finally stopped and she sat up to see where she was that she felt anything like a burst of rational thought. Across the hills the day was sinking away in deep ridges of purple and tawny rose, the upper air palest green, without a trace of blue. She could smell the smoke of fires, and when she got up she saw that the cart had turned off the road into the little street of a bazaar. Under a double row of thatched hovels, raised up on teak-wood piles, with extending roofs of palm-frond coming down to give shade in the street below, the bazaar was still there: low flat baskets of banana and orange and papaia and bright green lime, piles of vivid sweetmeat, sherbet-rose, bright green, turquoise, lemon yellow, half-moons of water-melon filled with flesh that was like juicy rosy ice, little lamps of papered candle already burning among glowing pyramids of fruit in the shadow. News of the exodus had not arrived. There was no panic in the solemn friendly little street with its growing fire-flies of light breaking one by one the purple bloom of falling darkness under the low palm leaves.

And suddenly the very ordinariness of it terrified her. She was trapped in its little backwater, lost from Paterson. The rejoicing sense of release was shattered by recurrent attacks of loneliness, of the fear that somewhere back on the road Paterson would presently be rushing on past the point where she would ever see him again, and by the final terror that he would think her dead.

She knew then that she had got to go back.

After Mrs Betteson had pushed the girl out of the car and had begun to fall out herself, she hung for a hideous moment hooked by the old-fashioned glacé leather belt of her dress to the handle of the door. She fought frantically to retain her spectacles. The entanglement with the door lasted about ten seconds. And as she hung there, ridiculous and terrified and yet not shrieking, she clapped both hands to her face, partly in instinct to save the glass of her spectacles from smashing into her eyes, partly to hide the final moment of her impact against the wildly rushing slope of sand that was going past her like a mill-race of sun-dazzling water.

And then she fell. She kept her hands pressed against her face, no thought in her head except 'My glasses, my glasses, my glasses!' knowing that without them she would never see. It did not occur to her that she might be killed. She did not cry out. She remained brightly aware of flying corridors of space, somewhere at the end of which there were great clashings of breaking glass.

She hit the sand ludicrously, bouncing. The speed she had gathered from the car had flung her a long way down the slope, well beyond the rock-shelf that held the road. She bounced several times, rolling, all the time pressing her hands to her spectacles, brightly conscious. And with her arms almost entirely wrapped about her head she fell a long way.

When she stopped falling she stood straight upright. She had slithered the last half-dozen yards or so on her back, digging her feet into the soft sand. When her feet struck shale and acted as a brake the impact stopped her, jerking her violently upward.

And in that moment she lost her spectacles. The effect of leaping up and then of jerking forward as if to fall on her face made her put out her hands. Instantaneously her spectacles jumped off.

At once she felt naked. The spectacles had clothed her. Now that they were gone she felt the sun on her tender eyes as painfully as if the spectacles had really smashed and driven minutely prickling particles of broken glass into her pupils. The effect filled her with dismay. She was not terrified. It seemed simply very stupid to have fallen all that way quite harmlessly and then to have done something so painfully silly at the last moment. She stood in a world of golden mist, groping. She had the great presence of mind not to move any further. She had lost her hat and already the sun had begun to bang down on the top of her head with the savage, vertical blow of a lump of dropped lead, but she felt mentally quite cool. Without the spectacles she was helpless.

Somewhere above her a rock began to fall. It fell in a series of irregular leaps. Its punctuations shattered the valley. Terrified now, she turned in the direction of the sound, looking up. And instinctively, seeing nothing but the same mass of sunshot mist above her, she fell down.

She put her hands almost at once on her spectacles. The rock went past her with a great whizz of air, hitting the dry bamboo a moment or two later with the sharp crackle of a scythe biting into the straws of dry corn. The spectacles lay on the sand, unbroken, and it seemed to her that a miracle had happened.

Spectacleless and hatless, able to see nothing and yet frightened of putting the spectacles on again, she began to tremble all over. The recollection of the falling rock terrified her more than the falling of the car, and in turn the loss of the spectacles more than either. Once before she had broken her spectacles and new lenses had had to be sent from Rangoon. For some days she had groped about the house, knocking things over, crawling about the garden like a mole, squintingly snipping with her scissors at a mist of green and orange and rose in her fight against tropical nature. All sharpness and beauty of colour in the flowers she loved had died. The sunlight had the flabbiness of wet custard. She could not read. She knew the terrors of temporary blindness, of being shut up in a world of colourless groping, of the most ghastly self-imprisonment and helplessness.

And for a few moments she knew them again now. She sat stunned. The rock had ceased falling. The long 'Ah!' of final explosive relief and wonder that Connie had heard was too far away for her to hear. She could feel for those few moments only the discouraging sense of that other helplessness: the sheer awfulness of the temporary blindness and the shattering knowledge that it might have come back.

Slowly, after a minute or two, she managed to put on her spectacles. They were speckled with golden-crystal grains of dust that had stuck to the film of sweat on the lenses as they fell. Automatically she wiped them on her dress.

Her trembling became better as she put them on. The despair at losing the spectacles, together with the terrified despair of recollection, had saved her from the terror of the fall. It was only when she put on the spectacles and could see where she was that she knew what might have happened.

She had slipped almost to the edge of a shelf of rock. The shale that had stopped her was vertically barred with tiger-fissures of sepia-red, worn away by the downward force of monsoon rain. Below the rock dropped away in two great yellow-brown steps of fifteen feet or so, and there bamboo and scrub and tree fringed the final declivity of sand.

Her instinct was to climb down. When she looked back up the cliff she was a little surprised to find that she could not see the road. It did not seem to matter. She had hardly time to think of it before she had begun to climb down the face of rock. It was so scalding hot to her hands that for a few seconds she could not hold it. It blistered her finger-tips so that she

played absurd painful scales with them as she tried to find a
hold. Through her cleaned glasses she saw every aggravated
fissure and vein of rock until it was like the buckled surface of
half-crusty, half-molten iron.

It took her half an hour to climb down to the last shelf of
sand below. It did not seem to her an extraordinary thing.
Armed now with the spectacles she felt she could accomplish
much more than that.

Resting at last, leaning back against the rock, she looked
down into the strip of hill-jungle below. Wisps of sun floated
through it like white splinters and down somewhere in the
middle of it the dusky, yellow column of dust from the
smashed car was still rising smokily in the sun.

For a moment a great creamy blur enveloped everything.
Sweat was pouring down her face and had begun to mist her
spectacles. And once again as she took them off and cleaned
them with the skirt of her dress, the helpless fog of weakness
enveloped her. Then as she put them on again, giving a vague
pecking sort of glance this way and that as if to be sure that
they were really clean and in focus, she saw an astonishing
thing.

Thirty or forty yards along the strip of sand lay Mrs
McNairn's parasol. She walked vaguely along to it and picked
it up. Until that moment she had not given another person a
single thought. Now the parasol brought everything rushing
back to her: Betteson, the Portmans, Mrs McNairn, the girl.
She remembered hooking the parasol into the handle of the
door and in those first calm but awful seconds, when everyone
else was either screaming or petrified, pushing the girl away.

She looked back up the cliff, but the deep long elbow of vivid
sepia-yellow rock still cut the road off from her. She had spun
down in a half-parabolic dive, the parasol rolling straighter,
more in the path of the car, to her left hand.

Standing there with the parasol in her hands, holding it by
the fabric because the silvered handle was almost white hot,
she could see where the car had ripped its way down through
the thin bamboo. Somewhere just above this point the trailer
had detached itself and shot separately away.

The calmness which had made her push out the girl and then clap her hands over her spectacled face took her steadily down through jungle of dwarf bamboo. Portman's heavy car had torn through the slender stalks, here sometimes as thin as the fawn-green grasses that undergrew it, in something of the way a rhinoceros tunnels through swamp-grasses. It had bored a perfect path as if it had really been driven through at great speed.

How far she expected to go or what she expected to find there she did not stop to think. In the hot air, closer than ever under the screen of bamboo, there was a powerful odour of showered petrol, and down through the barred flickers of vivid light the dust was still smoking. Then in front of her a great dark predatory jungle crow wheeled in out of the upper light, beating blackly down towards its own enormous shadow as it floated above the clearing ahead.

This shadow seemed to focus all her sight. It sailed upward as the crow passed over, and there was left in the clearing, where the sandy dust was renewed for a space of fifty or sixty feet, all bamboo thinned away, the wreck of Portman's car.

It lay upturned, on its side, the driving wheel underneath. Somehow a thicker length of bamboo had become interlocked with it and now speared up through the broken glass of the near side window, exactly like an arrow pinning the whole thing down.

A second later she saw Mrs Portman. The upturned door of the car had been ripped away and on the sand Mrs Portman was lying face upwards, murdered by full sun. From the car itself there was no sound of Portman and Betteson and Mrs McNairn, and there seemed to be no sound either from Mrs Portman until Mrs Betteson came close to her and crouched down.

'Oh! God help me, for God's sake help me, Oh, God help me! Oh God! Oh God!'

And instinctively Mrs Betteson opened the parasol and swiftly and tenderly held it above the screaming face.

13

The boy stood at the crest of the cliff, with Nadia and Paterson, looking down.

Some people were going back to Burma; some, like Mr Portman, were in too great haste to go on. The simple directness of the journey had become intricate with inexplicable motives and disaster. And still the act of the major remained less credible than the act of Portman. At least with Portman it was possible, now, to see the consequences.

Down the cliff there was nothing to tell that the car had ever been there except a single petrol can lodged in the cleft of a dead acacia bough. The yellow monsoon-skimmed sand, with its bars of copper shale, swept away, empty in the sun. All the people who had seen the car go over, with the exception of Connie McNairn, had gone. It did not occur to the boy that it could ever be otherwise. Already he knew perfectly well that no one was alive down there. He knew that if there had been a single flickering hint of life visible from the road it would have been very different. No one must be left to die. There must, because of Buddha's teaching, be no killing even of the maimed, even of the bullock with the broken limb, even of the milkless, useless goat, even of the dying cow, or the sickest buffalo. There must be no abandonment of the living at all. He knew that no one could be living down there, below the place where the car had gone over, simply because even the faintest chance of life would have driven the peasants to the best they could do at rescue. All this was very simple to understand; far simpler than the idiocy that had caused it all or the act of the major in doing the entirely opposite thing.

Paterson had quite different thoughts.

'Tuesday,' he said. 'If we got down there could we get back?'

'Nobody there,' the boy said.

'Never mind that. Could we get back?'

'Nobody there.'

Paterson did not answer. He stood for some time watching the gorge.

'All finished,' the boy said.

Paterson looked down. In the windless air the valley had the unreality of shapes painted on board, all colour toned down, bamboos like brush-strokes of palest fawn, rock and sand like unreflected washes of dull chrome and copper burnt out by sun.

'Find a place,' Paterson said. 'A path.'

'No path, Patson sir. No good.'

'Go and look.'

'All finished.'

'Go and look and then tell me.'

'All finish.'

'Nadia will go with you. Go and look.'

'Finish. All finish.' The boy shook his head, always smiling. 'No good.'

'Go and look.'

'Yes, Patson sir.' The boy walked slowly away.

Paterson went back to the car. Connie and Miss Allison were sitting in the back. The English girl had borne up well, he thought. And Miss Allison, who had been such a drooping, anonymous, self-effacing figure ever since she had walked out like a sleepy ghost from among the rickshaws by the hospital, had become remarkably alive. In a curious way both had control of themselves; they were almost artificially calm.

'How now?' he said.

'She's a little shocked, that's all,' the nurse said. 'She has no temperature. She needs a good lie down.'

'How far is this village you spoke about, Connie?'

'I walked in two hours.'

'I think I'll take you in there and then come back.'

'Come back?' She looked violently startled.

'I want to get down to this place.'

'You mean here? Is it necessary? Must you?'

'They may not be dead.'

The girl sat staring in front of her. It struck him at once that he had spoken too bluntly. The words seemed to shock her more visibly than the crash itself. All at once she looked terribly overwrought.

'The oddest things happen,' he said. 'You never know.' That sounded wrong too, and once again he wished he had never spoken.

Then suddenly the girl seemed to go to pieces. In a groping and dismal little gesture she put her hands up in front of her face as if sweeping away a web. Without any other warning she began to cry.

'It's all right, it's all right,' Miss Allison said. 'It'll be better if you cry.'

Paterson felt dry and embarrassed and got into the driving seat and put his foot on the starter.

'I'll take her to this village,' he said. He tried to speak impersonally, indirectly. The car started. He let it go gently forward. 'She needs sleep.' That remark, too, sounded obvious and artificial, and yet he could think of nothing better.

'Lie back,' Miss Allison said gently. 'I'll love you. Just cry. I'll love you.'

'I don't want to be loved!' the girl shouted. 'I'm all right! I don't want to be loved! I don't want that!'

She beat about with her hands, like a person frightened of being tied up.

'Let's get on and get out of it! I can't bear it!'

Her hands beat on the slender attentive golden arms of the Eurasian girl until she was free.

'Let me alone! I can't bear it!'

Paterson drove forward. Connie, free of Miss Allison, suddenly beat on his own shoulders in protest.

'Why do we have to come back? Why do we?'

Driving forward, he did not know what to say.

'If they're dead they're dead, aren't they?' she said. 'Why can't we leave it at that?'

'It's very hot,' Miss Allison said. 'You'll wear yourself out. Try and be –'

'I don't want to try to be anything! Why do we have to drag it all up?' She continued to beat on his back with her hands. 'It's perfectly idiotic! Why do we? Why do we?'

'It's the decent thing,' he said. It struck him that it was exactly the thing Portman would say. It was something else he did not mean and wished he had not said.

'I tell you they must be dead! I saw it. How could they get out of that fire?'

'Fire?'

He spoke sharply. It was the first he had heard of fire.

'It burned all afternoon. I told you that.'

No, he thought, you didn't tell me that.

'I saw it! I ought to know!' she shouted.

'Gently, gently,' Miss Allison said.

'I ought to know what I saw and what I didn't see!'

'Yes,' he said. 'I forgot.'

'Well, I can't forget! That's what I can't do. Don't drag me back into it! I've had enough!'

'All right.'

'I've had enough! I've had enough!' She was crying helplessly now, less hysterically and less bitterly, and she ceased beating his back with her hands. 'I've had enough.'

In the heat a great spurt of sweat had broken out of her face, mingling with her tears. Looking up into the driving mirror he saw the drenched and startled face staring straight at him. She had drawn up her body tautly. Her shoulders were stiff as if she revolted from the notion that Miss Allison might touch her. And her eyes, convulsed by hysteria and now shockingly transfixed, had something in them of that protuberant albino glare that he had seen in the eyes of Mrs Betteson.

'I hate the whole country.'

She suddenly jerked stiffly back on the cushions of the seat, her head against the arm of the nurse.

'I just feel I hate it all and I want to get out.'

'All right,' he said.

'I feel I never want to see any of it again.'

'I know,' he said.

Tuesday came up the road and Paterson stopped the car and got out. In doing so he caught another glimpse of the girl. She was still drawn tautly upward, her shoulders stiff, her dress pulled tightly over her body, so that her breast was like whipped sand, the two nipples standing out, pressed up, like rounded pebbles. She gave him an extraordinary glance of frightened curiosity and all of a sudden the whole front of her body seemed to collapse; the entire taut shape of sand crumpled and fell away. And for a second she looked scared as if she knew what he was thinking.

He was thinking that she was a liar; a very curious liar. There was nothing else for it. He walked to meet Tuesday. Then for a second the impact of his too violent thought bewildered him. He glanced across the valley, shading his eyes against the sun. Nothing moved across the ridges of moss-like forest repeating themselves into the farthest haze, except a few jungle crows planing above the virgin bleached bamboo directly below. There was not the remotest trace of fire.

'Nothing here,' the boy said. 'All finished here.' He smiled.

Nadia smiled too, and got into the front of the car.

Still troubled, Paterson walked with the boy to the edge of the road, twenty or thirty feet back from the car.

'You see anything?'

'Nothing. Nothing here.'

'You see fire?'

'Fire? No fire.'

Paterson arched his two hands over his eyes and stared down. The sun created dancing blisters of light. If you looked long enough, he thought, you could get caught up by oddest hallucinations.

'You stay here and I'll come back.'

'No good, Patson sir. No good staying here!'

'Just stay here and watch.'

'No good, Patson sir!'

'I'll be back in half an hour. Watch for fire.'

133

'Fire, Patson sir? Nothing here. No fire.'

'Stay and watch. Is there a path?'

'No path, Patson sir. Nothing.'

'No way down?'

'No way down. Nothing. No fire.'

'Stay and watch.'

'Patson sir!' The boy pleaded for a single second, with the most frigid, troubled smile, not to be left there. It seemed to thunder through him for an instant that Paterson might never come back. He seemed to stiffen for a moment where he stood, smilingly transfixed, mutely and awfully obedient in the face of this shattering possibility.

A moment later the car drove off. He stood watching it glitter down the road in the quivering sunlight as if he were seeing it for the last time. It disappeared beyond gaunt projections of yellow-brown rock. Dust rose in a sulphur-white column and poured down in front of his face, cutting off everything about him in sun-shot fog until slowly it settled on the road, the rocks and his own body, still clad in the football shirt.

Half an hour later, when Paterson came back, he was still lying flat on his stomach by the road. His body had something of the shocked rigidity of a sniper.

Slowly he pointed down at the convulsive white heat with one finger and Paterson, who had given up the thought of anything happening, stooped down.

'See something?'

'Down here, Patson,' the boy said. 'Look down.' He lifted the finger and aimed it at the mass of bamboo below with practical accuracy.

'Look, Patson,' he said. 'See? Down there.' He was smiling again. 'A little fire.'

14

The thought of fire had not occurred to Mrs Betteson until late afternoon; it came to her with pleasant suddenness as part of a recollection of that lamb of a boy.

It brought sharply to her the existence of the outside world: Paterson, Miss Allison, Major Brain, the Burmese girl and that lamb of a boy, all coming up the road somewhere in Paterson's car. She had been occupied until that moment with other things. Portman, Betteson and Mrs McNairn were dead in the car. She had covered their bodies with rugs from the boot and a white Chinese shawl that Mrs McNairn had been using on the journey to keep the dust off her dress that was so like a piece of solidified silken dust itself. In dying she had thrown up her arms, threshing about in terror, and had clutched at last the blind-roller in the rear window of the car. That last violent pull had stretched the coffee-coloured parallelograms in her armpits to the limit, ripping them away. There was a greater and more living agony in the flung-back arms, the natural naked hair and the clutching fingers on the blind than in her face. She had closed her eyes, and now possessed a kind of tired serenity that Mrs Betteson did not remember seeing before. On the front seat both Portman and her husband had died clutching the wheel and lay crushed by it, inextricable, so that she could not touch them. There was nothing she could do but throw rugs over them. One rug had on it a kind of Tibetan motif of dragons, vividly golden on peacock purple-green, and later whenever she had occasion to go back to the car she saw on the front seat not the bodies of Portman and her husband, but only the dragonish emblem, very living with its embroidered golden claws crawling over the bundled bodies of the two men.

Almost her first act had been to try to shut the only two windows of the car she could reach. Both had been open. Now the winding gear was slightly buckled, so that neither window could be wound to within more than two or three inches of the top. She knew perfectly well what would happen to the bodies within twenty or thirty hours.

In the boot of the car were stowed boxes of food which she had some difficulty in getting out. The boot lid had jammed; and after a great struggle to open it in the afternoon heat she decided to leave it until morning. In the back of the car was a single two-gallon petrol can of water. Mrs McNairn had always complained fussily about it because on the more violent stretches of road it had bounced about, hacking her shins. Portman had slung it in at the last moment because there was no room behind.

On the back window ledge, behind Mrs McNairn's tightly-clenched hands, she found Portman's rifle. It did not seem of very great importance. She had never fired a rifle in her life and she simply took it out and left it, with the water, by Mrs Portman's side.

None of these things gave her the comfort that she found in the possession of her scissors. They armed her, like her spectacles, with far more power than Portman's rifle. She had never been really happy except when snipping at something, either with the large tailor's scissors with which she attacked the more powerful vines and clematis and creepers and bignonias and bougainvillaeas of her garden, or with the smaller pair she used for snipping the seed-pods from carnations and gerberas and salvias and all the smaller flowers she grew. She kept them tied round her neck, always ready, by a piece of Betteson's pink-red office tape, and she did not know how many times Portman and his wife had laughed at them.

When she discovered the scissors still round her neck she, too, started laughing. As with the spectacles it was like clutching back at life. She found herself firmly grasping an essential thing.

The laughter was exactly of the kind she often let out in the garden, among the flowers, or on the verandah of the house, when one of the *minahs*, the starling-like birds she fed with scraps after every meal, hopped on one leg or walked tamely into the sitting-room or put its head on one side and talked to her. She loved the *minahs* more than any other bird. 'Talk like a parrot,' Betteson had always said, 'if you cut their tongue.' But the half-human language the *minahs* spoke on the verandah had always seemed to her clear enough. She always understood it; she did not want to cut their tongues, any more than she wanted to wound anybody, for greater understanding.

As soon as she found the scissors and recovered from the first laughing moments of the discovery, she went over to Mrs Portman. She carried her bodily out of the clearing into the broken shade of bamboo. Even there the sun came murderously through the lacy upper fronds, penetrating like an acetylene flare the flimsy silk of the parasol.

'I got my scissors. I found them. I still had them round my neck.'

Listening to that dithering voice, Mrs Portman lay motionless on her back, not speaking. She did not speak simply because her voice had lost its power, and she did not think of laughing at the scissors.

'Now I've got the scissors we can do things.'

Mrs Portman found her voice in a scream. As if not noticing it, Mrs Betteson said:

'And if I can once get the back of the car open I'll make you some tea. That'll do you good.'

Spectacles and scissors; and then tea. The thought of them all gave her new power. The outer reality of life which she had bungled for years did not oppress her. She had something else to face.

'Lie still. I've got some water. I'm going to wash you and make you comfortable.'

She took off her dress and kneeling on the ground began to cut it to pieces with her scissors. Her white underslip draped her shapelessly, half like a nightgown, half like the prodigious shirt she had so much adored on that lamb of a boy.

What she saw on Mrs Portman's body late that afternoon did not weaken the strength she had gained. She felt frozenly calm. She stanched the crushed intestines by making a cushion-like pad of her dress. Then she took off her underslip. Deprived of it she looked, in her long cambric drawers, like a picture of a bather from a faded magazine. Then she took off her corsets. They were pink, with laces. By laying them flat on the ground, wide open, and then by moving Mrs Portman very gently over until they were underneath her body, she provided a piece of taut pink armour for the pad that lay over the wound. When it was in position at last, she laced it lightly and tenderly until it was as comfortable and secure as she could make it.

After that Mrs Portman seemed to go off into a half-conscious doze. When night came suddenly, in a purple march that swept across the short horizon between the hills so swiftly that Mrs Betteson was caught unawares and found it too late to make another attempt to get the food from the back of the car, it was silent except for a little evening wind that crept down the hillside and stirred the grassy paper fronds of bamboo.

She sat awake all night with Mrs Portman. It was very silent and, unlike all other nights she had known in the East, it carried on the warm darkness no scent of flowers. For most of the time she sat thinking of her garden. She thought of the hibiscus and petunias and salvias and dahlias and zinnias she grew there, the wild rampant vines, the jasmine and roses, and of the *minahs* who talked to her on the verandah where the passion flowers ramped madly in the heat. Absently she found herself fingering the scissors, cutting away at something in the darkness, and sometimes she talked aloud, half to herself, half to Mrs Portman, of what she was doing or of the memory of what she had been used to do. Both things comforted her, wearing away the night. In the early hours of the morning she felt the falling of light dew on her bare shoulders, making her cold for the first time. She did not at first know what to do. There were no coverings except those that covered the dead in the car, and at last she lay down with Mrs Portman under the still opened parasol, where the dew could not fall, and they lay there together, half-sleeping or half-conscious, until she looked up and saw the first jungle crows gleaming above her, like wheeling aeroplanes of pink-black satin, in the powerful sunrise.

It took her half the morning to open the back of the car. When she had finished she looked, in her drawers, like a bather that had just come drenched, hair wet and plastered, bust dark with moisture, from the sea. She was dripping with great sweat as she staggered about with boxes of food. A kit of tools, a pump, a tin of oil and a pair of blue overalls of Portman's were with the boxes.

In her desire to be always cutting away at something she seized on the tools, rather than the food, as the things she needed most. Among the tools she found a hacksaw. It gave her the same delight, coupled with strength, as she got from the finding of the scissors and the spectacles. With the hacksaw she could make some sort of shelter, even a tent, simply by cutting bamboo. The practical idea of it filled her with delight.

Now and then, as she made the sections for the shelter, cutting down hard but half-ripened bamboo stalks and tying them with strips of torn material to form a frame, she left off to kneel down and talk with Mrs Portman. With great tenderness she wetted her lips with water, or gave her drinks of it in one of the cups she had found with the food.

And now, curiously, it was not the eyes of Mrs Betteson who had a wandering, flower-like fragility as they waved in their sockets, but the eyes of Mrs Portman, who gazed speechlessly upward, groping for comfort. In their weakness the faded pupils of her eyes could not hold themselves fixed on any one place for more than a broken second. The reflected fawn of the bamboo stalks gave them a tenuous flickering of unfocused disturbance.

'You're all right, aren't you? I'm going to get you some shelter. I'll get you in there, and then –'

And then what? Mrs Betteson did not know. She broke off suddenly.

Then as she went back to cutting and bending and shaping the bamboos Mrs Betteson knew what, really, it had been her intention to say: 'I'll get you in there and then I'll go for help.' That was it.

How? She knew quite well there was no way of getting help, and suddenly she dismissed the whole idea rather angrily. Far more important to rig up the shelter. She recalled suddenly how it was possible to split bamboo. She believed you somehow slit the end and then inserted another piece of bamboo in the slit, and then split the cane almost at a run, tearing it lengthwise.

With such light, flattened sections of bamboo she could weave a roof over Mrs Portman's head.

She tried it. Almost with machine-like accuracy, at the first attempt, the rod of bamboo split down. She was delighted. She recollected vaguely that it was even possible to split a bamboo stalk into several divisions at once, at a single run, but she was too delighted with that first success to bother any more. She ran excitedly about in her damp, white drawers. She had taken off her shoes for the night and had not put them on again. But now the sandy dust, fiercely hot, had begun to scald the soles of her feet whenever she left the shade, and at last she stopped to put on her shoes. It was only then, as she stooped for a moment, resting, that she felt the sweat running like tepid oil from her neck down over her chest and across her breasts, already so drenched with it that it wetted almost to transparency the stuff of her bodice, feeling too the first bitter, savage wave of thirst: the sensation of craving for liquid as if the glands of the throat were powerless or killed. She was hungry too. All of her body was hollow inside, the first delight of activity parched out for a second or two with pain.

It was not until afternoon that the shelter was rigged. It formed a box-like cabin of two sides and a top, about four feet wide and four feet high. The strips of slit bamboo were not closely woven; they let in light and air and yet like a venetian

blind gave shadow too. In the dead-still suffocating afternoon
hardly a breath of air ever moved and for a long time Mrs
Betteson sat at one end of the shelter, close by Mrs Portman's
head, mechanically fanning backwards and forwards a linen
map she had found in the back of the car. It moved the air
quietly over Mrs Portman's face. It fanned a little into her
own. Overhead many more jungle crows had gathered. Every
now and then a great shadow of one cut across the narrow
tiger bars of shadow and half-shade made by the roof of bamboo and like a racing cloud darkened Mrs Portman's body. As
the sweat dropped from Mrs Betteson's face it fell sometimes
on the already wetted handkerchief she held in her hands. Now
and then she wiped it across Mrs Portman's face. It gathered
more sweat there until it was warm and saturated. Once when
this happened and she got up and laid the handkerchief out to
dry for a minute or two in the burning sun, she took off her
saturated bodice too. It peeled from her body like the sticky
grey skin of a fish. She wiped her breasts and shoulders with it,
and then after actually wringing the moisture from it spread it
out, still muddily grey and damp, to dry. The sun hit her
naked back like a flattening blow from a metal press. It swung
down and seemed to pin her there. It seemed to shrivel still
further the already skinny flesh and she felt the sickening pain
of it run down her spine. In a second it woke with aggravated
pain all the nausea of thirst.

She thought again of tea. The idea struck across her mind
as violently as the sun had hit her shoulders. She had been too
occupied with the making of the shelter and too weary in the
heat even to think of it again. Now she was shot through with
a new excitement.

And once more, as with the spectacles and the scissors and
the tools, she found release in physical activity. Her long-
fingered, frog-like hands came suddenly into their own. They
were the hands which had repelled even Tuesday in their
skinny pawings of attempted affection. No one had ever
wanted their sloppy ugliness. Now they were taut and spirited.

'I'm going to make you some tea. How would you like

141

that?' She bent over Mrs Portman with whispered excitement. 'Don't you think that would be nice, eh?' She dithered and wiped the sweat from the yellow shade-barred skeleton of Mrs Portman's face. 'That would be wonderful, eh?'

How? Once again she had not the faintest idea. She groped for a moment with the idea of making the tea in one of the round biscuit tins that were packed in the food boxes. And then some association of ideas recalled with delighted abruptness that lamb of a boy.

She could not think of Tuesday without thinking at once of making a fire. She had loved, each morning and each evening, the business of gleaning for things to burn. Now the idea of tea was like the idea of a feast. She could not resist it. She felt it would do her good. She would make a meal with biscuits and perhaps a tin of meat and an orange: wonderful things.

And then the fire. She began to collect broken lengths of bamboo and pieces of the straw-like fronds. She had not put on her bodice again. She walked about in the heat naked except for her spectacles and her drawers. And Mrs Portman, slightly turning her head and seeing that odd, naked figure wandering about in search for bits of bamboo and straw, still as if in pure spectacled absentmindedness, saw it as a figure in a recollected and ghastly nightmare. It haunted her terribly as it went to and fro, white in the sun.

Mrs Betteson found three or four rocks and made them into a ring, piling straw and bamboo inside. She moved with confidence, remembering so well how that lamb of a boy had done it. Her spectacles flashed in the sun. When they grew very misty with the rising vapour of sweat she took them off and wiped them on her drawers.

It was only when she remembered how she had nothing that would light the fire that she began to be troubled. She stood vaguely trying to clear her mind. Terribly stupid, she thought, not to have remembered that simple thing. The thought cast her into dejection and she felt the sun hit her flatly, like a stab, on the top of her head.

Then she took off her spectacles to wipe them once more. For a second she felt hideously faint with thirst and sweat and the stab of sun. She groped in the mist of her short-sightedness, holding the spectacles idly against the stuff of her drawers, not troubling to wipe them.

And as she held them there, drooping and rocking in the heat, she felt the sun impinge itself through one of the lenses, magnified into a white pimple of scalding ferocity that made her suddenly cry out.

She bent down at once over her pile of bamboo and leaves and straw, holding her spectacles over it until their magnifying created the first orange flower of fire. In her excitement she fumbled and dropped the spectacles. They fell with a tinkle against one of the stones, and she let out a cry of joy and dismay as she groped and snatched them up. The dismay increased as she saw the thin crack the stone had made across the edge of the left lens – it had always been her weaker eye – but the joy increased too, as she rammed the spectacles on to her nose and gazed at the flame of her own miraculously created fire.

A few moments later the smoke had risen like a column of pearl-grey feather as high as the wheeling crows.

15

In the village Miss Allison had discovered beyond the narrow
bazaar a deserted hut, a single room of palm screen on teak-
wood piles, empty except for a few mats of woven cane on the
floor. On the steps of the next hut a saturnine Burmese
woman, more Naga in her ugliness than Shan, sat chewing
betel-nut. Her flat lips, scarlet with juice, shot grinning patterns
of bloody spittle into the dust below. In order to ask about the
hut Miss Allison had been forced, for the first time for many
weeks, to speak Burmese. And for the first time she did not
feel that it humiliated her.

There was something she did not like about the general appearance of Miss McNairn, and she had decided that Miss
McNairn and herself could sleep together in the hut. She carried among her belongings an orderly little leather case of
medical things: a few rolls of bandage, lint, adhesive plaster,
cotton wool, aspirin, quinine, iodine and so on. She had taken
a few drops of iodine in her water every day. She had also two
half-minute thermometers and a hypodermic syringe. The
syringe was useless since she had nothing to use in it, but she
had the idea of tactfully taking Connie McNairn's temperature. She had left her with Nadia at the far end of the bazaar.

Then, when she went back to find her, she discovered that
Connie was no longer there. And for the second time within a
few minutes she was obliged to speak Burmese. She was
forced to reach out and touch, reluctantly, each of the worlds
to which she did not belong: the world of the Burmese girl
whose pealing and almost shocking laughter had broken up the
camp silences each night as she lay down to make love and
sleep with Paterson, and the English girl who for most of the

afternoon had raved that she hated her country. In doing so Miss Allison felt herself not torn but strangely tranquillized.

She found Miss McNairn walking up and down the bazaar. 'What can be keeping Mr Paterson do you suppose? Why doesn't he come?' She advanced on the Eurasian girl with shrill demands, so that far behind the fruit piles rows of melon-like faces stared flatly in the smoky, fading light.

'He may have found something.'

'What could there be to find?'

'I really don't know.'

'Then why do you go on saying he may find something?'

'Perhaps he wanted to satisfy himself, that's all.'

'I think it's ridiculous, I think it's mad. It's all unnecessary.'

She shouted the last words and suddenly Miss Allison tried to change the subject.

'There's an empty hut at the end of the bazaar. I thought we could share it. The nights are cooler up here.'

'I'll stop in the tent, thank you. I always sleep in the tent.'

'Yes, I know. But I thought Mr Paterson might like it. He's had a terribly hard drive.'

'Why are you suddenly so concerned with what Mr Paterson does and feels and where he sleeps?' She, too, changed the subject abruptly. 'I'm going to buy some fruit.'

'I really wouldn't,' Miss Allison said.

'I want oranges, I'm thirsty.' She began pointing to small green-gold pyramids of fruit. The light was dying, purple and copper. In the dust a few small fowls plucked about, vivid green and scarlet and peacock-blue. Under the open-fronted eaves of palm the melon faces peered out, squinting.

Connie picked up oranges and said, in English: 'How much?'

'I really wouldn't,' Miss Allison said.

Behind the basket piles of fruit the melon faces spoke back, in Burmese.

'It's not a good thing to buy fruit in these villages,' Miss Allison said.

'Don't be so fussy!' Connie said.

'Much better to have a little of our own water. Let me get that. I'll put iodine in it.'

'I loathe iodine.'

'Most people do. It makes the water safe, that's all.'

'It's just fussiness,' Connie said. 'After all, I was drinking water all day yesterday and that had no iodine in it, and what's it done to me?'

Quite shocked, Miss Allison did not speak. Connie, angrily poised, fretful, rather pale in the gaudy cross-light of dying sun, stood with a green orange in her hands. All of Miss Allison's training became offended by the emotional English girl standing there shouting and angry as if she were going to throw the orange at the faces peering out from the shadow behind the fruit piles, and then she remembered the hysteria in the car. She pulled herself together and walked away.

Some minutes later she was surprised to see Paterson's car coming like a ball of dust up the road. Miss McNairn ran excitedly past her. The car was besieged by companies of cream-brown boys and in the front seat Tuesday sat god-like in the football shirt.

'You're soon back!' Miss McNairn said. 'You're soon back.'

Miss Allison heard, and said: 'What did you find?'

'There wasn't anything, was there?' Connie said. 'There wasn't anything?'

'Odd thing,' Paterson said. 'There was a fire.'

Connie spoke rapidly: 'I said so, I said so, I told you that.'

'What fire could that be?' Miss Allison said. 'Not the car?'

'Not the car, of course it would be the car?' Connie said.

Paterson said tiredly: 'It could be anything. The car still burning. A bit of jungle still smouldering.'

'The same thing really,' Connie said.

'Could it be anyone alive?' Miss Allison said.

'We're going to find that out.'

'Is it necessary? Not tonight? It's impossible,' Connie said.

'Tomorrow.'

'It means another awful delay. Must we?'

'Let's have some tea,' Paterson said. 'I'm done.'

He began to drive the car slowly down through the bazaar. In these few moments day had already gone. The little street was repressed in shadow, no light in it except the golden ray of the car's sidelights, which Paterson had switched on. More than ever the street of primitive open shops with its toy-like pyramids of pale-green lime and orange and its garish patterns of sweetmeat in magenta and rose and brilliant chrome had the look of something half-forgotten, a simple back-water, peopled by children, pecking fowls and staring melon faces, overlooked by the panic stream going north.

Miss Allison clung to one side of the car and Connie to the other, but neither of them spoke again as Paterson drove the car the entire length of the bazaar. And he did nothing to encourage them and was glad when he could stop beyond the farthest hut, the empty one discovered by Miss Allison, without having had to speak a word.

He lay flat in the dust while Tuesday made tea over the fire already built by Nadia. Lying on his face, he felt himself slip beyond the edges of physical tiredness. He was oppressed by a sensation of futility. It had begun to grow on the whole idea of the journey ever since Portman had gone ahead with the other car. Now it lay on all his thoughts like a mould, stultifying and sour. For a whole day he had reproached himself for allowing it to happen, for allowing Portman to override him, for allowing his own judgment to become the victim of the panic, the littleness, of the other man. It was a situation, he felt, that a good wholesale row could have prevented. He had simply let it drift into a tragic mess. He could even have prevented it by making love to Mrs Portman. And now someone was alive down there. Who? He could not get out of his mind the irritating and oppressive idea that it might be Portman. Perhaps Mrs Portman. Either one or the other would be ghastly. The Bettesons were simply victims; they were the sort of people who would automatically go under, with their constant surrender to fate and their luck. Nor was he troubled by Mrs McNairn. It was the Portmans who rose up to reproach him and he lay there wondering bitterly what would happen if it were Portman, and Portman alone, who was alive down there, the rest shattered to pulp, Mrs Portman with her selfish beauty and her perfect figure now no more than swollen flesh blackening in the sun.

The whole idea tormented him. It seemed to go repetitively round and round in his head without changing or inducing another thought. And he sat up with a violent start, as he had always done at first light in the bungalow, when the voice of Tuesday gently aroused him:

'Tea, Patson. Tea.'

As always the boy was smiling, fixedly and in that unprovoking way which was the most constant thing Paterson knew.

'Nurse Miss sent these too.'

The boy, not flinching from the thought that Paterson might throw the cup back at him, held four aspirins in his hand. For a moment Paterson was newly and more violently irritated. Women had the most damnably vexatious way of being helpful at wrong moments. He felt his head begin throbbing. It thumped like a heavy padded wheel, with the same changeless reverberation as his thoughts of Portman, just above his eyes. He shook his head sharply to and fro and then almost mechanically, suddenly irritated no longer, took the aspirins in the palm of his hand and sucked them down.

'Tea, Patson.'

He had forgotten the tea. He looked at the boy with a grin of affection, taking the mug from his hands. Half-blindly he drank the tea, into which the boy had dropped a slice of lime, and felt the hot fumes of it deliciously stimulating as he held his face there.

When he looked up again the boy had silently slipped away. He dropped the empty mug on the dust and lay down again, heated by the tea, too tired to think of getting up. For a long time he lay there in a sweat from the tea, thinking of nothing but Portman and the gorge where the smoke of the fire had sprung out from the mass of bamboo like a rising pigeon. It was dark and he could smell the bitter smoke of charcoal from the fires of the bazaar.

Then gradually as he lay there and the heat of the tea floated out of him and left him languid but refreshed, almost sweatless at last in the slowly growing coolness of real darkness, his thoughts stopped their repetitive wheel-like reverberation, troubling him no longer. The decision seemed very simple once it lay coolly there in his mind. He sat up. What he had to do was somehow to get down to the bottom of the gorge: no matter what it cost or how hard It was to do. Whatever was happening in the south, whether the Japanese were a hundred or fifty or only a dozen miles behind, whether cholera or typhoid or malaria were spreading up the road as fast as the migration itself – nothing of it seemed to matter very much. Whoever was alive there had to be got out; nobody would now make him go on from this place until that was done. Not that anybody would need to trouble to delay him very long. If he were not successful in forty-eight hours the sun, he knew, would do the rest.

'Bath, Patson sir. Bath.'

Tuesday was with him again, smiling. He smiled back, comforted by the wonderful thought that whatever happened the boy was always there: tea Patson, bath Patson, breakfast Patson; monumentally constant, complaintless, illuminated always by defeatless smiles.

'On other side of tent, Patson.'

'Thanks. I'll go.'

'Nurse Miss and Miss Con sleep in hut.'

'Right.'

'Something to do, Patson?'

'Yes,' Patson said. 'Find out about a path.'

'Yes, Patson.' Now there was no hesitancy, no hint of argument in the boy.

Paterson got up and walked over to where, on the far side of the tent and the hut, Tuesday had poured water in the portable bath. As he undressed he felt the evening air warmer than he had expected on his bare skin. He wondered about mosquitoes, thought for a moment how horrified Portman would have been, and then did not care. From the little village floated the breath, half-sweet, half-acrid, of flowers and evening fires of charcoal. Lights fretted the upper parts of the stilted houses and little curls of laughter spun down the bazaar.

He stood stretched and naked, rubbing his hands downward on his bare skin, catching the odour of all the day's stale and pungent sweat. And for a minute he was sad to be leaving. He thought with regret and a certain envy of the major, going back. Envy became touched with admiration as he remembered the major pushing his bicycle down the hill, alone, into the migrating stream of refugees, knowing as he must have done what, in time, would happen to him.

He sat down in the cold delicious water, looking up at the stars the major had thought were like fish. The stars reminded him of Nadia, to whom that notion of the major's had seemed so funny. In a moment she would come out to him; she would pour the water over his back and bring him, perhaps, a glass of gin with a little pressing of lime; she might even wash his hair and pour water over him from a bucket, so that it ran like a slow waterfall over his head and chest and navel, until at last all of the day was washed out from him, the depressing thought of Portman finally swilled away.

'Can I speak with you, please?'

Startled, he looked back over his shoulder. Standing ten or fifteen yards away was Miss Allison. She had put on a kind of white hospital coat, so that she looked like the spectre of something professional standing stiffly there in the darkness.

'I'm in my bath,' he said.

'Don't mind me. Men in their baths are just bits of anatomy to me.'

'Fire away. What is it?'

She came a pace or two nearer.

'It's about Miss McNairn. She's not well.'

'She's tired and hysterical,' he said. 'After all, she's just lost her mother.'

'That's just it. She doesn't think she's lost her mother.'

The thought cut crisply into his feeling of contentment. He

had taken the death of Mrs McNairn and the Bettesons so much for granted that now he was angered freshly.

'That's just letting her imagination get her down, that's all. That's damned silly.'

'She's running a temperature. A hundred and two.'

'Just hysteria and excitement. You ought to know that. You saw her.'

'I know. But it seems she was drinking water yesterday. The peasants gave it her after the accident.'

'The people are fairly fastidious about their water. I shouldn't worry.'

'I know. But you can't be too sure.'

'I think all she needs is sleep,' he said. 'Don't you?'

'I don't know. Perhaps you'd come and look at her?'

He did not know quite what to say and for a moment he sat with his hands on his knees, staring at the greenish brilliant stars swimming exactly as the major had said, like fish, in the night-purple water of the bath. It was almost the first time he had spoken with the Eurasian girl alone, and now suddenly he at once admired her and felt sorry for her. She seemed to have come to life out of that long repressed isolation and had confidence in herself at last.

'There's surely nothing I can do?' he said.

'You can tell her what you're going to do tomorrow. That's what frets her.'

'We're going to look for Portman and the rest. There's somebody alive down there. Must be.'

'I wouldn't tell her that.' The figure of the nurse had remained all the time at a respectful distance behind him, like a white spectre against the dark purple-brown background of palm thatch that formed the compounds of the houses. He turned with almost offensive sharpness to look at it.

'Why not?'

'She doesn't want anyone to be alive. That's all.'

'Did she say that?'

'No.'

'She's just hysterical and tired.

151

'Her one idea is to go on and get out of the country.'

'Very natural. Is that all?'

'No. She's tormented by the idea of her mother. She's afraid she'll be alive' – the nurse spoke with the rather correct blunt English of someone who does not speak it as a native tongue, so that what she said sounded stilted and incredible and unreal – 'and that it will be you who will bring her back.'

'Good God,' he said.

In a pretence of washing he thrashed about madly with his hands so that the stars were suddenly like golden-green shoals of darting creatures he could not catch.

He turned in time to see the nurse walking away. The thing was so absurdly unreal that he could trust himself only to speak briefly.

'I'll come in,' he said.

'Thank you,' she said. 'Be careful of mosquitoes. It's warm.'

'There are no mosquitoes up here.'

'I just killed one in the hut.'

'Yes? They never touch me. Hate the taste of me.'

'There's always a first time,' she said.

As she disappeared he swished water all over his body and up into his face, thrashing about again and again with his hands.

A moment later he heard the voice of Nadia, who had come up in silence to bring him the drink he wanted. At the sight of him sitting there angrily thrashing at the water she suddenly burst out laughing as loudly as when he had told her that the major had thought the stars were like fish.

He began laughing too, and took the drink from her hands. She was kneeling by the bath. She had smoothed and oiled her hair so that it was like a black and polished shell; there were fresh flowers in the side of it, a crimson one and a tasselled spray of milky cream, and there was a smell of fresh tanaka powder deliciously about her face. She kept laughing for a moment or two longer, her teeth white in the darkness, and then pressed her head against his water-sprinkled shoulder, half-kissing him, half-laughing with her mouth against his neck.

And as he sat there, his own mouth against her, the water gathering into drops on his body, the drink in his hands, he was disturbed once again by the thought of the major into a new regret, almost hatred, of leaving the country. He felt he wanted to grip very tightly, through the thin cream muslin, the shoulders of the girl; he wanted for ever the simplicity of possessing her. In all that happened neither she nor the boy had anything but that same complaintless constancy.

When, after a few moments, Paterson had finished his drink and she had gone back to the tent to get him another, he heard the first cry of jackals, northward, in the hills. It was a sound that always troubled him; and now it brought back another uncertain rush of thought about Portman and the accident to the car.

He was drying himself, standing up, when Nadia came back. She had brought not only his drink but another towel, a clean white shirt and long trousers.

She stooped without a word and began to dry his legs and feet.

Five minutes later he went to the hut that Connie and Miss Allison shared. The little bazaar had not closed. Simple candle lamps shaded by half-moons of paper illuminated all the fronts of the open-fronted raised-up huts. Orange and pink and almond green and yellow pyramids and circles of fruit glowed under a sky of grape-bloom. And pausing for a moment to look at it he saw Tuesday come floating out of it, bearing an armful of three or four papaias, with a bunch of small green bananas, the apricot-fleshed very sweet kind that he liked most, on the other shoulder.

He stopped, thought with pleasure for a moment of the papaias, sugared and cool, that the boy would prepare for him, and then asked about the path.

Yes, the boy said, there was a path. It went down into the gorge from the other side. It was a bad path and hard to find because every year it got washed away by monsoon rain and was not beaten out again until the dry season by hunters. It was very difficult but he had found a guide.

What guide?

A boy. He was a wonderful guide and he knew the path.

He'd better be wonderful, Paterson said.

He was very wonderful. He had only one eye, but it was a most wonderful eye to see things.

All right, Paterson said, the three of them would start at dawn.

He turned and went up the steps into the hut. A paraffin lamp with a tin reflector hung on the centre bamboo strut of one palm-thatched wall above Connie McNairn's bed. Miss Allison was washing her hands, with rather finicky surgical precision, in an enamel bowl. He stood for a moment looking down at Connie lying on the low, collapsible bed.

And then, before he could say anything, she said: 'I heard what you were saying. Just now.'

'I'm just going to give her a shot of something to make her sleep,' Miss Allison said.

'How do you feel?' he said.

'I heard what you said. It'll take days and days to get down there.'

'I don't think so.'

'I feel rotten. It's this place.'

'We'll be out of it the day after tomorrow.'

'When will we get to India?'

God only knew, he thought, and was glad to hear Miss Allison giving the preliminary jerking plunge of the hypodermic syringe.

'Oh! please!' the girl said. 'I don't need that.'

'You need sleep,' Miss Allison said.

'I don't need it, I tell you!'

Her eyes, directly inflamed by the paraffin lamp overhead, seemed to have expanded and were once again hysterically wild and large.

'I don't need it! I don't want it! I'm not having it, I tell you!'

Miss Allison walked to the bed and knelt down, the hypodermic syringe poised in her right hand. In her left she held a swab of lint. She made a rather hesitant movement as if to dab it on Connie's pale upper arm. Paterson stood away. The girl was wearing a nightdress of pale pink silk without sleeves, and for the first time he could see how long and white her arms were. He could see the entire shape of her body, half-naked, in its twisted resistance on the bed.

'And don't put your hands on me! I don't want that thing!'

Miss Allison made a second hesitant movement with the swab.

'Keep your rotten hands off me!' the girl shouted. 'Keep them off!'

She began flaying about with both hands.

'Mr Paterson!' the nurse said. 'Please.'

Even before she spoke he felt his own anger overcome him again. He turned and knelt by the bed. He saw in Miss Allison's eyes a glint of professional hardness. He picked the girl's flaying arms out of the air and laid them in one fiercely deliberate movement by her sides. The swiftness of it surprised and shocked her. It pulled the nightdress across her breasts, pinning under the transparent silk all the pulsating, excited softness of her flesh so that he could actually see her heart beating under the tautened skin. And within a second or two it was the only movement she made. He saw Miss Allison dab one arm with the swab, heard the suck of the syringe and watched the needle pin slantwise into the flesh. The girl did not move. He heard her begin quietly sobbing. He saw the syringe withdrawn and he released his grip on her arms that had been so like stretched elastic when he had first held them and that he still expected to spring up again and begin thrashing his face. But nothing happened. She did not move, and he pulled the thin cotton sheet up from the bed and covered her body, unexcited until she gave another great shudder, partly of release, partly as if she were suddenly drenched with cold.

'All over,' Miss Allison said.

He stood up. He felt suddenly as impersonal as Miss Allison looked. The lids of the English girl's eyes were half-shut, showing nothing but slits of exhaustion.

A mosquito went across his line of vision, pinging past his ear into the area of lamplight. Miss Allison made a dive in the air with her hands, unsuccessfully. He was surprised and said:

'You'd better give her a net. There's one in the car.'

'You'll need it. I have one,' she said.

'I never use one. They suffocate me.'

'Aren't you afraid of malaria?'

'Must keep the nurses in business,' he said. He grinned and took a last look at Connie before going outside.

Miss Allison followed him out. It was warm and quiet and the night had a thicker, more velvety blackness after the nearness of the lamp over the bed.

'I'll come and fetch the net,' she said. 'She'll be all right now.'

'What did you give her for an injection?'

'Nothing.'

'Nothing?'

'I had nothing to give.'

He did not know whether to laugh or not. 'All that fuss for nothing,' he said.

'Not for nothing. She believes she had it. It's enough.'

He laughed. 'If I were ill would you do that to me?'

'I might.'

'The thing is I'm never ill.'

'Some day,' she said, 'you might believe you were.'

He laughed again, suddenly feeling that he liked her: the combination of trained calm, the objective attitude and the rather stilted half-Eastern charm, with the high voice, that the crossing of colour always seemed to give.

'I'll give you a drink before you take the net back.'

Nadia was not to be seen, and Tuesday was sitting by the fire he had made, twenty or thirty paces away. In the firelight he was deep in contemplative examination of the little radio.

Paterson went into the tent and came back with gin and glasses. He poured Miss Allison a drink. He held up his own glass and wished her luck. And then, as if it were something she had long wanted to say, she said:

'I always think it was very fine of the major to go back.' She spoke as if it were something she had enviously turned over and over in her mind.

'Yes.'

'He'll have gone a long way by now.'

'I hope so.'

Silent and reflective for a moment, she drank, looked over towards where the boy was sitting with the box-like radio, devoutly listening, and then said:

'I wonder what's happening. I mean back there. In the town, at the hospital and everywhere. The Japs might be down the road for all we know. We never had any news.'

'No.'

Over by the fire Tuesday shook the radio like someone shaking a dice-box.

'What's he doing?' Miss Allison said.

'It's his radio.'

'If it's a radio we could get news, couldn't we? From India at least, or somewhere?'

'It doesn't work. All its condensers have gone. Hopeless.'

'Then why does he listen, poor kid, if it doesn't work?'

'He believes it does.' He grinned and raised his gin at her. 'It's enough.'

She smiled, and over by the fire the boy held the radio on his knees, looking southward. The illusion of hearing things had left him for a moment and now he sat with wide still eyes, dream-projected in the light of the fire, lost in the illusion of seeing things instead. For the first time he felt a little homesick for the places he knew. He remembered them with half-pleasant pain and saw them sharply in the darkness as he sat there with the dead radio on his knees: the bungalow, the room where he had splendidly waited at table in Paterson's shirt, the dusty compound, the jacaranda tree. And now, for all their sharpness, they began to seem terribly far away.

16

Just before nine o'clock the next morning Mrs Betteson saw the first vulture trying to get into the car. It was trying to force its neck into the aperture left in the front window. On the smooth cellulosed metal and on the glass it floundered like a seal on wet rocks, falling back into the sand. Then it sat there like a bald evil turkey, uncurling its powerful rubbery neck, giving ponderous flutters of grey wings as it got ready to spring. When it did spring it flew upwards and came clumsily to rest on the tilted bonnet of the car. Again the smoothness of polished metal would not hold it and it fell heavily down. Its talons scratched like files on the sheet metal, whistling.

As it sat once again in the dust, wings twitching, it was joined by another. They floundered for a moment and then rose, attacking the car. They could find no hold and fell against each other, grey bodies slithering on smooth metal. Flat on the air the sound of beaten wings, opened to break the fall and closed again, had a sound of exasperated power.

And then the two birds were joined by three others. In two or three minutes, after more attacks, they learned where they could perch on the car. They sat on the wheels, on the running-board, on the fenders and on the grill of the bonnet. They attacked once again the aperture of the window. They thrust into it necks that were like lengths of rubber hose. Exasperated, they made croaking noises as they began fighting for the aperture, three at a time, two from below and a third, head down, acrobatically, from above. The third had no sooner got its head into the window than its feet began to slide. The whole enormous body swung down by the neck, feet clawing wildly for grip. They beat the air with terrific lashings. For a second the bird hung by its neck, half-throttled, and then it recovered. Its feet found the handle of the door and pressed on it panically, bringing the whole weight of the body upward. The handle was forced down. It gave a click of release and went back and the vulture dragged its neck at the window and fell. But the door was open and the weight of it falling back was too small to shut it completely again. There remained about an inch of unclosed space. Instantaneously the birds began to claw at it, frantically, with enraged greed, claws whistling, until at last by sheer power the space was opened and the door was swinging back.

Mrs Betteson, sitting with Mrs Portman under the shelter of bamboo, watched it all through her cracked spectacles. She felt relieved and fascinated and revolted. But most of all she was relieved. She had expected it to happen in the heat of the previous afternoon and had almost brought herself to the point of opening the car doors herself, in readiness for what she knew would come.

Now there was no need to look. Over the end of the bamboo shelter she hung Portman's oily dungarees, so that the whole affair was shut away from Mrs Portman too. But every now and then, out of the corner of her eye, against her will, she caught sight of more birds arriving, like vast grey and crimson moths that shut their wings and became distended maggots, half-crawling, half-hobbling, as they disappeared inside the car.

She sat for some time like this, watching over Mrs Portman and then, in a hypnotic sort of way, the vultures. Mrs Portman's speech had not come back. As the sun rose the smell of decay rose too, and soon even the woman lying under the canopy of bamboo and dungarees knew of it and was sickened. And as the sickness rose up in her the light went out of her, so that the eyes, staring upward, seemed already dead.

Mrs Betteson sat heavily troubled behind her spectacles. The tea-making of the previous day had not been a success. She had wasted water because the tin can had tipped over; she had had to make two unnecessary extravagant boilings. And then, much worse, she had had sense enough to remember in time that Mrs Portman, with that injured stomach, certainly ought not to drink fluid in any quantity. And in the small doses Mrs Betteson gave her to wet her mouth she had not possibly been able to tell the difference between water and tea. So in a sense it had all been wasted. She had drunk the rest of the tea herself. It had tasted smoky and bitter. Still worse it had recalled Betteson, with his jibes at her cooking; the cooking that whenever she had attempted it had always failed. 'You couldn't damn well cook water, woman, you couldn't cook water.' Perhaps after all she had not been very good at practical things.

So at sunset she had let the fire go out. The last scalding hours of the afternoon had been full of wheeling jungle crows and the noise of the coppersmith bird. It had tapped with its metallic voice somewhere in the higher trees beyond the belt of bamboo. With its infuriating ringing repetition, worse even than the heat and the glare and the ripening odour from the car, it had almost driven her mad.

And now, suddenly, it began again. Once started, it was like the vultures and the sun. It would go relentlessly on until darkness, like something pecking with a little hammer at her brain.

It was that disquieting bird that decided her to make another fire. She had to do something with her hands. And she had no sooner begun to collect wood than she felt more cheerful. She was reminded, inevitably, of that lamb of a boy. She seemed to see his vastly amusing and smiling face as she roamed backwards and forwards about the clearing, collecting things to burn.

She walked backwards and forwards to the clearing fifteen or twenty times before she discovered what a pile of wood she had brought. It was not like the little pile of the previous day. It was already a jumble four or five feet high.

And suddenly it excited her. It offered all at once not simply release for her hands, but power and creation. She could build it up and there would be no end to it. It was almost fun.

She went back to kneel for a moment by Mrs Portman. She was surprised to find that her face had come to life again.

Then she saw that Portman's dungarees had gone from the edge
of the bamboo shelter. That in itself was strange. They lay six
or seven yards away. There was no wind and the dungarees
were heavyish with oil and could not simply blow away.

Then for the first time Mrs Portman spoke to her. Shocked
and weak, she spoke of the dungarees. A crow had swept
down, picked them up, then dropped them from a height of
ten or twenty feet in the air. She saw in the familiar dirty
trousers an association of terror with the dead Portman. They
came down like a dark floating ghost of the man.

The shock of it brought back her voice. And Mrs Betteson
was glad. It seemed to bring back a touch of beauty, through
the mere sparkle of spoken terror, to the face that had always
seemed to her so lovely, even in its aloofness, whenever she
had seen it on the flowered terraces of the swimming pool.

'Where have you been? Why did you go?'

'Making a fire.'

'Don't go. Stay here.'

'No. I won't go.'

'Stay here. Talk to me, will you?'

Mrs Betteson squatted down. She sat so that Mrs Portman
could not see the car, intercepting with her body and its flabby
drawers and bodice her line of sight.

She sat there for the rest of the morning, fanning the heat
from Mrs Portman's face, wetting her lips, gently talking. She
spoke of the marigolds and bignonias and orchids and hibiscus
she grew in the garden, the Swimming Club, the few pleasant
shops and the English tea-room that were only a short gharry
ride or rickshaw ride from any of the English bungalows, the
pleasant central gardens with cannas and lilies and zinnias
growing in their season between palms and shady delicious
margosa trees. She spoke once more of the *minahs* that talked
to her on the verandah; of all the pleasant, narrow, vanished
life of the town: a life that she had never taken part in except
as a flabby and unwanted spectator. And as she sat there talking, she thought of Mrs Portman – the beautiful and aloof Mrs
Portman, with her splendid figure, doing a swallow dive at the

Swimming Club. You hardly ever went to the club without seeing Mrs Portman there, in her pure white swimming suit of two pieces, her butter-smooth flesh several shades deeper brown than the despised Miss Allison's, her breasts like two white triangles of flower on that perfect background of unblemished sepia-gold, the rest of her body so taut that it had the carved purity of a nut. She was quite the show person of the town where figures were concerned. Betteson had once called her the goddess. It suited her very well. You never saw her there at the club without a man other than Portman ordering her a dish of ice-cream or a drink or tea or a chicken sandwich as she sat aloofly under the gay umbrellas at the side of the pool.

And as she sat there, mechanically fanning Mrs Portman's face, Mrs Betteson remembered an April evening when she had been walking across the grass compound of the club, behind the pool, where thick trellises of vine cut off the main buildings of the club; it was already the hottest weather and there, on the grass, in the first darkness of evening that still had in it the touch of the still smouldering orange day, Mrs Portman had been lying half-concealed with a man that was not Portman. Mrs Betteson had come flouncing across the grass and almost stumbled over the two of them. And then in the moment of turning away, mumbling something, she had heard the man swear suddenly: 'The bitch will get us thrown out of the club,' and then Mrs Portman: 'Lie still! It's only that poor idiot of a woman Betteson. Absolutely batty. She doesn't know what day it is.'

Down among the bamboos the coppersmith bird began again, ping-pinging with the maddening hollow sound of a child beating a can. Mrs Betteson got up and wandered about. And once again she began to pick up scraps and fronds of bamboo, moving slowly in the great heat. Each time she left the shade she felt the sun hit her across the neck as if she had been demoniacally struck with a hot iron. She piled the wood for the fire six or seven feet high.

When she had exhausted herself again she went back to Mrs Portman. She squatted down and fanned the air with a cardboard casing from one of the food boxes. She thought once again of Mrs Portman at the Swimming Club. Of course they would never speak of it. There would be no question of that. But all at once she saw the lovely figure lying on the darkened grass and it seemed to come out of the past to mock her bitterly. She could not bear the thought of its dying there now, irrevocably smashed, the beauty of it gone, in that putrid ghastly indecency of heat and decay.

She moved to touch Mrs Portman with the greatest tenderness and found herself crying instead.

She got up at once and moved quickly away. Tears and the mist of sweat began to film over her spectacles, so that she could not see, and she wandered out into the heat, helplessly. Something came down and struck darkly and swiftly the side of her face. She staggered about and saw the rising jungle crow that had flown down, with predatory cheek, to attack her. She stood trembling and crying in the sun, wiping her spectacles. The crow came down again, darkly swooping. She waved her hands and the flashing spectacles made glassy-gold circles about her face. And then in a second the crow seized the spectacles in its beak, pulling with frightening strength. She clutched the spectacles, weeping and terrified. She could feel the horny beak of the crow tightening on her spectacles and then on her fingers so that she could not let go. The crow was making a sort of guttural chawk-chawking noise, half throttled. She groped blindly and in great fear and then, directed by the sound, she had the crow by the neck. She felt its body warm and loathsome under the slippery feathers. The notion of losing her spectacles gave her suddenly the most murderous desperation and she seized the crow with both hands. It gave powerfully steely flappings with its wings against her face, but she clung with fierce craziness to its neck and in another minute she had fallen down, with the crow underneath her. Then she pressed down with her hands until the neck of the bird was buried in dust and she could hear the choked chawk-chawking of its big throat no longer.

It still had the spectacles in its mouth when it died. She took them away from it and put them on. In the struggle the cracked segment of the left lens had fallen out, so that now when she looked out from them that small upper triangle of her vision was blurred. Almost mercifully it cut off the hideous happenings in the car. She crawled on her knees, panting terribly, bathed in heavy and weakening sweat, bludgeoned by sun, crazily stricken and stupefied. And then the dead crow gave a great convulsive flutter of reflexed power with its wings. It frightened her so that she suddenly stood up. And then so that it should not happen again she stamped on the crow with both feet until it was nothing but black and crimson pulp in the hot dust beneath her.

It had happened so quickly that she was still crying as she stood there, beating the last quiver of life out of the bird. Almost immediately she felt that the whole gathered flight of crows were preparing to attack her. They began wheeling in vicious circles, about the height of the bamboos. They had begun to settle, like the vultures, on the car.

Trembling and crying, but without a sound, she decided to light the fire. She bent down against the mass of heaped bamboo and clenched her spectacles, focusing with the good lens the light and heat of sun. She almost laughed when it worked like a trick. Then as it began to burn she thought of something else. She remembered the can of oil from the car. She ran to fetch it and in the moment before the flames leapt up she poured it on. In the heat it was very thin, like honey, and it began to burn at once, darkening the flame with wreaths of dirty smoke. In anger she picked up the dead crow and threw that too, with the oil-can, into the fire. The smoke rose to the height of the wheeling crows and with the rising heat seemed to push them suddenly upward in a black canopy, cawing panically, out of range. In the car the vultures became aware of it too, and beat with talons and wings at the fire-reflecting glass, making gorged noises of quarrelling alarm, faces at the windows staring out like swollen and bloody turkeys, trapped and caged.

When she could bear the sight and smell and heat no longer

she went back to Mrs Portman. She felt a great sense of triumph as she squatted down. Even in the great heat of noon the smell of burning bamboo and smoke and feathers had the delicious pungency of a disinfectant, and she felt at last that she had beaten, even in a little way, the birds, the stench and the sun.

In the same moment she saw that a great change had come over Mrs Portman. It seemed to her all at once that she was dying. The grey light had come back to the face, which had no reality in its weakness, and there was no sweat on the dry skin.

The cloud of smoke closed over the two of them as she lay down. She had nothing to say and she simply rested her face against the face of Mrs Portman as they lay together.

Even in that moment she could feel the beauty of it. The skin was lovely to touch in its unblemished silkiness. Against it her own face had the clumsiness and ugliness of a misshapen knuckle-bone. She stroked her cheek backwards and forwards on Mrs Portman's cheek, partly in comfort, partly in the sheer tired joy of its tenderness. The face for a moment turned to her, but it had no strength and all that happened was that the lips rested, cold and lovely and speechless, against her own.

Out in the clearing the fire, dark and bright, burned itself away. Every now and then oil smoke rose above the height of the bamboos, keeping the wheeling crows away. It was thick enough sometimes to conceal for a moment, with churning orange clouds, the glitter of sun, and it burned like that for about half an hour after Mrs Portman had died.

It was not until then that Paterson, Tuesday, and the Naga boy who was guiding them saw it from about a mile up the valley. The Naga boy saw it first. He had only one eye; he had lost the other by running carelessly against a sharpened hunting spike hidden by elephant grass in another valley. It had made him very vigilant and he had spotted the crows some time before.

17

Paterson decided to remain in the village another two nights and a day, resting Mrs Betteson and Connie McNairn.

The boy sat for long intervals in the shade of a tamarind, deep in talk with the Naga boy. On his knees was the little radio set and sometimes he lifted his head to sing snatches of song. Beating his hands gently, drum-wise, on the sides of the case, and then singing to the rhythm he made, he indicated that these were the sounds that would emerge when the thing was working. All the time the Naga boy sat transfixed, thick bevelled lips open, his one eye gorging hungrily. The closed blood-rimmed slit of the other gave the effect of looking back over his shoulder. Sometimes he leaned forward to grasp the set with both hands. It was whipped away before he could touch it, and then Tuesday would hold it for long periods under his arm, hands locked together. Then the Naga boy crept on his knees, first behind and then in front of Tuesday, peering in wonder, ghoulishly. Once when he came near enough to breathe on it there were great polishings with the football jersey. It was held away, tighter and more defensively, as an untouchable thing. And then sometimes the Naga boy sat staring at the dust. He seemed to ponder over great schemes of possession. He talked with his hands. In the early afternoon he went away and came back with a Naga cross-bow. He began to demonstrate with it as Tuesday had demonstrated with the radio-set, jealously and grandly. He made long demonstrative speeches in which the Nagas were held up as great hunters, the cross-bow as a more wonderful and more necessary thing than a box that gave out no noise. He was careful not to talk of it with contempt. He spoke only as if the cross-bow were even more wonderful than that wonderful thing. You could do so much more with it than you could do with the little box. With it you could kill things. You could kill jungle fowl, pheasants, things to eat. The enemy was coming. You could kill the enemy. You never need be afraid. What use was the box? The Naga boy could not understand it. A useless thing without voices. All the time Tuesday did nothing but smile. Finally, holding the radio more and more possessively, he explained that there were voices. A long time ago he had heard them. Actually, from inside. And now, in his head, he could hear them still. They were not ordinary voices. They came from far away: Burmese voices, English voices, Indian voices singing, talking, playing music. Paterson had explained how they were real voices and how they came from far away. That was enough.

When the Naga boy finally walked away he waved the crossbow about with equal pride. The empty blood-rimmed socket of his lost eye gave him the effect of someone ghoulishly winking. The other eye rolled with hungry brilliance. He seemed always to have the air of naturally stalking something, with that curious one-eyed vigilance, in the glittering, shimmering air.

He did not appear again for the rest of that day. In the heat of the afternoon Mrs Betteson, Miss McNairn, and Miss Allison rested in the hut. Paterson overhauled the car. While he cleaned the plugs, checked the timing and set the carburettor, Tuesday worked under the chassis with the grease-pump and then checked over the tyre-pressures. He had become very adept with the gauge. Large-eyed, pale-brown faces crowned with greased black top-knots gathered about him all that afternoon as he pressed the gauge against the valve-nipples. They jumped and laughed at the little silver snake that hisses when he held its small fat head against the wheel. All the time he moved from wheel to wheel with the proud condescending calm of an engineer working among great mechanical intricacies. Sometimes, squatting down, he paused and looked aloft, squinting curiously, as if watching a bird in the burning sky above the hills. All the children turned and looked up, wrinkling flat eyes. And then, in the silence, at the curve of his hand, the tyre gauge would press against the wheel, and out of its great vicious hiss would come new shrieking laughter. He moved above it with the slightly bored, smiling air of a man long since used to the small terrors and mysteries of such things.

It was only when he actually took hold of the pump and began putting air into the tyres that he dropped the attitude of condescending lightness. The pump was a serious affair. He pushed the brown peering faces back. He became like a man who seeks elbow room for an important demonstration. The pumping, and the subsequent test by the gauge, were things demanding the most accurate delicacy. They demanded the reading of figures – twenty, twenty-five, thirty, the figures Paterson had taught him. These serious matters were above trifling. They were not of the world of little children pressing with dusty noses, peering with compressed brown eyes.

Sometimes he leaned back, resting on the handle of the pump, and spoke casually to Paterson in English. If the air gauge and the pump gave him something of the esteem of an engineer, the use of a strange unknown language turned him into a figure that was fabulous.

He was aware of this. His smile broadened marvellously. He knew himself to be the central focus of all the dumb laughterless eyes.

'Offside back is spare wheel, Patson. Change it back?'

'How worn is it?'

'Second spare, Patson. Not too good.'

'Better change it.'

'Yes, Patson, yes. Change it now. Change it right away.'

He rose with masculine offhandedness, wiping his hands on an oily rag. As he walked round to the boot of the car, to get the wheel jack, the little brown moon-procession of faces pressed about him tightly.

Aware of it, he peered for several moments into the boot, as if contemplating hidden workings. All the faces came to peer too. He picked up a wrench, weighed it for a moment in his hands, then dropped it. He wiped the sweat from his face with the back of his hand.

Then he picked up the jack. It was as if he had picked up an explosive weapon. It was as much as he could lift but he held it casually, as one used to holding such trivialities. He swung it about with easy importance and the children stood back.

When he lay flat on his face under the car, unscrewing the jack and fixing it there, all the children lay there too. They had something of the appearance of a row of fat piglets, sucking. They hunched and nosed about, pushing faces into the greasy shadow between the wheels. They snuffled and giggled and then when he emerged again, to begin the business of turning the jack-handle, they emerged too, watching him.

And then, as he saw the axle rise and the wheel lift itself from the ground and the children kneeling there to watch it all, he knew that he had scored a triumph. The tyre-gauge was simply fun. But the jack, the raising of the car, was a miracle. A wonderful thing. Wiping his hands once again on the oily rag, smiling, he knew that the whole affair had given him great prestige.

The faces were absolutely silent as he unclipped the wheel disc with the twist of a screw-driver and then unlocked the wheel-nuts, swivelling the wheel-brace, and then took the wheel away. He rolled it in the dust and rolled the new wheel into its place with one hand.

'Tuesday!' Paterson called.

'Yes, Patson! Yes, sir.'

'When you've got the wheel on go and get tea. I'm as hot as hell.'

'Yes, Patson, yes. Quick as hell!'

'Bad word!'

'Yes, Patson.'

Once again the short exchange of words raised him in the eyes of the watching faces. He put on the new wheel, swivelling the wheel-brace with careless deftness. All the time he felt that he was no longer a small boy. Now, because of Paterson, through Paterson, and by reason of the things Paterson had taught him, he was a person of grown stature. He was very happy and very important, he was immensely above the childish peering faces, the poor hill creatures who could not read the figures on a gauge or lift the two-ton weight of the great car with one hand.

It was not until some time later, when he went over to the tent, where he slept alone now because the three women had the hut, that he found the radio had gone.

In the morning Paterson drove slowly forward into curtains of sulphur fog. In the light that splintered whitely from the rocks the distances of earth and sky were impersonally fused. The ingrained crusts of forest looked shadowless in the haze. Where the road curved to circuit the shoulders of hills it seemed to be cracked off like the edge of a broken plate. It gave the effect of ending in air.

This suggestion repeated itself again and again: always the turning shoulder of rock, the broken rim of road, the declivity beyond it lost in yellow haze. Here and there from both sides and from the distance ahead the hill forest closed in, so that sometimes the road bored through tunnels of branching creamy feathers. Where the dust had continually risen and fallen without wind each frond of bamboo and fern and creeper and leaf, for fifty or sixty feet up, had become embalmed. Under the weight of it they hung down with the featheriness of cobwebs too lightly suspended. They broke and fell sometimes like dusty skeins.

On the naked backs of the peasants the dust settled with the fineness of creamy chalk. They walked in single file. They had the appearance sometimes of half-dressed dolls, skirted in purple and green and blue and vermilion or in hoop-wise stripes of several colours. They seemed to lean forward, woodenly, pressing against the fog. They walked now on both sides of the track, taking up several yards of it, so that there was no room for one vehicle to pass another. Where the forest was not like a fence on either side the road swung outwards, circuiting the shoulder of hills, and there was no way of passing. From the double defile of faces there was no one who looked up. They were concentrated in front of themselves with the dispirited muteness of tired soldiers.

In the car Paterson had rearranged the seating. There were now six of them. In the back Miss Allison sat between Nadia and Connie McNairn and sometimes as he glanced up into the driving mirror and saw them reflected there Paterson could not see much difference, under that high cream-dusty light, in the colour of the three faces. In the front the boy sat between himself and Mrs Betteson. He sat with one hand on each knee, the fingers half-open, as if he were thinking of grasping something. He seemed to be staring beyond the curtain of dust. Now and then Mrs Betteson glanced at him. It was a curious glance, not glassy or fussy now. The albino-like eyes seemed to have grown several shades darker; the pupils were like stamens of pale violet, delicately rigid and yet flexible at the same time. Underneath them the face had lost its air of creased neglect, the appearance of a crumpled garment that could never again be ironed smooth. And the stare she gave to the boy was affectionately free and yet restrained. It did not seem, as before, to pounce at him. It held him in cautious understanding. She did not once call him that lamb of a boy.

Poised between her and Paterson the boy was very afraid. He was afraid first that she would begin to gabble at him; then that she would fussily tangle him with questions and that he would have to reply. This in turn brought a greater fear of Paterson: the terror of his discovery that the radio had gone. He had never looked at the radio as a discarded thing. It had been given by Paterson and therefore it was a precious thing. He felt that to have lost it was to have offended Paterson. It aroused in him sensations that he was not, after all, good enough for Paterson. He recalled the affair of changing the wheel of the car: the ring of little faces, the idea that he was a great fellow. It seemed very cheap and stupid now.

In the back of the car Connie McNairn was also afraid. She was trying to think of ways to beat Miss Allison's thermometer. She had begun to feel more and more ill and sometimes, when the car rose on the edge of a larger pot-hole and hung suspended before bursting forward again, she felt for a second or so that her head was not part of her body. It seemed to float away, partially detached, on loose and distended wires. It became like the head of a broken doll pitching forward and then lolling into place again.

But in fear she was determined also not to be ill. She sat with her hands clenched at her sides. She was free of her mother and now, at last, in spite of everything, she was going to India with Paterson. And nobody, if she could help it, was going to prevent that; least of all Miss Allison.

She had watched the gradual strengthening of the Eurasian girl with fear. She had thought of her first simply as one of those girls. There were millions of them. They did not matter. Coming out of the darkness that first night, by the gardens of the hospital, anonymous and ghostly, with nothing to say, she had looked like the disinherited spirit she really was. It was she then, in those first days, who was frightened. She kept the palms of her hands face downwards. It was the palms, even more than the nails, with their awfully revealing colour, that she was afraid to let anyone see. She put the palest sort of powder on her face. In spite of the heat and discomfort she wore stockings. But it was no use. Anyone could tell.

And then she had put on her nurse's uniform. She had brought out the medical-aid box. That strange change had come over her. It was exactly like the change of the anonymous half-alive chrysalis into another creature. There was something wing-like, and to Miss McNairn quite maddening, about the white hospital cap she wore. It had given her a certain frigidity of stature and authority. And then the box itself. The hypodermic syringe. It was the expression of all the Eurasian girl's adopted power. And Connie McNairn's loathing of it, her determination not to have it stuck into her flesh, sprang out of that. It was only because Paterson had seized and held her down that she had given up resistance.

Then it had ceased to matter. Her fear was simply trans-

posed to the thermometer. No hypodermic could keep her
from India. It might even help her there. But the thermometer
could.

At first it had taken her unawares. Or rather Miss Allison
had taken her unawares. It was hospital technique, she supposed; rather cunning. 'Just hold that in your mouth for a
second.' Of course it was in there a minute before you knew.

And then they never told you what it said. It was your
temperature and they took the secret of it away. With the
hypodermic it was different. You knew you had that because
of the pain. There was no deceit in that. But they could cheat
you with the temperature.

And so, somehow, it had to be beaten. If the Eurasian girl
discovered a temperature of a hundred and three or four
Paterson could clamp down. Break the thermometer? They always had another. India could not be far away. She thought of
it always as being a little beyond the haze of hills, two or three
hundred miles away.

As she sat thinking of these things she felt more and more ill.
Her thoughts had more and more the swaying, jerky unsteadi-
ness of the car. And as she submitted her body to the motion
of the road, no longer holding it rigid, feeling as if incapably
sick on a roundabout that could not stop, she let herself be
thrown sloppily up and down. Several times she pitched over
and struck the shoulders of the Eurasian girl and then loosely
bounced back again.

Most of the time Miss Allison did not seem to be watching
her. She had grown indifferently tired of the hysterical acts of
the English girl who was afraid, or seemed to be afraid, of
the prick of a hypodermic needle. She was very likely one of
the kind that would bite the thermometer.

Instead, she began to be more and more troubled by what she
saw on the road. Whenever she saw a break in the defile of
walking people, men and women, Burmese and Hindu, Moslem and Madrassi, she leaned out of the car, facing the clotting
yellow dust and the sudden ferocious vertical blow of sun, to
see what had broken it. Sometimes a little camp had been

made. A few people were sitting about, listlessly eating, staring at the car. They munched with faces of dusty rubber. They passed out of her vision and became simply part of the heat, dust-hidden and impassive. And then sometimes she saw that it was not a camp. The knotted faces were staring at the earth. Once she saw on the dust the purple-rose feet of an Indian sticking vertically up from a crowd of Burmese waist-cloths and she knew that the Indian was dying and that the Burmese could not leave him until the breath had gone out of the body. All she could see as the car passed slowly forward were the pink undersides of the too-flat feet that had something of the undefiled tenderness of the feet of a child. The pink was the same dusky pink, but deeper in tone, as the colour of her own hands.

All the time there was nothing she could do. The car, part of the stream of traffic, was like a link in a chain. Fixed there, it could not be taken out until the road widened or the forest cleared. She could do nothing but sit there watching the other chain of living and dead that ran brightly between herself and the trees, and at the same time count the dead. There were twenty-three of them before noon.

Paterson camped at noon in the only place where it was possible to draw a car from the road. A small stream came down from the hills between knuckles of white rock, making a curve over which in the monsoon season flood water ran across reaches of crystalline sand. It had pressed the edge of forest gradually back, forming an open bay. When Paterson pulled the car from the road he felt the sand sucking at the wheels, binding them down.

Connie McNairn dragged herself out of the car and walked into the edge of the forest shade and sat down. Some part of her was determined to behave normally and she propped herself up by the trunk of a mountain acacia and began to read a book that Mrs Portman had left in the car. She felt very ill and could not see the words on the page. Yet the book, she felt, would give the appearance of not being ill. She could pretend

to read it and at the same time rest. When Miss Allison came
with the thermometer she would look bright and absorbed in
the book and say she was quite happy. In an hour they would
drive on. By evening they would be twenty or thirty miles
farther on; twenty or thirty miles nearer India, where she
knew no one except the friends up river from Calcutta and
where Paterson, if he had any respect, would have to look
after her.

As she sat there the light came off the whitened river sand,
painfully dazzling her face. It brought with it all the reflected
furnace heat of noon. It seemed to bleach the colour from her
face. She laid the book on her knees and opened her handbag
and took her lipstick out of it. Very shakily she held the lipstick in one hand and her mirror in the other.

She smeared dashes of bright lipstick across her mouth and
then looked in the mirror. The effect was ghastly. She took her
handkerchief and wiped a little of the lipstick away and rubbed
the crimson of it on her cheeks. It looked better when she had
powdered it. The powder was rose in colour and it toned away
some of the ghastly ivory neutrality that she feared and
hated.

She sat back and took up the book again and waited for Miss
Allison to come with the thermometer. It was useless to read.
She stared over the edge of the book to where, across the sand,
fifty or sixty refugees had camped too, making fires, eating,
sleeping under the shadow of bullock carts, washing in the
river. The odour of new cow-dung was wet in the hot air. Each
figure and each bullock and even the overladen carts seemed
suspended a foot or so off the scintillating whiteness of earth.
They floated between herself and the river like boatless sails of
violet and brown and green and yellow. She saw among them
Paterson and Miss Allison. They were helping Tuesday about
the fire. She saw Mrs Betteson and the Burmese girl coming up
from the river, carrying buckets of water. Mrs Betteson had
slipped off her blouse. She seemed to have no compunction
about it and she was half-running with the buckets, in bare
feet. The water swirled over the edge in a skin of silver glass

and spilled over her feet and she ran, laughing, until she almost dropped the buckets by the fire.

The girl sat there for some time and nobody came to her.

Very soon she lay down. She had begun to feel terribly ill. The heat seemed to thump down through the mass of branches above her like a gigantically painful press, hitting her. She could taste the heat on her lips.

She shut her eyes. Arms out, crucified by heat, she suddenly longed for Paterson and Miss Allison to come. Even Nadia, whom she despised, or the boy, too smiling sometimes in the football jersey. Even the stupid Mrs Betteson.

Under the blinding pressure of heat she felt the life run wetly out of all the pores of her prostrate body and in weak horror she let it go. She felt that she was going to die there, twenty or thirty yards from where people were eating and talking and sleeping and laughing, with no one to prevent it or help her or say a word.

The sound of footsteps startled her into sitting upright. She expected Paterson or Miss Allison.

It was Mrs Betteson, holding a cup of tea.

'Having a nap? We thought we wouldn't wake you.'

The girl sat groping through her dark spectacles. 'Half-asleep,' she said. She vaguely stretched her hands for the cup.

'Drink it up,' Mrs Betteson said. 'It'll make you hot but it'll cool you later. Tuesday made it.'

'That lamb of a boy?'

The girl meant it to be a sort of joke. Mrs Betteson simply said:

'I think he's in trouble. Unhappy or something. He's lost his tongue completely.'

The girl was not interested. She shook her head, trying to see straight, as she drank the tea.

Mrs Betteson sat down.

'It's quite nice and cool here.'

'Cool?' the girl said. 'I feel ghastly. '

Mrs Betteson looked at her. It did not seem to her that she looked ghastly. It was perhaps that her standards of comparison had changed. Mrs Portman had looked ghastly. The girl was neither as beautiful nor as ghastly as Mrs Portman had been.

'Where is Miss Allison?'

'She's doing what she can for a Burmese boy.'

'A Burmese boy?'

'Typhoid or something.'

'Typhoid? Oh no.'

'Typhus then. The same thing isn't it, only worse? The poor girl has had no rest or food at all.'

The girl shook her head and grimly sucked in the tea. She was not going to be ill. Nothing was going to make her ill. If you thought you were ill, hard enough and long enough, then you were ill. And if you thought you were not ill then, on the same principle, you were not ill.

She remembered suddenly that she had aspirins in her bag. Her mother had been addicted to aspirins rather as another woman might have been addicted to lipstick or cigarettes, out of boredom and habit, thoughtlessly. The girl was suddenly grateful for it and took four aspirins in her palm and sucked them into her mouth, washing them down with tea.

Mrs Betteson took no notice. If she had noticed it at all it would have been rather as she had noticed Betteson's Buddha. The aspirins had rather the same meaning, a charm against ill-luck. Betteson had been very unlucky in the matter of the Buddha. It had not availed him anything at all. But she did not notice and said simply instead:

'That girl will be the next one to crack up.'

'That's not surprising, is it? They always do. It's the way they're made.'

Mrs Betteson sat with her sprawling hands clasped over her knees, staring through her broken glasses at the bullocks drinking in the stream, and said:

'I think she's beautifully made.'

'I didn't mean that way.'

'It's the way I mean. The nicer way.'

'There could be more than two opinions about that.'

Mrs Betteson seemed suddenly not to be listening. She could not help being troubled first about Tuesday, who had hardly spoken a word all morning, and then about Miss Allison and the Burmese boy.

She stood up. 'I think I'll go and see how she's getting on. I could give her some help perhaps.'

'Help? How long are we camping?'

'I don't know. The car has to cool a bit. Do you want some food?'

'What is there? No. I don't want any.'

She leaned back against the tree again, irritated and tired, resigned at last to let Mrs Betteson go. She took off the dark spectacles that were misted and wet now with the sweat pouring out of her already from the tea, and as she did so, looking at the clear white sand with freshened eyes, she saw Mrs Betteson behaving in an astonishing and peculiar way. She was chasing a crow.

The crow had a sort of rocking lop-sided movement of cheeky greed as it came out of the sun. It made a slow, long swoop, wings quite still, glittering darkly down. And when the shadow of it beat over Mrs Betteson the woman began to flay about her madly with her clumsy hands. In her broken spectacles, mouth open, hands beating about her, she really looked, the girl thought, quite batty. She made screeching noises of anger that were so near madness and so comic, rather like the noises of a dismayed and infuriated fowl, that over in the shade of the tree the girl began laughing. She laughed for some moments, choking over the tea, bending her head, while Mrs Betteson ran screeching hither and thither, flaying the air with her hands.

And then when she raised her head again to look she saw another sight. It seemed to her even funnier than the first. Mrs Betteson had ceased chasing the crow. She had run instead to the car and had snatched something out of it. It was Portman's shot gun. She ran fifty or sixty paces with it into the centre of the clearing of dazzling sand and fired both barrels into the air. The sound split against the rocks beyond the road, and down in the stream a bullock charged madly about, stamping water. Green flames of parakeets descended from the trees, the cloud of crows sailed upwards and all the Burmese and even the hollow-bellied Indians crouching in filthy dhotis on the edge of shade looked up and began laughing, showing white mouths in moons of darkened skin.

All that afternoon the sight of Mrs Betteson firing the shot gun into the cloud of crows remained with Connie McNairn. It amused her so much that whenever she thought of it she felt better. The beating in her head, as though her skull were a tightened drum, gradually quietened down.

When they camped that night the situation was a repetition of what had happened at noon. The narrowness of the road gave them no choice of ground. Once again there was the clearing by the river, narrower now, and the confined shore of dust-like sand. The one tent was pitched by the forest fringe. She was to share it with Miss Allison.

When she discovered this, she crawled inside and arranged the bed and lay down. Once again she waited for Paterson or Miss Allison to come to her. Her head had begun to tighten up again; the angles of the little tent seemed sharply narrowed, rigidly confining her. Outside, the hollow voices of bullocks bellowed among the trees and a few Indians were singing wretchedly, with maddening, repeated quarter-tones, not fifty yards away.

They won't neglect me, she thought. Someone will come. Her stomach turned over and over in painless, weakening waves. A cooler tongue of air curled at ground height from the river, creeping in under the tent flap. She heard it stir in the dry fronds of bamboo and felt it blow coolly on her shoulders, making her shiver.

After a time she was aware of Tuesday, standing at the opening of the tent.

'Supper, miss. Patson says please come.'

'I'm not hungry, thank you, I'm not coming.'

'Miss?'

'I'm not hungry, thank you.'

'Tell Patson?'

'Yes. Tell Mr Paterson I'm not coming.'

As the boy went away she pulled the blanket over her shoulders. She had not undressed. But now she felt suddenly that her clothes, bundled under the blankets, had a terribly moist oppressiveness.

After a few moments she could not bear it; she got up and took everything off and then once again lay down, pulling the blanket over her. Her nakedness seemed at once to give her a feeling of great lightness. She had a feeling of floating emptily on long, slow waves of water.

And then all of a sudden Paterson was in the tent, talking.

'Are you all right? Don't you want to eat?'

He stood crouched over the bed. She saw his face in the rosy reflection of the camp fire.

'I'm all right. I'm all right really.'

'You ought to eat. You didn't eat at midday.'

The feeling of the two of them so confined in the close space of the tent, in the filtered light of fires, she herself naked under the blanket and Paterson bending down, suddenly made her tremble. Under the pressure of it she found herself telling Paterson a frantic lie.

'I'm all right really. I took my own temperature. It's just under a hundred. Not much.'

'You ought to eat. That's the trouble. You get over-hungry.'

The sensation of nakedness, the private physical sensation, coupled itself suddenly with the sensation of telling the lie. She felt both of them excite her.

Then Paterson stooped down. She actually felt him touch the blanket.

'Miss Allison has sleeping tablets. If I send them over will you take a couple?'

'Yes.'

Even as she said it she knew that that, too, was a deliberate lie. She would not take the tablets. She would put them under the bed roll and say she had taken them.

'You're sure you're all right?' he said.

'Yes. Just not hungry.'

'No hot and cold fits?'

'No.'

'No shivering?'

'No.'

'Nothing you want?'

She saw him put his hands on his knees, preparing to straighten up, ready to go. She did not want him to go. The sensation of intimacy, heightened by nakedness, became suddenly so strong that she felt her arms begin to tremble still more violently under the blanket.

'Perhaps I'd have some tea.'

'All right,' he said. 'There's no milk though.'

'I like it without.'

She felt herself gripping the blanket with both hands. All she had to do was to turn and let the blanket slip away. She would turn and it would slip from her shoulders and Paterson would see all that lay beneath it, and in a moment he would come in with her and lie down. The experience she had known about and wondered about so often as she heard the Burmese girl creep away from her hut in darkness would at last, in that simple way, become hers. She clenched her hands and felt her entire body quiver in its readiness to turn. She arched her body so that her breasts moved upwards, lightly, no longer timid in their movement of the blanket. For a second she held them rigidly there and felt the sweat of exhaustion and fresh excitement pour down her body, and then in a quiver of relaxation she drew the blanket not down but closer against her face.

Paterson stood as upright as he could in the tent, saying: 'I'll send the tea,' and even as he said it he looked embarrassed and she knew that it was all over. He turned almost immediately and, stooping, went out.

Long after the tea had been brought by Tuesday, with the sleeping tablets, she lay there and wondered why Miss Allison did not come. For some reason she felt her thoughts turn with fury on the Eurasian girl. The pain of her stupid illusion about Paterson seemed to find its outlet suddenly against the nurse.

She did not take the sleeping tablets. The tea grew cold and she poured it away. Outside the tent the infuriating melancholy singing, with its quarter-tones that seemed endlessly to repeat and never resolve themselves, went on and on, exactly like the pained echo of the most unresolved wanderings of her own idiotic mind.

It was half-past ten when Miss Allison at last came in. Most of the fires were out and the nurse came with a hurricane lamp. From the tent the girl saw the swinging light of it become motionless beyond the aperture.

'Is that you, Miss Allison?'

'Yes.'

'Where have you been?'

There was no answer. The girl heard only the sound of water pouring into a bowl. She waited for a minute, heard the splashing of water repeated a few times, and then said:

'Miss Allison.'

The nurse came slowly into the tent, drying her hands on a towel. Her mouth was open as if she were about to say something and had forgotten what it was. She wiped her hands slowly on the towel, as if terribly tired.

'I thought you might have come in to see how I was.'

'Yes. I meant to.'

Miss Allison stood staring, wiping her hands more and more absently.

'Well, anyway, Mr Paterson came.'

'Yes?'

'Yes. He took my temperature.' Her resentment and impatience against the nurse suddenly took exactly the form her emotions had taken with Paterson. She lied again: 'It's normal. It's ninety-eight.'

'Yes?' Miss Allison did not seem to be listening.

'He gave me sleeping tablets if I needed them, but I don't need them.'

'Yes?'

She wished suddenly that the nurse would not repeat that single questioning word in that infuriating way.

'It was nice to have some company. It did me good. I was here. In bed.'

Miss Allison slowly dried her hands and stood for fully half a minute staring before her without a word.

'He stayed a long time,' the girl said. 'It was nice.'

It occurred to her suddenly to reveal to Miss Allison, somehow, that Paterson was in love with her. The whole notion was abruptly checked by the sight of blood on Miss Allison's towel.

The girl sat suddenly upright. And as she did so the blanket fell away from her shoulders. Miss Allison blinked sharply as if briefly interested in the sight of the girl sitting there completely naked to the waist and then slowly, with terrible tiredness, began to cry.

'Are you hurt?' the girl said. 'What's that blood on your hands?'

'We delivered a baby. Two babies.'

'We?'

'Mrs Betteson.'

Connie, who did not know what to say, pulled the blanket up to her throat and Miss Allison walked about, still wiping the hands that were long since dry.

'A Madrassi girl and a Burmese.' Miss Allison began to rub her face with the damp, blood-stained towel, in an effort to dry her tears. 'Mrs Betteson did the Burmese, and I did the Madrassi.'

Miss Allison continued to speak with tears.

'The Madrassi girl died. Mine.'

'I'm sorry.' The girl felt that she spoke stupidly and suddenly her whole body shuddered and she felt weak again and sick.

'That makes twenty-four today.'

'Twenty-four what?'

But Miss Allison never answered. She walked in a dream of exhaustion out of the tent and outside, in the light of the hurricane lamp, she cried quietly, on and on. Her voice, in its too high, too tenuous and slender pitch, seemed to take up where the singing Indians had left off. It seemed to continue, in a way that did not belong to either East or West, the melancholy repeated song that went round and round, quiet and wailing in the hot darkness.

In the tent, Connie McNairn pulled the blanket over her head and pressed her face tightly on the pillow, so that she could not hear that wailing except as something heard through the cushion of a wall. After a time she fell into a half-doze and did not hear it again. She did not hear either the small echo of it that broke from somewhere in the direction of Paterson's car: the sound of Tuesday crying also, at last, out of terror and misery at the treachery of the Naga boy.

But Paterson, turning under his blanket, heard it clearly. He heard, too, the voice of Mrs Betteson, and wondered.

18

The Indian jumped on the car about noon the following day.

He came scrawnily out of the dust, like a starved spider. His dhoti hung about his lean dark legs like a deflated dirty bag. As the car came up, travelling at seven or eight miles an hour, he stood in the centre of the track, arms extended, as if he had been waiting for it to come. Then as the car went past he sprang on the running-board, gripping the handle of Paterson's driving door, gesticulating and wailing at the same time. He spoke partly in Urdu, partly in Burmese. The whites of his eyes seemed, in the glittering yellow dust, to have turned bright blue, and Paterson could see his heart beating against his shadowy ribs like a rabbit struggling in a sack.

'What is it?' Miss Allison leaned forward over the front seat. 'What does he say?'

'Something about his wife, I think. I can't get it. Do you speak Urdu?'

'No.'

'I used to speak it,' Mrs Betteson said. 'A few words, I mean.'

The Indian clung to the car with one arm, waving frantically with the other. Wailing all the time, he writhed darkly in the brilliant air as the car plunged at pot-holes.

'What does he say?' Paterson said. 'I get the word wife, that's all.'

'It's another baby,' Mrs Betteson said.

'Oh! I ask you,' Connie said.

'Where is it?' Miss Allison said. 'I mean, has it come yet?'

'They were at the camp last night,' Mrs Betteson said. 'They got on the way this morning and now it's happening.'

'It's probably her fiftieth,' Connie said. 'They have them like animals.'

'As a matter of fact it's her first.'

Paterson slowed the car down a little, putting it in lower gear. The engine seemed to grind out heat, thick and oily, more suffocating than ever. The car jumped a pot-hole and the Indian, half by accident, half in self-protection, fell off the running-board. For a second or two he ran by the side of the car, lifting his hands, supplicating.

'What does he want?' Paterson said. 'I can't stop here anyway.'

The Indian was riding on the car again, waving and wailing, his head in at the window.

'Push him off,' Connie said. 'It's the only way.'

She remembered Indians in Calcutta: the wretched, moaning, miserable Bengalis, always grizzling and begging, always holding up their hands. The more you gave in to them the more you could.

'The baby's going to be born,' Mrs Betteson said.

'I'll get out,' Miss Allison said. 'Don't stop.'

'If we're stopping for every baby that's going to be born on this road we'll be here till Doomsday,' Connie said.

'Don't stop,' Miss Allison said. 'I can make it.'

'Oh! why all the fuss?' Connie said. 'If we hadn't been passing, she'd have had it in the normal way.'

'It's a propitious day. The stars are right. That's why.'

Mrs Betteson spoke with unexpected and firm direction, straight at Connie.

'Not our stars. That's evident.'

'You should thank them,' Mrs Betteson said.

'I don't know what you mean.'

'Just that you don't have to have your babies by the roadside.'

'I don't have to have babies at all, thank you!'

Miss Allison at this moment opened the door and called to Paterson:

'If I'm not back you'll know I'm not coming back. Don't wait for me.'

'We'll wait.'

'No, don't wait.'

'We're camping anyway, and I'll come back.'

'There's really no need.' She held the door of the car open and Paterson slowed down almost to a standstill and she stooped in readiness to jump out.

'I'll come and look for you,' he said. 'About half an hour.'

'No need. Goodbye.'

Miss Allison jumped out of the car. The door swung back, hitting her box of medical supplies as she jumped away. The Indian leapt off the running-board at the same moment, and then Paterson leaned out of the window, looking back. He did not answer Mrs Betteson who, cut off by the back of the car from view, asked: 'Is she all right?' nor Connie McNairn, who said: 'I hope the stars are propitious for her too, that's all.'

Instead, he was fascinated for a moment by Miss Allison. She stood briefly embalmed by the sulphury cloud of dust raised by the car. With her face no longer visible, she became anonymous, together with the Indian, against the green frame of smoky forest, the leafy edges of the frame glittering in the glare of sun. And then the dust poured away. It seemed to shoot perpendicularly upwards, turning the sun to burning copper. Edges of gilded light poured in from another angle and illuminated Miss Allison, who smiled as she lifted her hand, and the bony Indian, his chest of hollow ribbing like a leathery basket, as he smiled too.

That was all. He saw it all in the space of a second or two before he turned his face to watch the road. The sight of Miss Allison confidently smiling, quite serene, gave him a shock of pleasure, so that he smiled back.

He put his foot on the accelerator. The car speeded up a little and when he looked back, twenty seconds later, he could see nothing of Miss Allison and the Indian in the opaque glare of dust except the two pairs of legs, the one bluish-bronze, the other flesh-tinted, walking away.

'She'll be all right,' Mrs Betteson said.

'We'll camp and I'll go back,' he said. 'How did you come to know Urdu?'

'Oh! it was an awful long time ago.'

'India?'

'I came out there before I was married,' she said. 'School marm. I still look like one in a way.'

She moved her spectacles up and down, twitching the bridge of her nose. The left lens with its broken segment still remained to give her the appearance of lopsided squinting.

'Would you guess I knew French and German too? I don't suppose you would. The most awful fuss is made about languages.'

'Yes.'

'I used to think them the most wonderful accomplishment. They're quite useless really. When I got married and wanted to have a family languages didn't help a bit.' She looked over her shoulder, as if still trying to catch sight of Miss Allison, and said: 'You know, that girl didn't finish her maternity. She was in the middle of the course when she left.'

With nothing to say in answer, he stared forward into the glare of light, watching for a place to camp in the restricting jungle on either side.

'She took it very hard last night,' Mrs Betteson said. 'She delivered the baby and then it died. I held it in my arms for a few minutes, but there was no hope. She took it very hard.'

From the back seat Connie McNairn said: 'How long do you suppose she'll be?'

'I see a place to camp,' Mrs Betteson said. 'Isn't that a place? Over on the left-hand side?'

'I said how long do you think we'll need to wait for her?'

'I'll try to get in between the two rocks,' Paterson said. 'There must just be room.'

'There's no shade there,' Connie McNairn said. 'Just rocks.'

'Have to put up with it,' he said. 'Watch out at the back.'

Over to his left the jungle split into a gap fifteen or twenty yards long, broken by bronze-red protrusions of a sharper fall in the escarpment. Under the brilliant rock there was no shade.

He pulled over and, as he stopped, felt the sun penetrate in an instantaneous steely blow the roof of the car. Heat came pouring in at the open windows with stifling power.

He switched off the engine, felt very tired, and then got out of the car and said:

'Tuesday can put up the tent to give a bit of shade while I go back.'

The boy, hearing his name, came out of the long silence that had held him, imprisoned, all through the morning journey.

'Patson?' he said, 'Patson, sir?' A little of the smile came back.

'Put the tent up for Mrs Betteson and Miss Connie.'

'Yes Patson, yes Patson.'

'I'm coming with you,' Mrs Betteson said.

'I should rest if I were –'

'I'm coming with you. Really.'

He looked at her sharply. The broken left lens of her spectacles seemed to give the most disarming sort of smile.

'All right. If you mean it.'

'I do mean it,' she said. 'I just have to get a thing or two from my bag.'

She had brought with her a sort of enlarged knitting bag of green fabric with a zip fastener and leather binding, and she went back into the car for a moment or two to get something out of it.

Paterson heard the sound of the zip fastener sizzling once, and then once again, and then she reappeared with the bag in her hands.

'I'll take the bag. It's just as easy. She'll probably need a towel and it'll be cleaner.'

'How long are you going to be gone?' Connie McNairn said.

'Me?' Mrs Betteson said. 'I shall stay as long as Miss Allison stays.'

'Don't wait for us,' Paterson said. 'Start eating. Have a good rest.'

'In the shade, I suppose.'

He did not answer.

Dutifully Nadia and the boy were going about the clearing, serene in the blistering heat between the enclosing rocks. He watched for a moment how the girl slid about the dust, saying nothing. The flower of the previous evening was still unbruised below her right ear, like a huge ear-ring of fuchsia vermilion petals, and she smiled for a moment as he walked away.

Connie McNairn stood for a moment looking at him too. Whether she was surprised or hurt or resentful or simply annoyed he never knew. She was not smiling; but in that moment he saw Mrs Betteson already disappearing behind the car, using little, impatient skipping steps as she went into the road.

He strode after her to carry the bag.

'No. I like carrying it. I like doing things. It can't be far.'

Her steps, skipping with bursts of eagerness, took her more into little bouts of running. Once or twice, on the narrow foot-track between the jungle and the traffic of carts and bullocks and peasants and bundled trucks coming up the road, she was ahead of him by twenty or thirty paces. Even at that distance the haze of dust, its fine crystalline particles harshly scintillating, seemed briefly to swallow her up.

Sweating already, he ran to catch her.

'This is no climate for running,' he said. He took her arm.

'Was I running?'

'Something very like it.'

He let go her arm and then, quite firmly, took the bag.

'Oh! no, really I can carry it.'

'It's very hot.'

'It's very kind, but I'm not hot at all.'

'No?'

'I don't think I shall ever notice the heat again.'

He did not answer. Already she was a few steps ahead and again he was striding out, swinging the bag, to catch her up. He was astonished by the weight of the bag; it was as if she had stuffed in it all her worldly possessions, with Betteson's heavy bronze Buddha for good luck.

Then he called suddenly after her:

'Half a minute. I had something to ask you.'

He had really nothing to ask but the words had the effect, for a moment, of slowing her down.

'What was it?'

And then he remembered that, after all, he really had something to ask her.

'Wasn't Tuesday crying in the night?'

'Breaking his heart.'

'In God's name, what for?'

'Couldn't get it out of him at all.'

The traffic thinned for thirty or forty yards, so that they could walk side by side.

'Tired, I expect. It's been a long way. I've lost count of the days.'

'Nine,' she said. 'No. It wasn't that.'

'Not tired?'

'No. It was something else,' she said.

He did not speak. He did not know what to say, and felt rather like a porter hurrying behind a volatile passenger fretting to catch a train.

'We must keep a look out for Miss Allison,' she said. She strode a pace or two ahead. She turned her head and squinted back at him through the broken glasses that seemed to splinter in the sun, and what she said shocked him:

'No, I think it was you.'

'Me?'

'I think so.'

'Something I'd said?'

'No, I fancy not.' She blinked and twitched the bridge of her nose so that the spectacles trembled. 'Just something you might say.'

He did not answer and let her go ahead.

By the time they found Miss Allison ten minutes later he was fifty or sixty yards behind her. He was supremely troubled by what she had said. The moment she reached Miss Allison she ran all the way back, fluttering and grasping her spectacles.

'The baby is born. I see the father holding it,' she said. 'I'll have the bag.'

Without speaking he let her take the bag. Once again she went on ahead to where, in the green shadow beyond the road, he could see Miss Allison's white dress. When she stooped she was screened from him by a mass of jungle fern. The sun, breaking in, caught the tender curled tips of green.

He sat down some distance from the edge of the road, out of dust range, in shade under the trees. The heat was simply less direct; it lacked only the finger fierceness of pouring down through glass. His shirt was wet with stains of sweat that were like shadows on his chest and he felt half-exhausted.

And sitting there, he saw Mrs Betteson take the baby from the Indian, who squatted over against his fire, cooking something in a pan. The Indian now and then raised his face, casually, and Mrs Betteson walked up and down. Absorbed, she swung the baby to and fro with extreme gentleness, talking. She walked up and down for five minutes before she saw Paterson sitting watching her, and then she came over to him, passing the Indian by the fire. He did not look up.

Paterson remembered how propitious the day had been, and said: 'What's wrong with him? The father?'

'Nothing. It's what's wrong with the child.'

'Is it –?'

'No,' she said. 'It's living. It's a girl, that's all. The day was very propitious and he hoped for a boy.'

She had wrapped the baby in a towel. It was very makeshift, and against its folded whiteness the puckered brown-red face was no larger than a doll.

Over by the fire the Indian had prepared his food and was eating it with his hands.

'So the day wasn't propitious,' Paterson said.

'No. He's not interested.'

'Is the mother?'

'If it had been a boy it would have been wonderful. Now she doesn't care either. The male child is what she wanted. The male child is the symbol. The male child could have made dozens of others.'

The bitterness in her voice was profoundly softened by the physical pleasure in her face, the pleasure of handling the child, of succouring for a short time, in the stifling shade, the first moments of a life that was not wanted.

'I thought it was women who had babies,' he said.

'Sometimes.'

The bitterness hit him crisply in the face. She turned from talking to him to talk once again to the baby. As she did so she walked away. He felt small and foolish and wished he had not spoken. He watched her walking up and down under the trees, between the ferns that still hid Miss Allison and the mother from sight; and then a bullock cart came up the road and he turned to watch that, too, as it passed. On the crest of its bundled baggage sat six or seven children, all Burmese, and one was weeping. He grinned and lifted a hand as the child went by, staring downward at him through grief-puckered Mongolian eyes, but the child did not cease crying and did not answer even when he called a greeting to it in Burmese.

And suddenly the sight of it recalled, and seemed to explain, the surprising remark of Mrs Betteson: the affair of Tuesday crying in the night. The child passing into the dusty distance on the road became suddenly for him the grief of a country. In a day or two all of them would be out of it; and for Mrs Betteson and Connie and himself and even, perhaps, for Miss Allison, it would be at last the thing they had striven for and wanted. But it occurred to him for the first time that for Nadia and the boy it was not like that. Like the child on the cart they were going out into exile.

Thinking of it, he became aware of someone coming towards him through the ferns. He looked up, expecting Mrs Betteson. But Mrs Betteson was sitting down at last with the baby, and it was Miss Allison who stood there instead.

He stood up.

'All finished?' he said.

'All well and normal. Before I got here.'

'Why did he panic and want you?'

'It was a propitious day and it was a first baby and he was very anxious. He wanted a boy.'

'The day wasn't so propitious after all.'

'No.'

She gave a sigh and stood gazing at the road, her eyes tired. In her white dress she seemed, in the shadow of jungle, very frail.

'Shall we go back?' he said.

She stood absently rolling down the sleeves of her dress, still staring in front of her. The palms of her hands were turned upwards by the movement of her fragile arms, but she did not seem to notice it and did not listen and evidently did not care.

He knew that she had not heard.

'Shall we go back?'

'Eh?'

'We ought to go back.'

'I'm not coming back.'

He did not speak. As she buttoned the cuff of first one sleeve and then another, her arms very beautiful in their extreme slenderness, he could not help wondering why she kept them covered.

'I've been thinking of it for some time.'

'Yes.'

'I ought never to have left the hospital.'

Over against the fire the baby cried in a small way and Miss Allison looked over her shoulder and back again.

'And then Major Brain went. I've never really felt the same since then.'

Mrs Betteson was walking up and down again, gently swinging the baby.

'You mean you're going right back?' he said. He spoke reticently. He understood the meaning of the decision for her and did not want to influence her, by argument, one way or the other.

She stared at the dreary lines of refugees passing between the dark edges of forest in the glittering sun through the perpetual yellowish dusty cloud.

'No. I thought only to the camp where we were last night.'

'I see.'

'I could do good work there. There's decent water and I could organize things.' She smiled. 'I'll get enough practice to finish my maternity.'

He felt suddenly touched by her fragility, the difficulty and strength of her decision, and then by her youthfulness. In the same moment all of them appalled him. He felt inconceivably shocked by the idea of leaving her there on a road that was hardly a road at all, in the insufferably rising heat, without the facilities of ordinary decency and ordinary protection against God knew what was about to happen. He felt the whole affair of the journey break like a rotten biscuit in his hands. Somehow he had to keep it from so grotesquely going to pieces.

'I think you'd do just as good work in India. Christ knows they're short enough of nurses there.'

'No,' she said. 'This is my country. If I've got a country.'

'We're bound to re-occupy it. You can come back.'

'It's sweet of you to argue,' she said. 'But –'

'I'm not arguing, for God's sake!' he said.

'Please don't shout.'

'I'm not shouting!' he said. 'I'm merely saying that no man in his senses could let you do this!'

'Then please go out of your senses.'

'Sometimes I think that's exactly what this damned trip will do to me!'

Little by little he had been raising his voice, not knowing he was shouting. He suddenly felt all the responsibility of the journey, fantastically aggravated by the behaviour of the four who were dead, and now newly and unnecessarily aggravated by the behaviour of Miss Allison, boil up to a maddening fester in his head. He remembered embittered resolves to take no notice, ever again, of people who wished to go on or wished to go back. He had reproached himself bitterly for the tragedy of the Portmans. He was not going to be forced into that avoidable ghastliness again.

He was checked in another bout of shouting because Mrs Betteson had arrived.

She rocked the baby soothingly up and down.

'What in the world are you shouting at?'

With great effort he calmed himself. He kept his eyes fixed on the red-brown, eyeless, puckered face of the Indian baby, of which he thought there were as many wretched replicas all over India, as there were two-a-penny plaster Buddhas all over Burma, and said:

'Miss Allison wants to go back.'

'That's understandable.'

'Not to me!' he said. 'You saw what happened when the Portman's argued me into splitting up.'

'Yes.' Dust from the road was already falling finely into the face of the baby, and with the corner of the towel Mrs Betteson wiped a little of it gently away. 'But it's not quite the same, is it?'

'It's worse.'

Mrs Betteson squinted up at him through the broken spectacles. The enormous boss of the good lens gave her glance something of the albino flowering fragility that so disarmed the boy.

'I don't see it.'

'All right,' he said. 'It's something I won't argue about. I'm just an ordinary fellow with an ordinary sense of decency and I just won't leave her here alone. That's all.'

'Must she stay alone?'

Once again she glanced up at him with the infuriating, half-innocent gleam from her one good lens, so that he did not know whether to think of her as intelligently innocent or intelligently mad.

'That's what she proposes. That's what I don't like.'

'I would like to stay with her.'

For an instant the shock of Mrs Betteson's remark expunged from his mind all his complex irritation. He realized that she was smiling at him. He wanted to exclaim flatly that she was as batty as everybody had always said she was, but he did not speak, and it was Miss Allison who said:

'You see, it's not quite as mad as you thought it was.'

'No,' Mrs Betteson said. 'There's two of us now.'

He wanted to say: 'Why don't we all stay?' but something about the cheapness of the remark deterred him and, even though he had never spoken it, belittled him too.

For some moments no one spoke again and it was so quiet, the baby not crying as Mrs Betteson rocked it gently up and down, that he heard somewhere in the deeper jungle a flight of parakeets break the trees with tittle-tattling voices and a fuss of wings and farther away still a coppersmith bird tink-tinking in the heat with maddening monotony.

All the heat of noon, even there under the trees, seemed to break out again, doubly aggravated by the breath of the Indian's little fire. But Paterson, to his own surprise, did not mind it. And he did not shout again as Mrs Betteson, roused by the voice of the coppersmith bird to an abrupt start, said:

'Of course, what I ought to have said was, if Miss Allison will have me. I ought to have asked her.'

Miss Allison smiled without speaking, and he knew that there was no need for her to answer. He spoke coolly for the first time.

'Perhaps the day was propitious after all.'

They all laughed. Tension was broken completely as Miss Allison said: 'The stars are always right for somebody. Today it's us.'

'The major's fish-like stars.'

He spoke almost to himself, but the two women, all tension relieved now, laughed again. They seemed quite happy.

'What about your things?'

'I have mine,' Mrs Betteson said.

He was aware of a new sense of humility and then Miss Allison said: 'I've only a few things. In a grey case. I won't come back.' Paterson said he would bring them himself or send the boy, but she said: 'There's really so few of them that it wouldn't matter.' She spoke simply, as if the formula for which neither East nor West could provide a solution had resolved itself at last.

'I'll come back,' Mrs Betteson said. 'It isn't far. I can carry the case. I can say goodbye to that lamb of a boy.'

'He'll come back with you.'

'I think Miss McNairn will be all right,' Miss Allison said.

It seemed almost over. The mention of Connie seemed a triviality. Mrs Betteson gave the baby to Miss Allison. The Indian threw dust on the fire and then trod on it, bare-footed, stamping it out.

'You took her temperature last night,' Miss Allison said, 'didn't you? It was practically normal then.'

'I did what?'

'You took her temperature. She said you stayed with her and took her temperature.'

'No.'

'I thought that's what she said. She talked a lot. I don't know — perhaps she didn't say it. I was very tired and upset and perhaps I wasn't listening.'

'She's highly strung,' he said.

Two minutes later he was walking on the road with Mrs Betteson. After what had seemed the suffocating shade of the jungle edge, the sun whipped down at him like naked flame. He felt it lick him callously on his bare neck. It caught his face as he turned to look at Miss Allison for the last time, stabbing blackly for a second at the retina of his eyes, so that he could see nothing but the white dhoti of the Indian still dancing on the smoking ashes of his fire. It was as if the jungle had shadowily swallowed Miss Allison up. And then he saw her. His sight cleared again and penetrated the yellow veil of glittering dust. With one arm she was holding the baby and with the other she was waving goodbye. As it waved slowly up and down, the arm seemed very slender and, against the darkness of jungle, unbelievably pale.

'The only thing that bothers me,' Mrs Betteson said, 'is the lens of my spectacles. If I lose it I shall be absolutely blind.'

As Tuesday joined the line of refugees to walk back to Paterson in the heat of the afternoon after trotting behind Mrs Betteson with Miss Allison's travelling case, he was confronted once more by the problem created by that curious act of the major's. He carried in his hands a crimson toothbrush bag.

First he thought of that mild and rather unsoldierly figure pushing the bicycle down the hill. Then he thought of Mrs Betteson and the nurse: the two ladies with travelling cases, standing at the roadside, rather as if they expected a train to come by and pick them up. And Mrs Betteson nursing an Indian baby.

He joined the line of refugees in a state of stupefied unrest. Nothing in his experience could explain the fact of Miss Allison and Mrs Betteson going back. Nothing could remotely explain the baby. He recalled that when the Portmans and Mrs McNairn had gone forward in the other car they had done so in miserable anger. Now the two ladies seemed calm and happy. The spectacles of Mrs Betteson, with their bulging, swimming lenses, had terrified him ever since the day she had kept him in the kitchen. Now the break in them seemed to charge her, as she swung the rabbity Indian child gently up and down, with the calmest sanity. He had expected her either to grasp him effusively, slobbering awful kindnesses, or to start crying and questioning him, floppily and stupidly waving her hands, as she had done the night before, about the reasons for his own tears.

All that had happened was that Miss Allison had asked him to put out his tongue.

For a moment he did not understand.

'Tongue,' Miss Allison said. 'Tongue. This.' She put out her own.

He understood then and shot out his tongue full length, swiftly. Mrs Betteson and Miss Allison laughed gaily.

'Wonderful,' Miss Allison said. 'That's fine.'

He kept his tongue hanging out for some seconds longer.

'That's all. Put it back. You'll need it some day.'

Slowly he curled in his tongue and then stood waiting, the beginnings of a smile on his face, with bright eyes.

Miss Allison held his wrist with her fingers and looked at her watch.

'Healthy as a monkey.' She smiled. He got the impression
that the two ladies were playing practical jokes; the impression also that they were, in another sense, serious; that in the
truest sense they were just starting on their journey.

'Give Mr Paterson these.'

Miss Allison had taken from her suitcase a bottle of quinine
tablets, a phial of iodine and a thermometer.

'Tell him it's all I can spare.'

Smiling, now understanding perfectly, he grasped the three
objects and began to stuff them into the back pocket of his
football shorts.

That set the ladies off again. As they laughed they saw his
own smile, defeated, fading slowly.

It was then that Miss Allison gave him the toothbrush bag.

'Put them in this.'

The Indian baby made small noises, tormented by flies. Mrs
Betteson fanned the air with her free hand and Miss Allison
put the phial, the bottle and the thermometer in the toothbrush
bag.

'You understand? It's all I have.'

'Understand, miss. Yes.'

'Don't break them.'

'Understand, miss. Yes. Understand. Yes.'

He took the toothbrush bag and slung its crimson cord over
his wrist. The smile lit up his face again. He wanted for a
moment to ask them his simple questions: why were they
going, where were they going, why after so long were they
going back? He recalled the major. He tried to link that strange
act of his with the stranger act of the two ladies preparing to
follow him now with their suitcases. The baby made its odd
noises again, struggling against the flies in the stifling air, and
Mrs Betteson broke a branch of leaves from the undergrowth
and fanned it slowly to and fro over the raw-red crumpled
face. The boy gave up the thought of asking his questions and
Miss Allison said simply:

'I think that's all.'

He stood for a moment, hesitating. It did not seem possible

that they were going, that the informality marked by the toothbrush bag was the end. His face was so oddly full of uncertainty that both Miss Allison and Mrs Betteson laughed again.

'Don't you understand?'

He nodded. He did not understand and Miss Allison said:

'That's all right then. Goodbye.'

All he could give was a half-smile in answer.

'All our love.'

The Eurasian girl spoke with tender affection, very amused, and Mrs Betteson said:

'Yes: all our love. We mustn't forget that.'

He remained for a second longer, staring at them with his bewildered half-smile as if hoping the entire hopeless mystery of the thing might still be revealed, and then he walked away.

'God bless,' Mrs Betteson said.

He did not understand. He heard the two of them laugh gaily again, but he did not turn and he had nothing to say in answer.

He was still thinking of it when he came back to Paterson's car. The problem of it puckered his face, erasing the smile. For the last hundred yards or so before reaching the car he walked with his head slightly down, staring at the ground.

It was only when he heard the clatter of petrol cans at the back of the car that he came to life suddenly again. He saw then that Paterson was pouring petrol into the tank. Petrol was slopping over the mudguards, over the wheel and over the dust and he could smell the strong odour of it and see the quivering vapour of it in the hot air. He watched for a moment while Paterson, caught in the trembling curtain of vapour, slopped half a can of petrol away.

And he knew even before Paterson began shouting his name that it was not only the vapour of the petrol that gave him the appearance of convulsive trembling. He was a little drunk too.

By mid-afternoon Connie McNairn began to realize that it was not the hotness of wind pressing in at the open car windows that dizzied her; or the behaviour of Paterson, naked to the waist, driving half-drunkenly. It was her own sickness, coming back.

Whenever she looked beyond the heads of Paterson and the boy to the hills that had now brought the visible distances down to five or six miles, she found the fragile contours swivelling against the sun. They seemed to slip away over the edges of earth; the gap which opened up between herself and them became like the opening of a pair of tired jaws, slowly yawning apart and then slowly closing again. The car seemed to plunge into the darkness that lay inside the opening and then with horrible sensations of sickness came quivering up into the sun.

She clung to the cord of the window with one hand and to the armrest of the seat with the other. She wanted desperately not to plunge down into the repeated hollows of sickness and now and then she tried to defeat it by closing her eyes. It gave her only the ghastly effect of falling away into darkness that had no end.

As the afternoon went on she became more and more frightened of being ill. The only thing that comforted her was that she was alone in the back of the car. She could keep the burning sickness of her stomach to herself and try to defeat the plunging dizziness without being seen. She knew that she had gone beyond any lying about the thermometer. She did not need a thermometer now to tell her that her whole body was burning or that the sweat of it seemed to pour inwards through the flesh, running scalding and loose through her bowels. The thermometer seemed useless and trivial now. In any case Miss Allison had taken it with her.

Whenever she thought of Miss Allison she was shocked by Paterson's act of letting her and Mrs Betteson remain behind. It seemed extraordinary callous. It had also something to do with Paterson's getting drunk. The drinking had begun quite suddenly when he had returned and sent the boy back with Miss Allison's bag. He had looked very weary and rather upset and did not want to eat the tepid meat and biscuits the boy had prepared. She had found him sitting on the running-board of the car, his face flatly pale in the reflected glare of sun-beaten rock, pouring out gin by the half-mugful. He had looked up at her and said something that sounded very like 'Cheers, damn you,' and then had raised the mug to her before taking the gin like water.

Then he had told her Miss Allison and Mrs Betteson were not coming back. She felt suddenly very glad; and then, before she could prepare herself for it, bewildered and horrified.

'But you're not going to let them stay alone?'

'They want to stay.'

'Yes, but that's monstrous. Leaving them there.'

'They're leaving us. They know what they're doing,' he said.

He sat with his elbows on his knees, the mug between his hands, and now and then he put his face into the mug.

'You mean they've just gone?' she said. 'Like that?'

'Like that.'

'But I never even said goodbye. I wanted to say goodbye. Couldn't I go back?'

'Don't interrupt my meal,' he said. The gin, in the terrific heat of noon, had worked itself quickly into his eyes. 'Cheers.'

'I don't know how you can sit there and not care about them,' she said.

'I love them.'

'You couldn't love anybody. You're just callous,' she said.

'I'm just an ordinary bloke,' he said.

He did not speak, but something about the way he lifted the mug, plunged his face into it and then looked up at her sideways, ironically, disturbed her for the rest of the afternoon.

Whenever she looked up into the driving mirror over the front seat she could see Paterson's face, tired, half-drunk, watching her with that same gin-fired irony until it became gradually part of the bewilderment of her sickness. Whenever she felt herself fainting into the gap between the car and the hills she tried to fix her eyes on to the reflection of the face in the mirror. Each time she lost it as she plunged sickly away; each time it was still there as she groped her way slowly back.

She looked at it in vain for a sign of comfort. The two eyes,

watery in the heat, the whites slightly bloodshot from strain
and weariness at the extreme edges, mocked her so much
that gradually she began to feel more frightened of them
than by the thought of being ill. She suddenly hoped that she
would be sick.

But she could not be sick. She lifted one hand to her mouth,
thinking of thrusting a finger into her throat. In the act of
doing so she saw Paterson watching her.

'Please, I feel ghastly,' she said. 'Please.'

'What nice little lie are you thinking up now?' Paterson
said.

She shut her eyes and lay back, too weak to answer. The
word lie seemed to pin her down like a hot needle. She remembered her mother. She remembered how it happened, in
the original event, that she had lied about Paterson. The fan-
tasy of it had long since seemed so real that she had accepted
it, as her mother had accepted it, as something true. She remembered how she had wanted the meeting with Paterson to
flower into something more than simple acquaintanceship. She
had written her mother a long letter about it – the wonderful
Mr Paterson who was coming out on the boat before her, the
new manager of the rice-mill; the desirable and gallant Mr
Paterson who had taken her out to dinner; the considerate Mr
Paterson who had promised to come down to Rangoon to
meet her. She had worded it all so that it seemed as if Paterson
was in love with her. She had wanted to contrive a situation
of delicious romanticism, presenting her mother with a pre-
designed affair, with something Paterson could not deny. She
had put the onus of it all on Paterson and gradually the romantic illusion that Paterson loved her had become, for her, a
reality. And Paterson, cornered by her lying into a situation
that had seemed to him one of pure friendliness, had gone to
meet her in Rangoon.

Her mother had never got over it. It was another blow in the
long run of hostile fate that had begun by preventing McNairn
from becoming a district officer. In a week Paterson had become, and remained, 'that unspeakable man who toyed with

my daughter's affections,' and in a month Paterson, as if to confirm it, had taken up with a Burmese girl.

It was all over and yet it was not all over, and now it came back to mock her. In another moment she knew that Paterson was not only drunk because of the act of Miss Allison and Mrs Betteson but because he understood, at last, everything about herself. She felt the shock of it become part of her intolerable sickness, the hotness of windy dust choking her as it pressed into the car, the chasmic distances into which she was trying not to fall. She knew suddenly that whether Paterson believed her or not she was still very ill indeed. The cords of her stomach went slack and the scalding wateriness inside her became nothing but ghastly vapour. As it floated away, leaving her blackly empty, she struck about with her hands, trying to grasp at the chromium edge of the front car seat, so that she should not fall.

In another moment the heat had suffocated her.

19

In the cooler air that dropped down with darkness from the narrow stream bed between deep gorges of forested rock the boy stooped over his small fire, cooking the evening rice in a pan. When he shook the pan to separate the grains of rice from one another and keep them from burning over the sharp, ochre-white flame, the clear wakened cast of light seemed to flatten his face into shadowless calm. He was not smiling and as he shook the rice delicately so that the grains kept separate and clean as a pan of soft brown ants' eggs, he thought first of Miss Allison and Mrs Betteson, incomprehensibly laughing as they looked at his tongue and felt his pulse and gave him the toothbrush bag of bottles and said goodbye, and then of Major Brain, many days ago, pushing the bicycle down the hill alone. He thought also of Paterson, getting drunk and still drinking as he sat in the tent watching Miss McNairn. He brought to all of it, to the women and the major, to Paterson and the girl, to the drunkenness and the sickness and the incomprehensible act of return, an amazed consciousness that had narrowed down.

When he had finished cooking the rice he mixed with it a little of the chopped meat left over from midday. He spooned a little more than half of it into two dishes, nicking off a grain with his thumb nail to taste its saltiness. He wanted the rice to have a perfection that would be tempting, and he saw with satisfaction each grain of it glistening like a separate egg as he spooned it carefully.

Then as he moved to take the two plates to the tent he saw his sister come from the car. She was carrying the papaia he had tried to keep cool for Paterson, and he could smell the sweetness of fresh tanaka powder on her body as she came past him. She carried the papaia absently, and when he called to her not to cut it for a moment, because he wanted to cut it himself and sugar it with the perfection that Paterson loved, she did not answer.

With the dishes of rice in his hands he waited at the aperture of the tent for a moment before presuming to go in. The hurricane lamp was burning inside; the big shadow of Paterson was thrust upward; and he waited for another second or two before speaking Paterson's name.

'Patson, sir. Patson,' he whispered. 'Supper.'

Even when Paterson moved his body a foot or so from the aperture there was no room for the boy to go in. He stood half in and half out of the tent, holding the plates of rice in his hands. He watched Paterson sitting on a beer-crate by the bed. The girl lay awake, and he could see the sweat of her face glistening in the lamplight.

Paterson screwed half-drunkenly round on the beer-crate. He was holding a glass in one hand and a gin-bottle in the other, and he stared at the boy as if trying to focus him. Then he seemed to fix him against the triangular aperture of the tent. He grinned. This grin delighted the boy. It was part of the universal kindliness that Paterson always exhibited in the middle stages of drunkenness. There was nothing in it to be feared.

Paterson put the gin-bottle and glass on the ground between his legs and then took the plates of rice from the boy. In return the boy gave him a smile of the most expansive delight. He had been filled with the stupendous notion that Paterson would knock him down. Now he grasped with incredible joy at a Paterson in which there was no longer any violence. He waited for some such mood in which to tell Paterson that the radio had gone.

'Like papaia? Nice papaia? Miss Conn like papaia? In five minutes nice papaia.'

'You bet. Bring big slices. Plenty of sugar.'

'You bet. Miss Conn too?'

'Miss Conn is very ill.'

'Papaia – cool. Nice cool.'

Paterson leaned forward, bending over the girl.

'Tuesday has a papaia.'

'I don't want to eat. I'd be sick again.' The boy saw the girl's mouth open and the tongue, brown and glazed, lick loosely at the dried lips. 'It's just that ghastly thirst.'

The words were so low that he did not understand them, and he understood only when Paterson turned to say: 'Bring it. Miss Conn would like it. It will do her good.'

'Good, yes,' he said. 'Splendid good you bet. In five minutes papaia coming, yes.'

'And plenty of sugar.'

'Plenty of sugar you bet!' he said. 'Plenty sugar!'

He went out of the tent with a smile that did not fade all the time he sat by the fire, carefully preparing and sugaring the rosy orange halves of fruit. Several times he looked up at his sister. She was not eating the rice he had cooked. She was half-lying, half-sitting in the dust by the fire. Her face had a look of troubled, dreamy patience and he knew that she simply waited for Paterson.

Absorbed in preparing the papaia, he did not eat his own rice either. The moment had come, he thought, when he must talk to Paterson. He could tell him of the radio.

He prepared the papaia with great delicacy. Sometimes on special occasions he trimmed the rind into the shape of a boat with a long, curled prow. He set it on crumpled leaves of plantain, so that it seemed to sail on pale disturbed green waters. A meal at Paterson's bungalow had often begun with these sugary boats, which guests loved because they were faithful and eatable copies of the boats they so often saw on the river below the town.

It occurred to him suddenly to prepare them now. Some of the delight he felt in his discovery of Paterson's kindly temper went into his hands as he carved the shape of the boats from the dark green rind. He forgot for a few moments the complexities of the journey. His narrowed consciousness narrowed still further, shutting out all that had troubled him.

When he had finished carving the boats he piled a little more wood on the fire. White flames broke out at once, candescently fierce in the clearing of jungle just wide enough to hold the tent, the fire and the car. In the bright light he ran over to the edge of jungle and grabbed handfuls of leaves from the lower bushes without knowing what they were. He crumpled the leaves and laid them on plates, putting the boats of papaia on top of them. Another thing that had so often pleased the guests at Paterson's was his idea of slotting a spoon and fork into the sides of the boats, as through row-locks, so that it seemed as if the boats were being rowed across their leafy plates by oars of silver.

He fitted a spoon and fork into each of the boats of papaia now, smiling with fresh pleasure because he had remembered these things. He gave the fruit a last touch of sugar and some of it sprinkled over the leaves, so that the crinkles of them were crested with sparkling grains of light.

When he finally took the two boats across to the tent, one in each hand, walking with solemn care so that they did not spill, his face gradually broadened to the limits of a terrific smile. It seemed to press his eyes to the narrowest of laughing slits. It forced back the flesh of the cheeks to the edges of his ears until the entire face seemed like a distended fruit itself, tightly ready to burst.

He stood for a moment at the opening of the tent and then went in. At the very edge of orange lamplight he glanced swiftly at Paterson. He was enormously relieved to see that he was still drinking. The kindliness of his half-drunken face had not faded, and it sprang up into a smile that became a guffaw as he saw the boats the boy had made and was now bearing in, like simple offerings, on their sugared plates of leaves.

'Well, for Christ's sake!' Paterson suppressed the guffaw and spoke quietly, as if not to arouse the girl. The two plates of rice, the boy noticed, had been eaten, and Miss McNairn was lying with her face to the tent wall, away from the light, as if she were sleeping.

Paterson took one plate from the boy, held it for a moment

as he looked at the silver-oared toy of fruit on the pool of leaves, and then leaned over with it to Miss McNairn.

'Connie,' he said.

The girl did not move.

'Connie,' he said. 'Look at this.'

The boy saw the face of Miss McNairn, yellow with sweat, painfully turn itself to the lamplight.

'Look,' Paterson said. He spoke like a man of indulgent tenderness speaking to a child, coaxing it, all anger at her stupidity and lying and hysteria gone. 'Look what Tuesday brought for you.'

The boy did not see any kind of reaction on the turned face except a more brilliant and ghastly gleam of sweat.

'Going to India by boat now,' Paterson said. 'There in no time. See?'

She seemed to stare straight at the boat, the bloodless lids of the eyes drawn narrowly down.

'Tuesday made it for you. See? It's your boat,' Paterson said.

Her hands began to loll about on the covers of the bed. On her face the only new response was the quivering of her tongue, darkish brown and more glazed as it pressed itself out again.

'Connie,' Paterson said. 'See the boat?'

In his attitude of leaning across the bed he suddenly swayed, unbalanced, drunkenly. The boat slipped and seemed for a moment to fall partly out of his hands.

'Rough,' Paterson said. 'Rocking.' He tipped the boat sideways again, almost letting it go, grinning as if to rouse her. 'All at sea.' The girl, hearing but not seeing, tried to open her lips in a smile.

The boy saw in these things a new complexity. Miss Conn was very ill. The boat was there to be seen and yet she did not see it. She did not respond to the clownish motions of Paterson's hands.

Presently he saw in the face of Paterson, turning in the lamplight, a reflection of all he was thinking. The drunken tender nonsense, the coaxing indulgence, had suddenly gone. He saw once again only the face overwrought by all the heat, the dust, the glare, the anxiety and the tragedies of the journey. It was all at once a strange Paterson he saw there, holding the toy-like boat of fruit, the essence of decency lost for a moment in bewilderment, the clownish, friendly, drunken face troubled without a trace of anger. He had an awful thought that it was ill too. He saw one of Paterson's hands leave the boat and drag itself down his face in a single broad sweep of the opened fingers. The eyes were very bright and the spark of friendliness remained. All that the boy loved was there in the moment of helplessness, the little boat that was still held in one hand, the remembered foolishness, and yet the beginnings of something that frightened him were with it too. He saw in it a reflection of the girl's sickness. A shot of feverishness seemed to leap up and replace with minute burning brightness the gleam of final foolishness in the tired eyes.

A moment later Paterson seemed to recover himself and was out of the tent, carrying the boat of papaia unsteadily in both hands. The boy followed, carrying the other.

To his astonishment Paterson began cramming the fruit into his mouth, very fast. The fork fell to the ground as he dug the spoon into the sugared flesh. The boy, in increasing bewilderment, picked it up. Paterson had dropped the plate and the spoon. He was holding the half-circle of papaia with both hands, gnawing at it with venomous greed, and the boy watched him pressing the raw sweet flesh against his face, burying his mouth deep between the rind as if desperate for its coolness. The juice ran sugarily down between his fingers and in a few seconds, one boat finished, he took the other, slobbering his mouth into it with the same sobering greed until it was finished and he stood empty-handed, wiping his face on the sleeve of his shirt.

'Now,' he said. 'Now.'

He made another great effort to wipe the stupefaction out of his face, this time with both hands, dragging and pressing them down, so that they were wet with sugar and sweat and the

211

remains of the orange flesh of fruit that had smothered him up
to the eyes.

'Now,' he said. 'Get the other lamp.'

The boy stood so amazed at this demand that he could not
move.

'Go on,' Paterson said. 'Get the lamp.'

Rolling about, he wiped the last melting sugariness from his
face with his two hands. Amazed, the boy was glad to see
Nadia coming over from the fire.

'Got to get Miss Allison,' Paterson said. 'The nurse.' He
wavered unsteadily from one foot to another. A paroxysm of
the old anger flared up. 'Bloody swindle. Ill all the time. Jesus.'
The anger spluttered out. 'Poor kid.' Nadia came from the fire
and he staggered to meet her, his speech breaking into Burmese.
He began telling her how ill the girl was and how he would go
back for Miss Allison. The boy, still standing there disregard-
ing the order about the lamp because he did not understand
what lamp or what he was to do with it, saw him lunge helplessly. He saw this helplessness with relief. It meant that in a
moment Paterson would fall down. He would fall flat on his
face partly through drunkenness, partly through sheer fatigue,
and then Nadia and the boy would cover him with blankets
and he would sleep and in the morning it would be all right
again.

But Paterson did not fall down. The boy waited for it to
happen but nothing happened, except that suddenly Paterson
ceased staggering from one side to another, helplessly, and
found his direction. He turned, stood for a moment absolutely
still, and then went straight for the car.

In a moment the boy understood what he meant to do. He
saw it with horror. He seemed to see Paterson driving the car
drunkenly along that small road by night, recklessly going
back.

He shouted to the girl as he ran past her to the car. And at
the car, looking back, he saw that she had turned Paterson
slightly away. He was staggering stupidly again, wiping his
face with his hands.

At the car he thought of two things, the ignition key and the rotor arm. He decided on the rotor arm. He lifted the bonnet of the car and held it up with his head so that he could use his two hands in the darkness. He worked by touch and in thirty seconds or so had the arm unclipped and detached, just as Paterson shouted: 'Where the hell is that boy?'

After that he no longer cared. He heard Paterson bawl his name again and this time he answered: 'Here, Patson, yes.' He opened the door of the car at the same time. With the rotor arm tucked in his football shirt, he felt calm in the possession of simple power.

Paterson blundered into the car and lunged and sat down. He found the dashboard light and switched it on. As the greenish-scarlet glow shone up into his face, turning it sickly, he glared sombrely through the driving screen, ramming his foot on the starter and then, cool and alert for a second, remembered he had not switched on. His hand deftly switching on the ignition was the last of his coherence. The girl climbed into the other door of the car and sat beside him, waiting. From the other open door the boy watched him ram his foot hard on the starter, turning it madly. Its grating revolutions cut into the night in which there was no other sound until Paterson fell forward on to the wheel and pressed into life the shrieking horn. The two sounds ripped ghoulishly across the warm silence and seemed to tear through the cushion of invisible jungle and strike the rock-faces and reverberate back.

The boy waited until the sounds had stopped. Then he reached over and turned the ignition key and shut the door of the car. Paterson fell away from the wheel and the girl held him firmly as he slid away.

The boy got out and then stood for a moment, listening. The shrieking of the horn had impressed on the esries of rocky valleys stretching away in the humid darkness a great quietness. He listened to it for some seconds longer with relief and then walked away.

He opened the lid of the luggage boot and laid the rotor arm inside. He went over to the fire and stirred it with a rod of bamboo, feeding it with branches until it flared. Then as the fire burned up he put the little pan of rice back against the flame, shaking the grains gently, adding a little water and then shaking again, to keep them apart. As he did these things he felt more than ever that the situation was his. The problems of the earlier evening, of the radio set he had lost, the pain of dispossession, the difficult necessity of speaking to Paterson, had become resolved. They were replaced by more urgent things. He saw them quite calmly now: how he would eat, sleep a little, watch by Miss McNairn, and then, an hour or more before dawn, set out to find Miss Allison. Now at last it was his turn to go back.

When the rice was ready he squatted before the fire and held the pan before him and ate his meal. His face was tonelessly flattened by the light of the fire. The stars were very bright in the black soft sky and were themselves like glistening grains of rice above the hills. The rice was very good and he was very hungry, ravenously and boyishly hungry, so that he ate the portion that was his sister's, knowing she would not want it now.

By the time the sun came up, in one single rapid burst of purple-salmon light unbroken by cloud, he had walked five or six miles back along the road. For two days the traffic of bullocks and peasants had been thinning out, and now as the light strengthened he could see the track-marks, clearly imprinted but never very straight, left by the car tyres in the fluffy dust, first pink and then yellow as the sun rose. He kept his eyes fixed on them in the rising light as he walked. He had a curious way of walking on the balls of his feet, slightly pitching forward, in a bouncing sort of run.

As he went forward, not meeting until about an hour after sunrise the first of the loaded bullock carts, he thought repeatedly of one thing. It was the word typhoid. He had heard Paterson shout it. It did not mean anything to him and he could not pronounce it physically. Yet in a curious way he could still hear it, as spoken by Paterson, in his mind. He knew that it was something of great importance and that somehow he had to remember it and then when the time came repeat it aloud. In order to do this he kept his tongue half-curled, as if in readiness to spit it out. This seemed to thrust his flat mouth forward, in almost comic determination: so much so that as he bounced past the first of the bullock carts a peasant woman riding on the back of it lifted her face and laughed. She seemed to see something extraordinarily funny in the striding bouncing boy.

Some time later, on the jungle edge, at a point where the small ten-foot stream came skimming down over bone-white rock, he passed a group of Nagas, three women and four men, squatting by a fire. Another woman was at the stream, scooping water in her hands. They watched him with fierce opium-dilated eyes, the woman at the water squinting one eye against the heightening brilliant sun as she followed him round. A jungle crow circled the clearing in spirals of glistening black, waiting to scavenge. He flushed a blue and emerald cloud of parakeets and turned to watch them sprinkle low over the stream, breasts iridescently reflected, like fish. They disappeared into elephant grass, touching the tips, and the woman at the same moment turned away, spitting at the stream, the spit like an arrow of glass in the sun.

Suddenly he was nervous of the squinting woman, the opium-eyed Nagas silently watching him from the fire, the solitariness, the quietness after the parakeets had passed. There seemed to him a sinister link between the watching woman and the darkly-waiting crow. Gradually he felt a haunting notion that the Nagas, the eaters of opium, the head-hunters, were waiting for him to come back.

And then, when he reached the place where the Indian baby had been born, where Miss Allison had given him the toothbrush case and the two women had laughed so much as they said goodbye, there was nothing there but the dark ring of the Indian's burnt-out fire and a handful of charred rags still brown at the unburnt edges with blood.

He stood for a moment undecided. Then he recalled the

camp of the night before the Indian had leapt on to the running-board of the car. It was several miles back.

Remembering it, he bounced on.

It took him more than another hour to reach the wide clearing where the Indians had gone on singing dismally into the night after the two babies had been born. The shore of sand by the widened river seemed exactly the same, with its crowd of camping Burmese and Indians, its bullocks and buffaloes, carts and fires, as when Paterson had driven out of it the day before.

He wandered across it, looking for the gleam of Mrs Betteson's spectacles. The thought of them had suddenly begun to comfort him. By the river bullocks were being watered and women were washing clothing on white rocks. A dark Indian stood in the middle of the stream, soaping himself down, still in his dhoti. There were no white faces. Above it all went the swinging, swimming crows at which Mrs Betteson had rushed with the gun.

It was only when he began to speak to people about the Englishwoman with her spectacles, recalling the babies that had been born, that he got from a Karen woman the news that Miss Allison and Mrs Betteson had moved farther back.

He stood in the centre of the camping place, suddenly a little tired after the long walk, very thirsty and undecided. In the crisis of indecision he was troubled also by a recurrent thought of Paterson. He was worried by the idea that he ought to go back.

'How long,' he asked the Karen woman, 'since they went? The two women?'

She told him how they had moved off that morning, before sunrise. He did not know what to do and stood calculating the distances, the time, the journey back. He saw how, if he went on, it would be evening before he could overtake the two women, and then another night and day before he could get to Paterson. The word typhoid faded from his mind, to be replaced by the haunting image of Paterson ramming the sticky sugary papaia into his mouth in a drunken and desperate effort to sober up, and something about it all, the strange Paterson, rather helpless, a fraction feverish, bright-eyed, forced the boy into his decision without process of thought.

He turned almost at once and began to go back. He was delayed for a moment by an impulse to drink. He decided against it. Reflecting on the bullocks, the washing women, the soapy Indian, he decided to wait for clearer water, farther up stream.

He had been walking for about half an hour, less buoyant now, not running, when he recalled the Nagas camping by the river. He was fretted once again by a presentiment of something sinister.

He saw the smoke of the Naga fire while he was still five or six hundred yards away. He stopped for a moment, watching. The squinting woman, the solitary crow, the ring of Naga faces by the fire shocked him into thin waves of terror.

They passed in a second or two. He decided to cut away, through jungle, skirt up past the camping place and follow the stream.

On the far bank of the stream he found deep patches of elephant grass, bordered on the water edge by dwarf bamboo. He walked for a short distance in the stream-bed, cooling his feet. Concealed by grass, he walked quite quickly until the course of water curving slowed him down.

At the curve of the stream a rock projected. It burnt the palms of his hands as he rested them against it. Then as he peered beyond it, to where flood-water had pressed the jungle back into a shore of sand between the stream and the road, a slice of rock, fractured by heat, cracked from under his hands and fell away, splashing loudly into water, and in the same moment he saw the five Nagas, just as he had passed them, squatting by the fire.

All of them looked up. Sharp-eyed, they watched, back-glancing, for something to appear from the direction of the sound. One of them wore a straw hat in the shape of a cone. The tip of the cone seemed to have exploded under pressure of his hair, and the hair had bristled through, volcanically, in fierce stiff sheaves.

217

The Naga with the strange hat got to his feet with a sudden twist of his legs that brought him upright in one movement. The boy was near enough to see the dilated glassy glint of his eyes turning sunwards.

Forty or fifty yards away a flock of small blue parrots broke from the trees and the Naga started walking. He seemed to walk straight at the boy. He came for fifteen or twenty paces, quite swiftly. The boy felt the heat of the rock burn the palms of his hands and under them the dust crumbling from the fresh-broken fissures, sprinkling slowly down into the water. He felt another splinter split away and he desperately held it with both hands, very frightened, so that it should not fall. He heard the feet of the Naga kicking the sand ten or a dozen paces away and suddenly felt himself stooping, ready to run.

And then one of the women called something from the fire. Her shout stopped the Naga in three or four paces. He stood still, listening, and then grunted and went back.

Some distance further upstream the boy discovered that he still had in his right hand the slice of rock that had splintered away. He had been too scared to let it fall and now, long and thin and axe-like in shape, it seemed part of his hand.

Now he was very thirsty and coming back to the stream, he crawled down to the edge and lay on his belly, hands outspread, his face in the water. He lay for five minutes or so, washing the sweat and dust and fear out of his face, still grasping the splinter of rock in his hands, until at last he felt rested and could walk away again up the sandy edge of the stream.

A projection of rock, like a sepia-yellow nose, shelved down from the escarpment side of the river and cut him off at last from the low edge of the water. It rose to ten or fifteen feet above the river grasses. He crawled up the face of it. It was very smooth and without fissures for the seeds of grasses and vines and creepers that lay dormant in scorched declivities until woken to fecundity by the monsoon.

At the top of this rock he lay flat on his face, staring over the edge of the rock, at the water. What he saw in the deep pool below the rock was exactly, for a moment, like a reflection of himself. It was the face of a boy.

He lay staring incredibly at this image in the water for about ninety seconds. Lying flat on the rock was like lying on a heated grid of iron. It stung the tender places on his feet and shins so that now and then he flung his feet in the air. This violent motion of his legs threw spidery leaping shadows on the rock. The rest of him seemed dead. He was altogether paralysed by the fact that the face in the water had one eye.

The Naga boy was fishing. He was working very quietly, squatting navel-deep in the dark green rock-shadow, working with a drag net attached to a six-foot pole of cane. Casting and dragging the net, he kept his one eye fixed levelly down at the stream. This reflected one-eyedness, the slit of the other like a blood-shot gill, gave the face something of the appearance of a sinister fish.

Tuesday lay for another fifty or sixty seconds before going over the edge of the rock. He went over in a springing dive that was half a fall. In the second before going over he saw the reflected eye of the Naga boy, roused by the shadow on the water, squint in alarm, the white of it flashing like the turning belly of a frantic fish.

The next moment he hit the brown body violently. In the moment of impact he heard the bamboo cane crack in two and felt the splinter of rock in his hand slice the averted flesh of face below the dead eye. He hit the face again as they went together under the water. He saw the streak of blood vein the water surface with scarlet and he struck down, through water, for the third time. The splash of water seemed to wake the Naga boy and he turned in the water, kicking, coming up strongly. For a second or two he was tangled in the net. The face swam as a scarlet web. When it broke free it gave a sort of cat-scream, wild with pain. This scream seemed to give the boy the most terrific and desperate strength and the two of them went under for the second time, tangled in the net.

Under the water Tuesday hit the Naga boy for the fourth time. He felt the body slacken for a moment and he tried wildly to hold it under. His hands slipped on the naked flesh and the Naga boy turned, fish-like, coming up for air, and in that moment Tuesday struck at him again. The hand holding the stone cut through the water dully, not hitting anything, and in the act of swinging he felt the sharp edge of the broken bamboo cane shoot up into his groin like a sting.

He felt himself blindly weeping with rage as he struggled upward into the sun for breath. All the accumulated misery of the thing, his hatred of the boy's one eye, his fear of Paterson, the ghastly wretchedness of his dispossession went into another blow. It hit the Naga boy as he surfaced. The rock flew out of his hands. It struck the boy just above the ear so that he began groaning ferociously again, struggling fiercely in the bloody entanglement of the net. Suddenly he swam free, making frenzied strokes. In five or six thrashing strokes he was on the bank, turning a raw, scarlet face, screaming murder across the pool.

And then suddenly he was running. It so violently shattered the mesmerized weariness of Tuesday, still standing in the water, that he too clambered out, pulling himself up by the rock. He stood for a moment sickly coughing for breath, the cough waking the pain in his side. Then in full terror of the thing, the freezing renewed terror of the five opium-glassy Nagas waiting by the stream, greater than any pain, sprang up at him.

He clawed up on his feet at once and began to run, wet and bloody, up the bank of the stream. To his astonishment he fell down. The sting of pain in his groin, coming back, piercing up through his belly, towards his heart, paralysing the action of his right leg, struck him helpless. He lay in the sun, feebly surprised, watching the blood ooze out of his side, staining the brown and salmon stripes of the football shirt with vivid pattern.

After a few moments he got up and ran again. And like this he kept on for some time, running, terrorized, watching the blood run out of his shirt and then falling down. After about half an hour he was back on the road. By that time he had rolled up the edges of his shirt and balled them into a thin pad that stopped the blood as he squeezed it against his side. Every now and then he would fall down again and then, with scared misery, with a curious dry triumph, get up again and run on.

20

The boy spent some time the following afternoon beating a needle with one stone against another, turning it to the shape of a hook. It was a slow and delicate business because the heat from the fire died quickly and the needle took some time to whiten in the flame. When he had finished he found a yard or two of string in the car and made a paste of bread in his hands.

Twice as he went down through the jungle to the stream he fell down. The pain in his groin leapt up, stalled him, seemed to paralyse suddenly the muscles of his thigh and heeled him over. But when he walked on his energy was not suppressed. He was gay with the idea of the fish he would catch. The fish was for Miss McNairn. Miss McNairn was very ill and lay in the tent and could not eat the things he took to her. He had taken her papaia and rice and tea and it pained him to have these things neglected. It pained him also to think of Paterson, still half-drunk as he sat by her bed, and of the journey to India that could not be continued. In a simple way he had a contribution to make to these things.

In the heat of the afternoon the fish did not bite much and he lay for a long time on his belly, dropping little seeds of paste into the stream, before he felt the pull of the string. He let the loop of it tighten on his little finger like a knot before pulling up and then he saw the fish turn in the water, struggling in the way the Naga boy had struggled, turning and diving round, and then swiftly he pulled it up. It was seven or eight inches long and it died almost at once in the hot air as he held it in his hands. In that moment he saw a sun-bird turn on the forest edge, disturbing a flock of feeding blue ring parrots – their flashing flight across the stream struck him once again with the recollective terror of the Nagas and the one-eyed drowning boy.

He ran most of the way back to the camp, carrying the fish under his shirt, falling down only once in the same unpremeditated curious way. The sun was falling away rapidly to the copper rim of lower hills and it was purple dark, swiftly, by the time he had the fish gutted and washed and cooked, first in water, then to finish it in a saucer of butter and shavings of green lime.

As he sat cooking the fish his sister sat on the other side of the fire. She asked once if the fish were for Paterson. Absorbed, watching the two thin fillets of fish bubble in the pan, he did not answer, and it was only when she spoke a second time, asking the same question but now in a different way, that he troubled to raise his face in answer.

'The fish is for Miss Conn.'

'She will not want it.'

'No?'

'No.'

On her face was a flat smileless sort of scorn for the fish he had caught.

'It's all I could get,' he said. 'It took an hour.'

'She won't eat it.'

'It's very good. It will help her.' He squeezed lime into the pan. 'She will eat it.' The juice struck the butter and bubbled.

'She won't eat it.'

'Why?'

'Because she is dying. That's why.'

This brutal fatalism struck him into painful astonishment. He looked up from the bubbling strips of fish into the face of his sister. She was not watching him. She was staring deep into the fire, and he knew suddenly that what she said was not a simple statement of fact, to be taken as true or untrue, but as something she hoped and waited for.

'Did he say she would die?'

'No. He knows, though.'

'How does he know? Is it because I didn't get Miss Allison?'

'She would die anyway.'

'How do you know? When will she die?'

'Soon.'

He realized that she spoke indifferently; that she did not care. He lifted the pan from the fire and let the two buttery slices of fish, garnished with bright emerald yellow sauce of lime and butter, slide on to the enamel plate he held in his other hand. Nadia did not even look up.

'It stinks,' she said. 'The fish stinks. It smells like a frog.'

'You're a frog,' he said. 'Squatting there.'

'Don't take it to her.'

'I shall take it. It will do her good.'

He stood up, obstinately proud of the fish. He gazed down at her in brotherly contempt, not thinking of her as a woman but only as a sister, behaving with the unromantic stupidity of sisters.

And then she looked up.

'Take it, then,' she said. 'Take it. But don't fall down.'

He was taken off his guard and gave a little exclamation, partly of surprise, partly of fear that she had seen him fall.

'Fall down?' he said. 'Who is falling down?'

'You've been falling down all day.'

He was frightened of Paterson knowing the truth and said: 'I twisted my foot on a rock when I went back for Miss Allison. Why do you trouble about it?'

'If you twisted your foot why was there blood on your shirt?'

'I cut my hand.'

'Which hand?'

'How could I show you which hand? I'm holding the fish.'

'Don't take it to her,' she said.

She sat inscrutably watching the fire. Above the smell of the fish and the fire he suddenly caught the fragrance of the powder on her body. He understood all at once why she spoke as she did; why she spoke of death as if she did not care; why a little thing like the taking of the fish to Miss McNairn angered her beneath her calm.

'I am going to take it,' he said.

'Does he know?'

He was troubled; he knew quite well that she spoke of the wound.

'No.'

'If you only cut your hand and fell down and hurt your leg why don't you tell him?'

'It's a little thing and nobody but you would think it worth bothering about.'

'You keep falling down.'

'It's nothing,' he said.

'If it's nothing it will not matter if I tell him,' she said.

Once again she did not look up. He waited for a moment, watching her sitting by the fire, seeing her only as a sister. A wave of fear shot over him and died away. The conviction that it was right to take the fish to Miss McNairn, even if she were dying and even if because of it his sister spoke to Paterson of his wound, impelled him suddenly to walk away.

By that time it was already quite dark. Over in the tent the hurricane lamp burned, casting a triangle of shadow, orange on the dust outside. He stood on the edge of this triangle, feet together. He was quiet and subservient, holding the fish before him on the plate, with both hands.

Through the open aperture of the tent he could see Miss McNairn, lying on the camp-bed and Paterson, arms folded over his bare knees, sitting on a box beside her.

'Patson sir,' he said. 'Nice fish.'

He saw Paterson lean forward in the lamplight.

'Bring it in,' Paterson said. 'Come in.'

He could feel the plate still warm on the palms of his up-turned hands as he stooped to go into the tent. He could smell the warm butter, a little sickly in the humid air, as the plate, in the act of his stooping, came nearer his face. On the bed Miss McNairn lay flat, face upwards. Her eyes were bruised low into her face. Her skin had something of the brightness of the oily butter on the plate. Paterson leaned over and said to her: 'It's Tuesday. He has fish for you, of all things.'

She made troubled and hazy attempts to focus the boy. From her horizontal position she seemed simply to look far beyond him, a few inches below the level of the plate, to the dark triangle of the tent aperture. The boy knew that she did not see him and said: 'From the river. He is just fresh,' and took another step, hopefully, nearer the bed.

She began to try to speak in reply. The boy saw her lips, cracked like old scarlet enamel, open a little. All that happened after some moments of waiting was that the tongue pressed itself forward between them, like a brown slow slug. As the lips moved again the tongue receded.

Then came a word. He did not know what word it was. It seemed to hang on her mouth like a thin blob of water that would not fall. He waited for it to fall and all that he saw there after a time was the brown dry tongue, re-emerging in some new and pained attempt to finish the word or join it with another.

He stood watching her with eyes that shone in the lamplight. He wanted to step forward and lay the plate on the bed. He stood as if waiting for her to wake up.

For some time he remained like this, the plate cooling in his hands. The girl struggled to focus him and then to speak to him from the bed, until at last he heard Paterson telling him to sit down. He was not surprised by this. He was troubled only by the problem of whether to sit on the bed or squat on the floor. He decided to sit on the floor. And then as he moved his body to crouch down he felt the needle of pain in his side. The brief shot of paralysis crumpled him. He suddenly found himself sitting on the bed with a croak of pain.

To his great surprise it did not bother Paterson. At the same time it seemed to wake the girl. She made flabby and disjointed movements with her arms above the blankets. The plate of fish, cooling now so that he could see a little congealing of butter on the fork, lay between her hands and his own. He saw her grasp the edges. Her hands could not hold themselves still and shuddered several times so that the fork on the plate rattled feverishly. This sound had its echo in her mouth. She seemed to be trying to speak to him and after a second or two he heard a word. The pain in his side eased off and he leaned forward a fraction in order to hear her better. He thought the word sounded like 'You' but he was not sure and in another moment her face, drenched in sweat, seemed to shrink away.

He did not know how to interpret all this, and smiling at last, looked at Paterson.

'She means you,' Paterson said. 'She wants you to eat it.'

'No,' he said. 'No.'

'You eat it.'

'No,' he said. 'For Miss Conn.'

'She doesn't want it.'

'Patson eat it?'

'No,' Paterson said. 'You eat it.'

'Very good fish. New from the river. With butter.'

'You eat it,' Paterson smiled. 'It will make you fat.'

'Yes,' he said.

He waited. For perhaps half a minute Paterson leaned over Miss McNairn, wiping her face with a towel. It seemed a wonderful opportunity to disregard the odd desire of Paterson's that he should eat the fish. 'Is the light too bright?' he heard Paterson say.

He was glad when Paterson turned down the lamp. It lessened the stare and the brilliant, torpid face of the girl. He felt secure from her strange efforts to speak; from Paterson's persistence; from the curious obligation that he, of all people, should eat the fish he had brought.

At that moment Paterson said: 'Come on there. Eat it.'

'Miss Conn?'

'No,' Paterson said. 'You.'

'Patson eat it.'

Paterson did not answer. The boy saw then that the girl was still holding the plate. He did not know what to do. He looked with a precarious and wretched glance from her face to Paterson and then back again.

He picked up the fork and, not wanting to eat, his sickness rising full and sour in his mouth now, gave Paterson one more glance before stabbing at the fish hardening in its pale congealing butter. From her horizontal position the girl seemed to be watching him. Her eyes were nothing more than cracks in the purple-brown bulges of her swollen lids. This stare seemed to be fixed on him with a sort of horrible affection. He wanted passionately to rush out of the tent, away from it. It held him hypnotically as he raised the fish in small mouthfuls, chewing at it dryly.

And soon, as he slowly ate the tepid fish that had no taste now except the sickliness of butter and a touch of acid sometimes from the lime, he became aware that there was no sound in the tent except the small click of the fork on the enamel plate each time he put it down. This sound began to take on a terrible monotony. It affected him so that little by little he was afraid to touch the plate with the fork. At last he let the fork lie on the blanket. Then slowly and quietly, relieved from the repeated tiny sound that seemed to clatter with ghastly echoes through the confined space of the tent, he ate the last of the fish with his hands.

When he put them down again he found them held by the girl. The plate, released by her, slipped slowly off the blanket, taking the fork with it. They fell together, striking one of the metal-faced supports of the camp-bed, then clattering against each other.

The sound magnified the silence infinitely. In turn the silence seemed to grip him, pressing him down. He was held by the girl's hands into a curious squatting position on the bed, inextricably locked with her. He wanted to be sick. The fish seemed to have swollen and lodged in his throat and would not go down. From the hollow of his stomach fresh waves of nausea rose and met it. He held the misery of it with his mouth tightened.

All the time the eyes of the girl seemed to be fixed on him tenderly. Once they seemed to open a little, so that he could see the curve of the pupils. For some reason he got the impression from these partially opened eyes that she wanted to see him better. He moved his head forward in the lamplight, lowering it slightly. She caught hold of him with her hands. He was embarrassed and frightened and troubled by the rising nausea of his sickness and terrified by the youngness of her face and he did not know what to do. In this confused moment he felt her pulling him slowly down. She pulled him with great difficulty to within about six inches of her face, so that he could smell the terrible breath of her fever and the rottenness of her sweat. A second later the stab of pain hit him in the side and the spasm of death going over her became part of his own pain, neutralizing and making it a small thing, so that at last he was free.

When he released himself and went out of the tent, taking the plate and fork with him, without a word, his sister was still by the fire, waiting for Paterson to come.

'Miss Conn is dead,' he said, and slowly his sister smiled.

Paterson sterilized the thermometer and took the boy's temperature, once that evening, after Connie McNairn had died, and once in the morning, before they started on. He made the boy bath himself and then stood over him, night and morning, while he washed out, with a solution of iodine, his mouth and throat and nose. He was taking no chances, he thought, and it was the best, in a simple way, he could do. The temperature was obstinately normal both times.

When he had finished with the boy he sterilized the thermometer and took the hurricane lamp and went over to where, by the car, the girl was already lying under the blankets. He set the lamp in the dust by her face and saw her black eyes move, clear and quick, wide awake. After the dilated dying eyes of the girl in the tent, they seemed wonderfully vigorous; he could not believe in the beauty of their bright wakefulness. He knelt down and put the thermometer in her mouth and pressed his own mouth against the turned flank of her hair, feeling for a moment very tired, the veins of his body sere and empty, his mind sleepy and yet terribly grateful that she was there. She took the thermometer out of her mouth and said, 'I am well. There is no need for this.'

He smiled and put it back and held her wrist, watching the hands of his watch, feeling her blood beating steadily and strongly. For a full minute the small, stray pulse of it seemed to spread out down the forested valley. It broke on the dark hills and seemed to become, in an odd way, the reverberation of a car engine, accelerated into shattering revolutions somewhere very far away. Occupied with her temperature, he did not take much notice of it. Then he took the thermometer out of her mouth, holding and turning it in the light so that he could see the mercury. He saw the glint of it on the normal mark, heard the engine churning and revving furiously again and sat there for a moment listening, wondering what it could be.

'Am I well?' she said.

'Very well.' Thank Christ they both are, he thought, and felt relief flooding through his dried veins as he listened to the engine suddenly, in an explosive roar, dying away.

'And now you.' She moved to take the thermometer and put it in his mouth. He wanted to say 'not without sterilization' but the word had in Burmese no equivalent that he could remember and he said 'Not without washing,' instead.

She laughed a little and said, 'Am I not clean then?' He caught the fresh fragrance of her face and did not know how to explain what suddenly seemed like a trivial and superfluous thing.

'Put it in your mouth,' she said.

'It should be boiled first,' he said and she began laughing again, her eyes brilliantly black as she flicked the thermometer and teased his face.

'Because you eat it?'

'Because there could be disease on it.'

'I have no disease,' she said. 'I am very well. You said so.'

'There could be disease on it. That's what I said. There could be disease on it and if it were not washed away I could get it into myself.'

'Are you afraid of getting the same disease as I might have?'

'No.'

'Then put the thing in your mouth,' she said, and held the thermometer between his lips, pressing the tip of it softly in.

He opened his mouth to say 'There is no need. I am well. Like you,' but in the moment of opening it she pressed the themometer in. He found himself taking it on his tongue, curling it under and holding it there. For about thirty seconds she did not speak and then she said, 'You were not afraid of the disease you might get from her,' and he understood suddenly all her teasing, all the laughing that was really fear.

Somewhere far down the valley the car engine woke again with a roar. He sat with the thermometer askew in his mouth, listening. He was puzzled by the sound of it and did not for a moment hear her say 'You have not answered' and then became aware of it and took the thermometer out of his mouth.

'I could not talk with the thing in my mouth,' he said.

'Are you afraid? Say it now.'

'No,' he said. 'I am not afraid.'

'If the disease is in my mouth, will it be in yours now?'

'It could be.'

'If the disease was in her mouth and came to yours, could it come to mine?'

'No,' he said.

'Why not?'

'Because the thing has been washed.'

'Are you afraid of dying?'

'I don't want to die.'

'What does the thing say?' She took the thermometer from his hand and held it in the light of the lamp, turning it. 'Where does it say you will die?'

'When the little mark goes up to a hundred and three, or a hundred and four, or a hundred and five.'

'What is it now?'

He took the thermometer back from her, flipped it several times in his fingers. Then he turned it in the light so that she could see the line of mercury. He saw it gleam like a silver hair streak and heard, far down the valley, for the third time, the noise of the car. He listened again to it, momentarily preoccupied.

'What does it say?'

Suddenly he came to himself. Tranquillized, no longer quite so tired, the hideous affair of Connie McNairn shrouded over, he felt some of the life in him come back. He looked casually and dryly at the thermometer. And then, teasing her, he told her how bad it was for him. 'A hundred and ten,' he said. 'Very terrible. I shall die. No one can live with that.'

She began crying even before he had finished speaking. Instantly he felt he could have cut out his tongue. He lay down beside her, outside the blanket, speaking to her softly; he felt miserable and angry with himself and said: 'It was not that. I didn't mean it was that. There is no danger. It is not that,' but she did not answer. After some moments he moved the lamp away and undressed himself and put the thermometer where he could find it in the pocket of his shirt. As he tucked it away curiosity impelled him for a moment to look at it and he saw the mark at a little under a hundred and one. He felt abruptly impatient at the whole affair, and then vaguely remembered something about typhoid, or perhaps it was typhus, and keeping the patient's temperature down. He wished suddenly that Miss Allison had never gone back. She would have told him whether or not it was true that if once the patient's temperature had soared it was all over. And then down the valley the car roared once more. It shattered all the brittle consciousness of his personal fear, bringing him back at last, quietly and tenderly, to the girl. He crawled under the blanket and lay beside her. Her body was naked and warm under the blanket and he felt once again as he held her there that the naked simplicity of it stood for all he loved and hated losing in Burma, just as in another sense Connie McNairn, far more than the Portmans or Betteson or her mother, stood for all that was being extinguished there. And suddenly he wanted passionately to survive. He wanted the three of them to survive. Only through survival could the journey have any meaning. And if it had any meaning it was that one day the three of them, inextinguishable, would come back.

In the morning the road climbed for some distance steeply away from the stream, into hillier country. Traverses of bamboo, roughly built across gradients, had been beaten by traffic into useless tinder. From the crest of a rise in the road the country was revealed simply as one crest after another, the jungle tightly fissured like a cauliflower, the high plateau separating it from India still nothing but a shapeless mass in the high haze beyond.

And then soon the road wound down again, steep in thick dust, back towards the river. In half an hour traffic was congealing on the slopes: first coolies and villagers who shot out of the way as Paterson hooted, then carts, then whole groups of Indians and Burmese, mostly women and children, squatting on the road. He managed to push the car forward, using low gear as a brake, the radiator steaming, for another half-mile. Then the impasse of carts and bodies became complete, stopping him altogether. When he leaned out of the window and asked for reasons, he was greeted with pointing arms. It was always the same answer:

'The bridge.'

Finally he left the car in gear and got out and walked ahead for about a hundred yards. Beyond the next turn of road, he saw the bridge. It was one of those bridges, fragile in appearance as if knotted of sun-bleached rope, built for the dry season with teak piles and bamboo, that the waters of the monsoon regularly wash away. It had never been built for the continuous traffic that had now broken four or five yards out of the centre of it, so that it hung above the gorge like the fractured back-bone of a fish.

Paterson stood for some moments watching coolies working to repair the middle of it. They seemed tiny and casual, like drugged ants in the sun. Among them a vaguely familiar figure was arguing loudly. Bunches of refugees were waiting at the bridge end, infinitely patient, as if resigned to the fact that what was not repaired today would be repaired tomorrow. He

saw a car there too. Under the bridge the water was too deep
and fast for wading, and a few improvised boats of bamboo
were being paddled over, festooned with emerald silky sails
made of large leaves of plantain.

He walked down to the end of the bridge. It was a reason-
ably good bridge for reasonable times. But now, he thought, the
times were not reasonable and it curved down to the centre to
a drop of thirty feet above the water, and down below he could
see the partially submerged wreckage of a bullock cart that had
gone over.

He walked on to the bridge. With a double stamp of his feet
he sent across it a quiver that abruptly aroused, in the middle
of it, the arguing coolies. He had produced the effect of someone dangerously rocking a boat.

Immediately a figure came roaring back towards him across
the bridge.

'What the bloddy hell are you playing at? You want the
whole lot to go? What the hell are you up to?'

The sweating, maddened figure of the Dutchman came rolling along the bridge track, swaying the whole structure violently.

'Oh! it's you. Please for God's sake don't do that. You want
the whole lot to go?'

'How long has this been going on?' Paterson said.

'Two bloddy days!'

'They're pretty simple to repair. Usually. What went
wrong?'

'They repaired it and then a bloddy cart went over – too
soon! before it was ready! Two people drowned. A hell of a
thing. It may be a week now.'

Paterson took a step or two forward along the bridge. The
Dutchman was a pink ball of sweat. 'Don't swing it! Don't
rock it, for God's sake!' he shouted.

'All right,' Paterson said.

He walked slowly out to the centre of the bridge. He paused
now and then to lean over and look down. It seemed to him
that the original collapse had been a minor affair; a thing

easily done and easily repaired. But the fall of the heavy, cum-brous bullock cart had cracked, like a matchstick, a diagonal centre support. At a point where stress was greatest the big supporting bar now stuck up like a fractured bone.

He began to speak to the coolies, who were lashing fresh lengths of bamboo across the central gap. They were not happy, fearing the Dutchman would come suddenly blunder-ing over, as the cart had done, before the repair was ready. They spoke with unassailable fatalism, as men to whom one day was exactly like another. Karens mostly, friendly, chatter-ing, inclined to embellish the story of the cart that had gone over, they told him: 'Ten people killed. Ten or twelve. Three or four bullocks. Many killed. Thirty altogether.'

He nodded once or twice; they saw that he understood them and crowded round him. They pointed over the side of the bridge to the smashed support, repeating the story of the fall-ing cart with new embroideries of horror. He looked down. Under the bridge a raft of bamboo floated across stream, poled by a Karen in a waist-cloth of brilliant purple-rose. Bundles of white and yellow and red and brown, heaps of half-naked chil-dren, festoons of shining plantain leaves swam suddenly into the blinding reflected ball of sun. The intolerable shocking pool of light, like a flash of magnesium fire, consumed in a moment every scrap of colour on the little floating raft. The whole bridge seemed suddenly to sway, the water with its contor-tions of light and sickening distortions of fiery green and purple and white and rose flooded away down a gorge that opened up, cavernous, a thousand feet below. The sun seemed to hit him from both above and below, partly forcing him, partly dragging him down to the water. He tried to grip the edges of the bridge, failed, saw the reflected column of the poling Karen, purple and brown, clear itself in a rapid flash of all the distortions that drowned it, and then with a great effort pulled himself upright.

At the same moment the bridge gave a great shudder. He said something vaguely to the Karens, felt very sick and walked back across the bridge.

The Dutchman was waiting.

'Well? What do you think? How long will they be? What chance of getting over today?'

'Damn all, I think.'

'The bloddy fools!'

Paterson walked off the bridge. To walk on hot, solid dust was to feel for a moment that that too could give way under his feet and let him fall. An Indian, a dark red skeleton, ran along with him, begging for rice. The Dutchman shouted. The Indian hung on, trotting, one hand on the grey hairs of his breast, the other curled like a pink claw. Before Paterson the hazy perspective of dust and trees, squatting figures, carts and sky, suddenly cleared and he said: 'These people have to be got over. Have to be organized. Somehow,' and the Dutchman shouted:

'Yes, but how? Look at them. Waiting for a bloddy miracle.'

Paterson, his head clear again, stopped and looked back. The Indian stood by, panting.

'The bridge will never take a car.'

'No? It's going to take mine! Where are your people? Don't you want to get them over?'

'Back there.'

'Well, we have to do something. There are all sorts of rumours about soldiers coming up.'

'These people are full of rumours. They love rumours.' Paterson stood watching the bridge. 'Their whole life is a rumour.'

'Is what? Is what?' the Dutchman said. 'Is what?'

'We can build rafts for the lighter traffic. That'll clear the road.'

'Yes, but what about the cars?'

'The bridge can be fixed. Probably in two days.'

'Two bloddy days!'

Paterson turned from watching the bridge to where, on the stream edge, two peasants and a woman were lashing bamboo into a raft with vine cords and strings of green bamboo.

'Might get it done in less if we feed them,' he said.

'Feed them? Feed them? Why the hell should we feed them? They have food.'

Paterson began to walk up the track. The wave of sickness had gone. He felt very English. Obstinately, phlegmatically, purposely, deliberately English, he remembered the Dutchman's rumour of cholera and suddenly hated the excitability, the shouting anxiety, the sweating gusto of the man. He realized that his faintness had come ot hunger. He had not breakfasted. He had not been able to face, after the ghastly necessity of burying Miss McNairn, even Tuesday's cup of tea and the burnt biscuit that passed for toast. The sickness had started then. Now he felt oddly empty and slack and yet hungry also out of weariness and nausea, and he wanted a drink and food. He said deliberately: 'I'm going to eat and have a nap for an hour. I'll be better able to think things out.'

'Tea!' the Dutchman raved. 'Tea!'

They were within sight of the car. Aghast at what seemed to be Paterson's indifference, the Dutchman exploded and then was speechless. Then as they came nearer the car and he saw Nadia and the boy sitting on the running-board, patiently in charge of it, he realized that something was wrong. He remembered another car. He recalled several people, a very pretty woman with a good figure, another odd-looking creature in spectacles. The absence of them all astonished him.

'Where are your people? Didn't you have another car?'

'They went back.'

'Went back? Went back?'

The Dutchman, flabbergasted, stopped for a moment wiping the sweat off the hairs of his chest with a perfectly clean, well-ironed handkerchief folded in a white square.

'You can't mean it. You're joking. You're joking. There was cholera back there. Didn't you know?'

Paterson did not speak. The Dutchman made several noises of throaty disbelief, mopping the hairs of his chest at the same time. And then, speaking more slowly, not knowing whether Paterson was fooling, lying or simply being obstinate, he said something about 'You can't be too careful. You don't look too

well yourself,' but Paterson, who had been giving orders to the
boy to get tea and what food he could, turned with indifference
to ask:

'What did you say about cholera?'

'It was raging in Shwebo. Everywhere.'

'How many cases?'

'Oh! that I don't know. Some cases.'

Ten or fifteen yards beyond the car Tuesday had started a
fire. Paterson felt suddenly tired, physically tired from the
nausea of the morning, mentally tired of the agitation of the
Dutchman. 'Have some tea with us.' He suddenly flopped on
the dust, in the little shade that came down at the rear of the
car.

'No thanks,' the Dutchman said. 'I'm going back there. See
what I can do. What does it matter how many cases of cholera
there were? There was some cholera. Everyone said so. You
can't be too careful.'

He turned, mopping his over-hairy breast with his handkerchief and said:

'You can't be too careful. You don't look too well yourself.'

'I'm all right.'

He did not want to talk. His head was raging again, torment-
ing him. His stomach felt full of nausea and from the river the
air came up, dust laden, in stifling waves.

He lay on his face. After what seemed a long time he turned
to find the girl looking down on him, holding a mug of tea.
Looking up, he felt as if a web had woven itself over his face.
He sat up and wiped both hands across his face, but the net
persisted and the girl seemed to recede beyond it, taking the tea
farther and farther away from his upstretched hands.

At last he was holding the mug. He clenched it with both
hands, very tightly. He felt that if he let go of it he would fall.
The web had cut off the road, the bridge, the glittering bonnet
of the Dutchman's car. He could see only the girl's face,
watching him, and the mug, like a cylindrical section of a
post, to which he was holding desperately. He heard the girl

speaking, but the words of Burmese he needed to answer her were somewhere beyond the web and his mind could not grasp them. He fought at this web for some moments with a sensation of angry and confused pride, desperate that it should not defeat him.

Finally, when he emerged from it, he saw the girl holding the thermometer. The tubular shape of it, enlarged by its nearness to his face, recalled the bridge. He tried to wave it away. A second later it was in his mouth. He suffered it to be there with surprised and unresisting anger. He was aware at the same time that she was gazing at the watch on his wrist.

He tried to resist all these movements, first by words, then by standing up. Nothing happened. The thermometer was taken out of his mouth. He tried to pursue its progress with his hands. They seemed glued to the sides of the mug and there was no strength in them and he did not move. Then for another moment the web cleared. He saw with shattering brightness the girl put the thermometer into her mouth and hold it there.

The sight of this simple act filled him with terror. He felt the thermometer splinter as he wrenched it through her lips. It was as if she had been holding it with her teeth. Silver beads of mercury were spilt like seed. They mingled with the blood of her mouth where the glass had torn it. He came to himself with horror, speaking for the first time, muttering tenderly about her pain. And then as he staggered to his feet he was overwhelmed by the simple significance of the thing she had done. He felt belittled and humiliated by it and suddenly he dropped the mug and held her against his face. He tried to wipe away the blood by little convulsive movements of tender sorrow. 'Little one. Please. Little one,' he said.

Five minutes later, glad the thermometer was broken, his brain freed of the disturbing web of nausea, he staggered back to the bridge. The sun seemed to hit him ferociously as he walked. It descended with regular flattening blows, hitting the top of his skull like a sword. In these painful pulsations colour sometimes died. The river turned grey, with grey masses of jungle on either side, grey scrambled bodies on its banks, grey needles of timber forming the bridge, grey water swirling away the rafts of grey feathered plantain leaves. Each time this happened he battled against it, shaking his head ferociously, until colour came back.

The Dutchman strode off the bridge. His face appeared to Paterson like a grey bag of rubber. He was full of rumours, gathered from the Karens. That troops were coming up the valley.

These troops, he said, were Japs. There was fighting in Shwebo. There was fighting in Mandalay, Mojok, Myitkyina, Bhamo; there was butchery and rape; the towns of the plain had gone. The British were running. In two days the retreat would be over. The Dutchman was obsessed by a certain fixed notion of time. Everything had happened, was happening, or was going to happen in two bloddy days.

'In two bloddy days the Japs will be here, at this bridge,' he shouted, 'and then where will we be?'

'Probably at this bridge.'

In irony Paterson felt some of his self-possession, his phlegm and all of his Englishness come back. He was relieved that his power of colour came back too. The Dutchman became very red. Fierce pellets of yellow sweat darted off his blond eyebrows as he shook them at Paterson.

'Well, what do we do? What do we do?'

'Stop getting windy.'

'Windy? Windy? I don't get that. What is windy?'

'We need two gangs. We'll repair the bridge with one and make rafts with the other.'

He walked out on to the bridge. It swayed deeply once again. But now the swaying was no longer an integral part of himself and his sickness and he did not care. The Dutchman followed. He did not like the word windy and growled suspiciously, sweating.

Paterson stood in the centre of the bridge and spoke with the Karens, offering rice in return for work. He would make a first dole at five o'clock. He thought perhaps they could work by night, by the light of fires, by hurricane lamps, perhaps by a couple of lights plugged in from the cars. He spoke briefly. In ten minutes the two gangs, twenty to thirty-five in a gang, were lined up. They had kukris for cutting timber. He sent the smaller gang down into jungle to cut bamboo. He explained the size of the rafts, the weight they were to carry, and knew that they would do the rest. He took the second gang along the escarpment, telling them as they went what timber he needed. He hoped perhaps they could cut some of the timber that day, haul it out by darkness and float it into position by dawn.

He did all this, and then began to select trees for the Karens to fell as near the water's edge as possible, without realizing that Tuesday and the girl had been with him all the time.

They walked a pace or two behind him, one on either side. Turning and becoming aware of them for the first time, he saw blood on the girl's mouth. The breaking glass of the thermometer had scratched her two lips as they tightened to hold it from him. The blood had run down her chin. Under the chin and down the throat it made a fading, darkened line that she did not seem to know was there. It troubled him as if he had caused it; he was touched by her complete obliviousness of it and wanted to wipe it away.

All that afternoon and on into the evening, as the Karens cut timber and bamboo for the rafts and the bridge, the thin scarlet line of blood was there on the girl's mouth and throat whenever he turned. Each time he meant to wipe it away. And beside it, always, was the smile of the boy. At five o'clock he left off directing the timber cutting. He called the first relay of men for the rice-dole. They filed past the car as he measured out the rice in a mug. Down on the river the second gang, hauling timber to the water's edge, were singing, and then the Dutchman appeared, agitated, with a new story that convoys of Japanese transport had already been seen, not five miles back, on the road. 'You can hear it coming!' he said.

'Can't hear a thing,' Paterson said. 'Have some tea.'

'You can't hear it for that bloddy singing.'

'Just a rumour. They love them.'

'You think so? So much the worse if it is. It's always the bloddy rumours that make people run.'

'You should know.'

'And suppose they do run? And this bridge not finished? What do we do then?'

'Walk,' Paterson said.

'Talk bloddy sense, please!'

The last of the Karens went past, taking his rice. A message had gone down to the gang on the river and suddenly the singing ceased.

'Now listen,' the Dutchman said. 'Now listen. Well? Can't you hear that?'

Paterson stood by the car, listening vaguely, suddenly tired. He felt himself sliding down by the car until he sat on the running-board. He still had the mug for the rice in his hands. The half-filled sack of rice stood by the running-board, a foot or so away. Sickness, gathering again in the form of a web, grey and nauseating, came running back. He could not see for a moment the colour of anything in front of him; he felt as if he would pitch forward on his face. With a great effort he dipped the mug into the sack of rice. He let the grains run out of it in a brown stream, gripping the mug desperately and letting the rice run slowly so that it should seem as if he were doing a normal thing. A long fiery vein of revolting and weakening sickness poured down through his bowels, leaving him terribly cold as it passed, the coldness ghastly as it blackened him out. All of his life seemed to be pouring out through the slow, thin, brown stream of rice and then the Dutchman said:

'There. You can hear it now.'

Ashily Paterson stared at the last grains of rice, making a desperate effort not to fall forward, flat on his face; and then he listened.

From some distance down the valley he could hear the sound he had heard the night before: the sound of transport, heavier now than ordinary cars, climbing the gradient in low gear.

'You hear it, you hear it?' the Dutchman said. 'What do you make of that?'

He did not know at all what he made of it. Stupidly he struggled to say something rational, to appear normal, and once again not to fall down. The last of the rice had slipped out of the mug. He scooped at it slowly. It occurred to him that, after all, the Dutchman might be right; that the Japs might be coming. He tried to count the number of days he had been on the road, but their own fatalistic recurrence, one exactly like another, had obliterated them. He could not tell if there were one or twenty. The Dutchman said something about the sooner they get the cars over on the rafts the better, and then the second gang of Karens came up the hill.

Once again, gripping the mug, staring at the bewildering myriad grains of rice, Paterson struggled desperately not to fall. It struck him suddenly that the Dutchman was ready to panic and he realized that the sight of him madly rushing his car over by raft would only have consequences that were disastrous. Mass panic would bring down the bridge. At the same time he might be right. He tried once again to calculate how long the journey had taken, but the days, running together, repetitiously, fused by sun and dust, had no meaning or number.

The gang of Karens appeared and filed past him. For some time he had the impression that he doled rice. His hand moved automatically. He found himself staring on a succession of waist-cloths, of many tones of purple and red, towards each of which he raised a doling hand. He heard voices, answered them, and once argued with the Dutchman that no advancing force, Jap or otherwise, would send up its invading spearhead by truck. He argued that they would have heard artillery; that there was no sound of planes. The Dutchman, oddly, did not seem to resent these things.

Some time later he discovered that the mug was no longer in his hands. He knew all at once that it had never been. Looking up, he saw the last of the Karens filing past the car. The rice was being doled by Nadia and the boy. The Dutchman, with whom he had argued so passionately, was no longer there. He struggled to his feet. He called to the Karens, in a voice curiously disembodied, something about the bridge, and then a second afterwards could not remember what it was.

Later still he was under the bridge. It was growing dark. He could see the faces of the Karens, as they swarmed about the spidery structure, trembling there like berries of orange and ripe copper in the setting sun. He was doing something about superintending the hauling of a teak spar. This spar was thirty or thirty-five feet high. Catching the sun, it flamed at the tip with a bruise of dusky purple. It was a gigantic matchstick supported and swung and tipped into its place beneath the bridge by the little Karens, shouting and laughing in and above the stream. He knew that the spar had to be strapped to the fractured support of the bridge, as to a broken bone. Then in some way that he did not understand, unaware of climbing the bridge, he found himself lying above the fractured spar. He was lying face downwards, looking at the stream. There were pools of faces, giant frogspawn jellied and gleaming everywhere below him with black eyes. He was aware of the Dutchman, waving emotional arms. Upwards, out of all this, swung the spar.

Then a heap of timber broke suddenly into flame on the bank beside the edge of the bridge. White flame painted the river, the spawn-like faces, the huge matchstick of the upward swinging spar, the wide hands of the Dutchman. Gazing down, hugging the wooden pile support with his legs, he reached with both arms to grasp the spar as the Karens thrust it upwards. It suddenly seemed of extraordinary length, stretching far down to the stream below as if to the shaft of a well. An eye of water gleamed up at him. He felt terribly and helplessly sick. The eye turned itself over the whole circumference of the world, glittering above him like the first green star. He thought swiftly of the major; then of Miss Allison and Mrs Betteson; then of Mrs Portman, cool and beautiful, angry and frustrated, trying to seduce him; then of Betteson and the dying girl and the rest. He conceived suddenly that he owed them something; that in a horrible way he had failed them. The spar swung upwards; the Karens shouted; the bitterness of sickness left him for a moment, leaving him in a sweat of remorse, cold as he clung above the water.

An instant later he was falling. He was determined at the same time not to fall. His terror was transcribed suddenly into conscious alertness. He felt his hands gripping the bridge until the blood froze in the finger-tips. The thought of falling became identified at the same moment with dying, and in the same way he was determined not to die. Far down the valley, across miles of darkened jungle, he heard once again the grind of gears that might have been a hostile army. It seemed to exemplify all the weariness, the horror, the heat and the ghastliness of the long retreat. All along the road lay the dead. He saw them as a long line of unheroic agony, putrefying, vulture-ridden, jackal-ravaged, the dead of all colours and all creeds, yellow, red, white, brown, Eurasians, Europeans, Asiatics, babies, women, children, men, the dead of typhoid and typhus, the dead of malaria and enteric, the dead of exhaustion and starvation, the dead of cholera perhaps, the dead that were simply dead. He felt his fingers slipping on the spar, knew suddenly that in another fraction of a second he would fall, be one with all the dead who were nameless, and would never know, in that unheroic moment, what had really happened.

A moment later he was aware of what seemed like a great weight on his shoulders. It pressed him against the spar. The notion of falling passed. In the light of the fire the bridge became pale yellow, more than ever spider-like, a web into which he was securely wound. The conscious thought of dying, together with the fear of falling and the determination not to fall, was smoothed out. He was not lonely. The voice of the boy was gentle, comforting him greatly.

'Patson sir. Patson. Patson sir.'

He became vaguely aware of the arms of the boy winding tightly about him, folding him to the spar.

21

In the morning, some time after the Dutchman had been ferried over on the raft, the car disappearing into jungle on the far river bank in a ball of dust, the boy unhooked the trailer from the car. He had spent considerable time cutting poles of bamboo and slicing the green skin from others in thin peelings that were like string. The girl had unloaded the cans of petrol and water. Now with the poles of bamboo and the string of bamboo they worked to build a skeleton roof on the trailer. They covered this roof with a thatch of banana leaves, leaving the sides and ends exposed, to give a little air. When this was done the boy unbolted the steel draw-bar and took it off entirely. With two poles of bamboo for shafts he made the trailer into a little cart. Underneath the cart, at the forward end, he slung a length of wire that could be unhooked at one end. It was long enough to hold four cans of water.

For more than an hour there had been congestion at the bridge. By ferrying himself over the Dutchman had avoided it. He had not found it necessary to put his trust in the repair. Now the refugees were pressing forward; they stirred dust that hung over the glassy water in the early sunlight like a haze of salmon and gold. The rumour that the Japs were coming had increased. There was no singing from the Karens still working to strap up, with fresh spars, the under-structure of the bridge. The grind of heavy gears coming up the road could still be heard, and now and then an Indian voice, more nervous than the rest, let off a screaming lamentation that echoed with melancholy piercings against the forest wall and down above the water.

In the early light the bridge was a web beaded with colour.

Later the sun began to kill the greys, the yellows, the whites, the neutral shades of bullocks and clotted faces. At the same time it intensified the purples and shades of red, so that the light played tricks of refraction, the massed line of colour quivering up and down.

By nine o'clock the boy and his sister had the trailer ready. It had the appearance of a small, green-roofed house on wheels. They had covered the inside of it with blankets and had laid the half-sack of rice like a pillow at the head. Underneath were slung four cans of water, a frying pan, a kettle and Paterson's folding camp-bath.

The boy, recalling moments of triumph with the tool-kit, pumped air into the tyres of the trailer. He realized he would need the pump too, and then that he would need tools, and he strapped the pump with the tool-kit, laying it so that he would not forget it on the trailer. Paterson lay on the floor of jungle in shade, covered with blankets, away from the road.

All the time he worked on the trailer and the tyres the boy was preoccupied by a sound. It was the rising sound of gears grinding up the long bend of road. It had been growing louder and closer since dawn. Now he judged it to be rather less than a mile away. Sometimes as he stood in the road and looked back, watching for whatever it was that was labouring in low gear, he remembered the Nagas, looking with terror for the opium-squinting faces and the one eye of the boy. This terror sometimes held him transfixed, so that he stood on the roadside as if not really seeing the faces, the bullocks, the long column, dusty and patient, seeping through to the bridge.

He was still standing there like that when the British sergeant leaned out of the cab of the first army truck that came up the hill. The sergeant, red with sweat, was very astonished at the smiling face above the football shirt. He greeted it with pained and cheerful irony, calling it to the attention at the same time of his mate, the corporal.

'Puts years on you, don't it, kid?'

The boy smiled.

'Speak English?' the sergeant said.

'Bloody footballer an' all,' the corporal said.

'Yessir. Yessir,' the boy said. He nodded swiftly. The smile was cheerfully broad on his face.

'Speaks English. Cheerful as hell,' the sergeant said. He had himself a kind of rude buoyancy, tempered only by the irony and trial of retreat. It cheered him still further to see the dusty and indomitable boy standing by the trailer, proud of the faded stripes of the football shirt.

'Going far?'

The boy smiled enormously.

'Free trip anyway,' the sergeant said. 'Don't cost a sausage.'

The smile on the face of the boy broadened as if this joke were comprehensible.

'What holds us up?' the sergeant said. 'Not that we care.' And then, looking ahead, he saw the bridge. He gazed at it for some seconds as if it were a congested rabbit-hole. He called it to the attention of the corporal. The corporal made noises of great horror and together they gazed through the windscreen at the spidery fragility of the bridge, calling it several degrees of murder. 'Gawd help us,' the corporal said. 'Pray for us, mate.'

'We got two chances,' the sergeant said. 'If we don't go through we go under.'

'Always go back,' the corporal said.

The sergeant greeted this with spasms of splendid laughter. 'Order the bastards out!' he said, and the corporal, lifting the canvas screen behind him, yelled into the back of the truck: 'All change here for Bakerloo, Waterloo, and bloody Cal.'

'Waterloo it is an' all,' the sergeant said. 'If we make this we can make bleedin' Everest.'

'And if we don't make it it's bleedin' ever rest for sure,' the corporal said.

These ironies were lost on the boy. He watched the truck disgorge its load of khaki men. They shouted incomprehensible greetings at him, teasing him about the origins of the football shirt, calling him chum. He stood unmoved, smiling, relieved at last to know that the truck was the thing he had heard grinding all through the night, his fears dispersed by their laughter. They filed past him, coming one by one into sight of the bridge. 'Let her go, sarge,' they said. 'Gee mare! Gee up. Only gotta die once. Over she goes.'

'Single file on the bridge!' the sergeant roared. 'And look slippy! Else I'll have every bastard on the peg.'

'Oh! sarge!' they said. 'What peg?'

'You'll see! Wait till I get you to bloody India!'

'Somewhere,' the corporal said, 'I've heard that before.'

They waited for some moments longer. The sergeant leaned his chest on the wheel. The boy remained gazing up into the cabin, still smiling, proud of these contacts, fascinated by the ironic banter of words he could only half understand.

The sergeant leaned out of the cab.

'Bridge any good?'

'Bridge good,' the boy said. 'Yessir.' He had suddenly great faith in the bridge. It had been repaired by Paterson. It was Paterson's bridge. He was very proud of the bridge. 'Yessir, yessir. Good. Yessir.'

'Mother,' the sergeant said. 'Here we come.'

The sergeant let in the clutch, revving the engine, and as the truck went forward, he leaned from the window, grinning.

'Pick up the bits,' he said.

'Yessir!'

'See you in India,' the corporal called.

Triumphantly the boy understood these words. He felt that a great light flashed on him. He waved.

'Yessir! In India! Soon!'

The smile on his face expanded with glorious understanding. The sergeant grinned back, sticking his thumb out of the cabin. The boy shouted.

'Goodbye sirs! Goodbye misters! Goodbye!'

He stood for a moment longer watching the truck creep slowly forward to the bridge and the khaki file of men that were passing over. He waved his hand once more and then went back to where Paterson, in a sweating stupor, lay on the floor of jungle, waiting to be lifted on to the little cart.

A few moments later they lifted him on to the cart and the girl stood over him, pressing the blankets under his body. The boy spoke with echoes of triumph, smiling down.

'English soldiers!' he said. 'Trucks. Big sirs!'

Paterson, sweaty-eyed, his entire vision grey again, did not answer. He seemed to be watching the hills.

The boy and his sister took hold of the bamboo shafts of the trailer and pressed their bodies against the bamboo cross-bar and dragged it towards the bridge. Ahead of them the truck was half-way over, raising dust that cocooned against the sun. The entire spidery mass of the bridge swayed, like slender steel, curving down and recoiling as the truck passed over. The coolies who had built it stood watching and there were noises of ironical cheering from khaki figures on the other side. The hand of the sergeant, cheerful from the driving window, waved.

Then as the truck went over the cocoon of dust descended, slowly revealing the sun and then below and beyond the sun the clear line of mountains. And suddenly the boy saw the mountains, near and revealed at last, as something he could reach out and touch with his hands. They did not seem for a moment any higher than the branches of the jacaranda tree back in Paterson's compound. And then as he turned, filled with grave triumph, to look at Paterson, he knew that Paterson saw it too, and all across his face broke the enormous smile.

A few moments later they too were over the bridge.

More about Penguins
and Pelicans

Arnold Bennett in Penguins

THE CLAYHANGER TRILOGY

Clayhanger

Arnold Bennett's careful evocation of a boy growing to manhood during the last quarter of the nineteenth-century, with its superb portrait of an autocratic father, is set in the Five Towns. Bennett, who believed inordinately in the 'interestingness' of ordinary people, was never more successful in revealing the 'interestingness' of an apparently ordinary man than in Edwin Clayhanger.

Hilda Lessways

In *Hilda Lessways* Bennett relates the early life of Hilda Lessways, before her marriage to Edwin Clayhanger. Her involvement with the enigmatic, self-made man, George Cannon, and his enterprises takes her from the offices of an embryo newspaper in the Five Towns to a venture into the guest-house business in Brighton.

These Twain

In many ways this is the most accomplished of the three novels, for Bennett, drawing together the threads of his trilogy, presents already-established personalities in confrontation.

Hilda is now married to Edwin Clayhanger and the two, with Hilda's son by her disastrous 'marriage' to George Cannon, are living in Bursley. As they cope with immediate tensions and with old wounds they are forced continually to reassess their relationship.

Henry James in Penguins

The Wings of the Dove

Milly Theale, the 'dove' of the title, knows when she visits Europe that she is shortly to die, which lends urgency to her eager search for happiness.

What Maisie Knew

'One of the most remarkable technical achievements in fiction. We are shown corruption through the eyes of innocence that will not be corrupted' – Walter Allen in *The English Novel*.

The Awkward Age

Thrust suddenly into the immoral circle gathered round her mother, Nanda Brookenham finds herself in competition with Mrs Brookenham for the affection of a man she admires.

The Golden Bowl

Henry James's last, most controversial novel in which Walter Allen has found 'a classical perfection never before achieved in English'.

The Spoils of Poynton

Here both the characters and the setting are English. The novel opens with some of the triviality of drawing-room comedy and deepens into a perceptive study of good and evil.

The Turn of the Screw and Other Stories

For James the whole world of Americans, Cockneys, upper-class snobs, writers, dilettanti and intriguers allowed him to indulge his greatest obsession: observation.

Graham Greene in Penguins

Brighton Rock

Set in the pre-war Brighton underworld, this is the story of a teen-age gangster, Pinkie, and Ida, his personal Fury who relentlessly brings him to justice.

The Power and the Glory

This poignant story set during an anti-clerical purge in one of the southern states of Mexico 'starts in the reader an irresistible emotion of pity and love' – *The Times*

The Comedians

In this novel, Graham Greene makes a graphic study of the committed and the uncommitted in the present-day tyranny of Haiti.

The Quiet American

This novel makes a wry comment on European interference in Asia in its story of the Franco-Vietminh war in Vietnam.

The Heart of the Matter

Scobie – a police officer in a West African colony – was a good man, but his struggle to maintain the happiness of two women destroyed him.

The End of the Affair

This frank, intense account of a love-affair and its mystical aftermath takes place in a suburb of war-time London.

Our Man in Havana

Agent 59200/5 Wormold invented the stories he sent to the British Secret Service from Cuba ... and the results surprised him most of all.

H. E. Bates in Penguins

'One of the most vividly evocative writers of English ... able to conjure up in a handful of words whole landscapes and moods' – *Listener*

The Purple Plain

An aircraft crashes miles from help in the Burmese wilderness. Assailed by heat, thirst and pain, three men set off on the long trek towards safety. 'It haunts you, alike for the queer and mounting suspense and for the masterly portraits of the three men' – *Sunday Times*

The Scarlet Sword

Kashmir, 1947. Partition has provoked political crisis and the fierce Pathans and Afridi of northern India come sweeping down from the hills to take part in the riot and massacre. A small Catholic mission is in their path, and for ten days its inhabitants suffer the nightmare of murderous attack and occupation.